"Don't go," she begged in a whisper, raising her liquid green eyes to Ken, her plea little more than a tremulous exhalation.

"Audrey...."

The soft utterance brought a sudden realization of the audacity of what she had asked, and with an effort Audrey pulled herself together and stepped away.

"I'm sorry," she apologized, and the tiny smile she summoned flitted uncertainly across her mouth. "We're not kids anymore. I can't expect you to hold my hand during all the scary parts."

The dark brown eyes, so filled with tender understanding, rose to focus on the distressed verdancy that could not conceal the loneliness within.

"We're not kids anymore," he whispered thickly, but the words were absorbed in the gentleness of his kiss....

ABOUT THE AUTHOR

As a former free-lance illustrator, Laura Parris has worked for Hallmark Cards and the U.S. government before turning to writing full-time. Laura often turns real-life occurrences into fiction form, and some of the events in this, her first published romance, have truly happened. Laura and her husband make their home in Virginia.

High Valley of the Sun

LAURA PARRIS

Harlequin Books

TORONTO • NEW YORK • LONDON
AMSTERDAM • PARIS • SYDNEY • HAMBURG
STOCKHOLM • ATHENS • TOKYO • MILAN

Published June 1984

First printing April 1984

ISBN 0-373-16060-7

Copyright © 1984 by Laura Parris. All rights reserved.
Philippine copyright 1984. Australian copyright 1984.
Except for use in any review, the reproduction or utilization of
this work in whole or in part in any form by any electronic,
mechanical or other means, now known or hereafter invented,
including xerography, photocopying and recording, or in any
information storage or retrieval system, is forbidden without
the permission of the publisher, Harlequin Enterprises Limited,
225 Duncan Mill Road, Don Mills, Ontario, Canada M3B 3K9.

All the characters in this book have no existence outside the
imagination of the author and have no relation whatsoever to
anyone bearing the same name or names. They are not even
distantly inspired by any individual known or unknown to the
author, and all the incidents are pure invention.

The Harlequin trademarks, consisting of the words
HARLEQUIN AMERICAN ROMANCE, HARLEQUIN
AMERICAN ROMANCES, and the portrayal of a Harlequin,
are trademarks of Harlequin Enterprises Limited; the portrayal
of a Harlequin is registered in the United States Patent and
Trademark Office and in the Canada Trade Marks Office.

Printed in Canada

Chapter One

"Boring! protested Audrey's weary brain as she absently tucked a stray strawberry-blond curl behind her ear and blew the eraser crumbs off the storyboard before setting it on the floor beside a stack of TV cards that rested against the wall.

But, it was a job. A steady job, she added for reinforcement, stretching across the drafting table to reach the stack of copy on the desk. In the process, she exposed an expanse of long, curvaceous leg and her left hand automatically tugged at the navy cotton skirt, although there was no audience to appreciate or take offense at the unintentional view. The small agency handled pedestrian local accounts and the hackneyed ads were a far cry from the elegant, expensive accessories she had done for fashionable Goldwater's department store, nor did the demands on her talent begin to approach the clever, colorful teaching manuals Audrey had designed for the Indian Pre-School program. Yet, at its best, she reminded herself, free-lancing had been a sporadic source of income, and given her ex-husband's nonsupport and her marital history of financial instability, security was what Audrey needed most. But, why did it have to be so dull?

If it was dull, Audrey chided herself as she thumbed through the copy, that was her fault. She was being paid to come up with creative ideas. "Anyone with minimal talent can make a decent presentation for a memorable product," a graphics professor had once said. "The test is in making the mundane memorable."

"Test, nothing," Audrey muttered to herself when she saw the discount furniture, lighting company and used car ads. "This was an ordeal that demanded supernatural imagination!"

Audrey glanced at the large chart above her drafting table and confirmed that according to this week's calendar, the lighting account was the next order of business. When she pulled out the information Nancy had compiled and paper clipped, her green eyes fell on the note attached to the bulky manila envelope beneath. The broad, imperious black strokes were a calligraphic self-portrait of her boss, but it was not Barney's bellowing handwriting, nor even the crisp Helvetica typeface that spelled out the name of the prestigious account the Longworth Advertising Agency stood a miraculous, if remote, chance of acquiring that attracted Audrey's attention. It was the subject of the message:

Meeting - Ken Walker
10 A.M. - Friday

Ken Walker? An eyebrow flickered upward and Audrey opened the package. She knew Ken had studied architecture, but who would ever have suspected that he would be connected with—in charge of, Audrey almost gasped aloud when she scanned the cover letter—Nava del Sol, the most important, innovative residential experiment in the nation?

"Good ol' Ken," she mused. It had to have been eight years since she'd seen him. Maybe longer.

A wry smile curved her lips. She wondered if Mike knew. She had a dim recollection of her brother having mentioned Ken recently, but it had made no impression at the time, for she and Ken had never gotten along well.

The last time she had spoken to him had been at the homecoming game, Mike's and Ken's last year in college. Ken, the traitor, had gone to ASU, and it was during halftime of the traditional ASU-UofA rivalry match that Audrey had rushed up to them, ecstatically waving her brand new engagement ring. Ken had, quite uncharacteristically, said nothing about her plans. Instead, he had irrationally launched into a tirade against a penalty imposed on his team. He and Audrey had become embroiled in a fierce argument over conflicting loyalties, and after one exceptionally caustic remark, she had stormed out of the stands. Ken had gone on to graduate school in Hawaii and had stayed in the Islands to work, although he and Mike kept up a correspondence, of sorts, over the years.

"Well, back to boring," she sighed, shoving the unread literature back into the envelope without another glance and setting it aside. Her features assumed a pose of concentration and a small frown furrowed her brow as Audrey read the copy and the key phrase that was to be played up in the ad's headline: "Light up your life."

Add "trite" to "boring," taunted her mind while she moved the trio of cutouts of the featured lighting fixtures around until she arrived at a pleasing arrangement, *and you get:* "Pizzaz!" she gloated in a burst of inspiration, for her practiced eyes knew that, with the proper emphasis, she could delete the sarcasm from that conclusion.

Mentally discarding the delicate line drawing she had initially conceived, Audrey capped and put away her Rapidograph pen and picked up a handful of felt markers with assorted nibs. Then she began a bold drawing of the featured chandelier: an elaborate, Mexican-style wrought-iron affair with glass chimneys. Working in strong, sure strokes, she did a large rendering that filled the 18" x 24" pad. When she was aesthetically satisfied with the starkly dramatic black and gray graphic, Audrey superimposed a sheet of layout paper on which she outlined the appropriate size in the lower left-hand corner, extended the diagonal, then experimented with various croppings, using a hairline rule and triangle to drop the vertical until she had achieved an alignment that created a recognizably abstract background design from a portion of her drawing.

After making a rough tracing, she took the layout to the "lucey," a compartment housing a lightbox over a projector, and reduced it to size. Returning to her drafting table, she measured out the exact placement of the crop marks and blue-penciled the horizontal notation: "reduce to 4-column width & screen to 30%," set that drawing aside and taped the reduced layout to the drafting table, placed another sheet of layout paper over it, and lightly penciled in the abstract background design. Working from the arrangement she had decided upon, Audrey blocked out the headline and copy blocks, sketched in the three fixtures, chose an appropriate typeface to complement the style of the drawing, and "spec"ed the type for the copy.

The mechanical tedium of designing an ad complete, Audrey carefully rendered the chandelier, one table lamp and one floor lamp to size, using the same bold style as the background with its exaggerated, deliberately artificial shading. "Not bad," she thought and gave herself a mental pat on the back as the drawing shaped up. Not a bad job, either, she concluded, her disposition improving with the ad.

Longworth Agency was a small operation, consisting of the owner, Barney Longworth; Jack Stevens, art director; and Nancy Miller, secretary and (what had in the past been referred to as, "gal Friday," but with the advent of the women's movement had been euphemistically elevated to) administrative assistant. The petty little jobs and discriminations prevailed under the two chauvinists, however, and those annoying "go fer" tasks that smacked of servility, still fell with irritating frequency and contempt to the two women, Audrey's title, graphic consultant, notwithstanding.

"What's in a name?" Audrey always snickered to herself when her title came up in conversation. "A boost in pay," she wryly conceded, having, quite accidentally, discovered the lucrative difference it made when she stopped calling herself a "free-lance artist." Her job had not changed one iota, but the semantic promotion had doubled her hourly rate, a peculiarity of the business world that never ceased to amaze and amuse her.

She was putting the finishing touches on the drawing when Jack approached the drafting table and leaned over her shoulder. He was a thin, balding man, his plain, undistinguished features pockmarked with the scars of adolescent acne, yet, from his swagger and deportment, it was apparent he fancied himself quite a catch.

"Not bad," he concurred, removing the final layout from Audrey's table. "I'll take it from here."

He returned in a few minutes with a stack of weekend grocery ads.

"These have to be pasted up for the four-thirty pickup," he informed Audrey as he dumped them on her table.

Disgruntled though she was, Audrey worked quickly and efficiently and had completed almost half of them when Barney came into the art room to discuss the upcoming solar campaign with Jack.

"That's just what that ad needed," Barney complimented Jack on the lighting display ad, and Audrey's temper flared when the loutish art director accepted full credit.

Nancy entered as Barney left, and with an apologetic smile, the attractive blonde placed three sheets of copy changes on the corner of Audrey's drafting table. To Audrey's complete dismay, the alterations were in those ads she had just completed, and one major change was going to necessitate an entirely new layout.

"It's almost three," said Jack, drumming impatiently on the corner of Audrey's table. "If you don't have that ready for the messenger, you're going to have to run them over to the newspapers yourself."

"Why don't they get these changes in sooner?" she complained, not doing a very good job of suppressing her irritability. "They know well enough when the deadline is."

"Your job is to get it done," he snapped, "not grouse about the clients." The nondescript little man glared at Audrey with undisguised dislike and resentment. "I won't have time to get to that lamp account, and I might try another arrangement, so redo those fixtures as individual drawings and have them on my desk by noon, tomorrow."

Audrey lined up the grocery copy, not trusting herself to look at him.

"I'll need the layout back," she said in her most professional voice.

"Just do the drawings," Jack responded testily. "I'll decide how I want to arrange them."

"What about the size?" she asked, knowing that the placement would affect that.

"I'll have them photocopied, not that that is your concern," he snidely cut her off.

It would be a needless expense to the client, and Audrey seethed as she watched him strut into Barney's office. What an insufferable boor! She was beginning to suspect that Jack was really quite incompetent and possessed of very little creative ability. What he lacked in talent, though, he more than made up in pure gall. If she had any sense, Audrey conceded, instead of resenting Jack, she should try to learn his art of self-promotion. Everything about him was so detestable, however, Audrey knew she would despise herself if she detected his influence rubbing off on her, in any way. Besides, she reminded herself, she had been hired to work for, not against Jack. She would just have to learn how to swallow her pride when necessary.

If she was no longer her own boss, Audrey had to admit that ego-gratification had not been particularly profitable, hence her presence here. Barney had had no objections to her continuing to free-lance, as long as it did not interfere or conflict with her work for him, and she looked forward to eventually augmenting her income from the agency. Perhaps, she was looking at this all wrong. If she found free-lancing assignments more interesting and challenging, she should probably consider the agency job her supplemental source of income.

Everything always came down to a matter of "perspective," her favorite art history professor had been fond of saying, and Audrey had only recently come to appreciate the validity of that observation. Certainly her divorce had attested to its veracity. Once she had recognized Alan's perception of life, she had been able to forget the bitterness, and she sincerely wished him the best. With any luck, the best would keep him well out of her life.

She collected the ads for the messenger at a quarter to four, but Jack appeared at her table with yet another page of corrections.

"I already did those," said Audrey, barely glancing at the sheet of copy he handed her.

"The signs for the canned goods were wrong," he pointed out. "Also, I spoke to the client and he agrees that we should use cents instead of dollars and decimals. Looks like more of a bargain that way."

"When did he decide to do that?" Audrey suspiciously asked, fully aware that the grocery ads were so regular they were prepared and approved days in advance.

"It just came to me, in a flash," Jack smirked. "Now, get those changes made and those ads out to the papers or you'll have to answer for them not getting printed."

Audrey stared forlornly at the stack of ads on her table and began to sort through them for the ones requiring renovations. "Naturally," she muttered to herself, the chain of stores that had opted for the changes ran ads in four different papers, and because of the size differences in each ad, it necessitated four separate pasteups.

Faced with no alternative, Audrey redid the dreadful ads that defied any infusion of life, their primary purpose to supply people with a basis for meal planning and budgeting. It was an immutable fact of life, as routine and essential as dishwashing, but Audrey kept it first and foremost in her mind. While her own quest for a comprehensive shopping guide had resulted in a subtle improvement in the ad format since she had begun handling the account, that did not have anything to do with artistic fulfillment by any stretch of the imagination.

Audrey cast a furtive glance at the clock, willing the uncooperative minute hand to remain at twenty-two minutes past the hour. Impervious to her emerald glare, the wretched wand obstinately crept in imperceptible increments to the numeral six, and that integer's very shape seemed doubled over in derisive laughter. With a punctuality destined to badger the harried woman, the messenger appeared at Audrey's elbow and annoyingly tapped his foot.

"Come on, lady," he complained, "I gotta lotta pickups to make before five."

"Here, take these and I'll bring over the rest." Audrey handed him the completed ads without looking up.

"You got those marked on the tickets, lady? I ain't gonna be responsible for stuff not gettin' there."

"Oh, never mind," snapped Audrey. "I'll take them all over."

"Suit yourself. You still gotta sign that I came by here so I don't get docked."

Audrey signed the clipboard he presented, thinking of several things in addition to docking she would like to see visited upon him—and Jack—then returned to the task of peeling off the erroneous information and carefully realigning the corrections.

It was five twenty-five when she finished, and all but one of the newspaper offices were clear across town. It figured. One small local paper was handled by a printer housed in the same building as the agency, but she called each of the others to tell them she was on her way. They reluctantly agreed to wait until she arrived, and Audrey knew it was not out of the kindness of their hearts, but due to the fact that the grocery ads constituted such a large portion of the newspapers' advertising budgets. None of them was especially gracious and in silence Audrey endured their snide comments about her efficiency, too tired to come up with a retort.

Ken Walker crept into her thoughts as she drove east to the babysitter's home, pushing aside some of her petulance. Or, more specifically, providing a new focus. She had known Ken all her life, yet, oddly, she could not picture him. Just a vague impression of brown hair and gangling arms and legs was all she could conjure. But then, she shrugged, he had been her brother's friend. His best friend, true, but Ken had never had any use for Audrey, and the feeling had been more than mutual.

It was six thirty when she pulled up in front of Mrs. Haskell's house to retrieve Bonnie. The babysitter was decidedly put out and the baby was cranky and weepy, her pudgy little face streaked with grimy tears.

"You said five," harrumphed the plump, disheveled woman, pushing a greasy strand of hair back behind her ear with the back of her hand. "I got my own family to tend to, y'know."

"I'm terribly sorry," Audrey apologized, scooping up her teary, soaking-wet sixteen-month-old. "They just made so many last-minute changes—" she started to explain as Mr. Haskell came into the room.

"Look, lady, five o'clock comes around, and them brats is s'posed to clear outa here," said the heavy-set man as he unbuttoned his filthy mechanic's shirt. "I don't wanta come home to a lotta squallin', smelly brats. After five, it's gonna cost you two-and-a-half times the hourly rate, startin' with a full hour. This here's a business, jest like yours, even if it ain't got no fancy title. My wife earns every penny."

"Yes, I'm sure," mumbled Audrey. She paid the woman, shifting the soggy toddler to her hip to open her purse.

"Next time, bring more diapers if she's gonna go through 'em, like that."

Audrey mumbled something that passed for an agreement. How was she supposed to know how many diapers Bonnie would go through on a given day? She placed the baby in her carseat and buckled her in, but she was so angry and tired she snapped at the child when Bonnie tried to wriggle out under the restraining bar.

"Sit there!" she ordered, plunking her upright and testing the slack on the belt. "I'm sorry," she quickly apologized as she planted a kiss on the little curly red head.

Poor kid. It wasn't her fault. Audrey drove home, bathed her daughter, and fed her. Later, after she had cleaned the kitchen, she went in to look at the beautiful, slumbering child. She would have to find another sitter... not that Mrs. Haskell was all that bad. She had three children of her own, and Audrey sympathized with anyone who could manage seven babies in various stages of mobility and still run a relatively neat home. Her husband was an impossible oaf, but Mrs. Haskell was good to Bonnie, for the most part. With a sudden pang, Audrey wondered whether she was rationalizing, and she worried about the care Bonnie was actually receiving. One never really knew. But, then, there were times when she was not that good to Bonnie. Tonight in the car was a good example. Everyone had bad days, she tried to console herself, but she was not fully reassured. Free-lancing had had all sorts of advantages, even if they were not monetary, she acknowledged with a rueful sigh.

Audrey started a bath and went through the day's accumulation of bills while she waited for the tub to fill. Money certainly wasn't everything, but when one didn't have any, it made a very convincing case for itself. She looked at the balance remaining on the bankcard bill. One more year, she calculated, then that would be paid off. She tried to remember what they had purchased, but it had been over a year since the divorce, and Audrey had not used the card since. No doubt it had been some expensive piece of photography equipment Alan could not live another day without. She wondered how he was financing his propensity for expensive toys now, but she did not really care. She didn't even care that he had categorically refused to send the $150 a month for Bonnie's support. Against the advice of family and friends, Audrey had refused to pursue the matter and, instead, had put into effect the legal barriers to Alan's interference in Bonnie's life. She was a beautiful, charming, intelligent child, and it had been his loss.

Perspective, she reflected. Her vision had cleared significantly once she accepted Alan for what he was... Peter Pan, a charming, lovable child, totally overwhelmed by the prospect of responsibility.

For three years, prior to their marriage, while Audrey was still in college, Alan had held a good job as a successful automobile salesman, although he had never finished his junior year at the university. But a series of costly mistakes and a dubious transaction for a buddy had put an end to that career. Fortunately, Audrey had quietly built up a decent reputation in her field that sustained them for three and a half of their four married years, while Alan searched. For what, Audrey ceased caring. He was a dreamer not a visionary. Something had drastically changed Alan that last year, and Audrey suspected it had been the arrival of Bonnie.

He could not tolerate her crying, the smell of the formula, the endless, noisome diapers, and her constant spitting up. He persisted in draping the infant like a rag doll over his forearm when she had finished eating, and no amount of explanation would deter him from carrying her in that fashion. The inevitable regurgitation he looked upon as a personal affront.

Alan had never wanted Bonnie, but he was not mean, just irresponsible. He left her unattended on the dressing table at three weeks of age to catch a replay of a football game, and she had rolled off onto the floor. True, he had been upset and worried, but also, to Audrey's disbelief, thoroughly annoyed.

"Even newborn kittens have more sense than to roll off high places," had been his asinine protest to Audrey's near-hysterical reaction as she examined the tiny infant from head to toe. He had stormed out of the house and returned much later that evening, sufficiently elated from an afternoon of drinking with his buddies to think Audrey would leave Bonnie in the house, alone, while they rejoined his friends. When she refused, he called an old girl friend and left to meet her. Three days later he had come home, bedraggled and unshaven, his clothes filthy and covered with makeup, announcing that he had quit his temporary job and was on his way to California. To Audrey's surprise, she had not been angry, but relieved, for she no longer cared what he did, so long as he did it somewhere else.

She had taken Bonnie to a friend's home and come back to help him pack. Her assistance was not needed. Maura, the girl with whom Alan had spent the previous days, was already in attendance, selecting those items she wished to take with them. Audrey kept her peace, finding the situation laughable, protesting only when Maura prepared to help herself to Audrey's china and cookware. To Maura's disappointment, Alan instructed her to leave "that junk," then both cheerfully waved to Audrey who stood in the doorway, suppressing a bitter laugh as they pulled away in the car on which she had made the down payment.

As she thought of the bright-red sports car, Audrey smiled sadly. Charm was a commodity Alan had ceased wasting on Audrey, but his credit had been worthless, and in a rare exhibit of that disarming talent, he had cajoled Audrey into signing for it. It was the last, meager gesture either had extended to the other, and it could not salvage the wreck that was their marriage. Besides the house payments, Audrey had been stuck with the charge accounts. She would be damned, however, if she would pay for that car, and it had been the only obligation she had insisted the lawyer force Alan to accept.

Audrey climbed into the tub and quickly skimmed the newspaper. There was an article about the Nava del Sol solar project and she read it with interest. She would have to go over that solar energy information her brother had sent her, too, she remembered, momentarily digressing from the article. The newspaper had quite a few complimentary things to say about the thirty-year-old chief architect and she reread the glowing adulation several times. Ken Walker? There was no picture, but there was no doubt he was the same Ken Walker she had known all her life. Tall, bossy, opinionated Ken. Her brother's best friend and her lifelong tormentor.

He had harassed Audrey continuously for making the honor roll every marking period of her academic life. "The little brownie," he had derisively dubbed her. Jealousy, that's all that was, she sniffed, tossing the paper across the tiled floor and plunging her hands into the water to rid them of the black ink smudges from the newsprint. His abominable grades had set an all-time record of consistent lows. The class clown, the zero, she had always considered him. But then, Alan had been the hero and look at how he had turned out.

The "hero" and the "zero," she grimaced as she pulled the plug and rolled her eyes heavenward. Someone up there had a very warped sense of humor.

Audrey dressed for bed and looked in on Bonnie one last time before she turned out the lights and checked the doors. Good ol' Ken. She climbed into bed and wondered sleepily how he would fare with Jack and Barney. That was an awfully big project. The biggest thing in the state. Why had Ken contacted the Longworth Agency? And in Tucson? Surely, Harkness and Walker could afford any of the more impressive agencies in Phoenix where their architectural firm and Nava del Sol were located? Jack would probably find some way to con her into doing the work for him, and at that thought, Audrey was suddenly wide awake.

"Oh, my God!" she gasped aloud, sitting bolt upright. "I can't handle anything that big!"

She lay back down. They wouldn't want her help. At least, Ken wouldn't, for Mr. Almendaro and the last project on which she had assisted Ken, to disastrous results, had come vividly to mind, though those high school days were so long ago.

Audrey's brain was a fertile field that lacked a gardener, Ken had once said, and her ability to carry on one conversation while thinking about something totally unrelated...a quirk that came to light whenever she absentmindedly verbalized one of these non sequiturs...had been a constant source of amusement to Mike and Ken. That Audrey could (and would) interject extraneous ideas without breaking stride evoked a grudging admiration from the two boys, although they seized upon every opportunity to take what was already out of context and hurl it into orbit in a futile effort to break her of the habit. It was their buffoonery, though, that disconcerted Audrey, not her meandering stream-of-consciousness with which she was quite comfortable. Therefore, the memory of "Almendaro" rankled Audrey, yet, conversely relieved her of anxiety. Whether Ken wanted her assistance or not did not matter. She was not disposed to give him any.

"So there, Ken Walker," she muttered as she fluffed her pillow, giving it an extra thump. "Why didn't you stay out in the Islands?" she wondered drowsily as she drifted off to sleep. Definitely warped were the fates.

The next morning Audrey deposited Bonnie at Mrs. Haskell's with a full box of disposable diapers, relieved to find the woman in a better frame of mind.

"Sorry about last night," Mrs. Haskell sheepishly smiled, giving Bonnie a big, welcoming hug. "My hot water heater went out yesterday, and Carl got home early, cranky as a wet cat, and well, it was just one of those days," she shrugged helplessly.

"I understand," smiled Audrey. She patted Bonnie on the back before she kissed her cheek. "And, he was right about the overtime. I should have thought of it myself."

"Oh, that's okay," Mrs. Haskell flushed in embarrassment. "'Course, we can always use the money, but I don't think it's a good idea to be late too often. Carl is very peculiar about things. And, it is his house," she defensively added.

"Of course. I'll really try, but with this job, it can be very difficult. They have their deadlines, too. Maybe,"

Audrey thought aloud, "I should try to make other arrangements. I honestly can't make any promises about my time."

"Now don't you worry." Mrs. Haskell patted Audrey's arm reassuringly. "We'll just make the best of it. I've grown very fond of this young 'un."

A smile of relief wreathed Audrey's face.

"Thank you," she warmly replied. "I can't tell you how much I appreciate that."

With a small wave, Audrey climbed back into her battered station wagon and arrived at the office ahead of Jack and Barney. While she worked on the chandelier drawing, Nancy made coffee.

"Whew! Just look at all that stuff!" exclaimed the secretary when she brought a cup to Audrey.

"What is all that?" Audrey absently pointed to the enormous stack of blueprints and folders that had sprouted overnight on Jack's desk.

"The information on that Nava del Sol project. It came in last night." Nancy opened a manila envelope. "Boy, this account ought to put us on the map."

"Us, the agency, or us, the state?" laughed Audrey.

"Both!"

Audrey wandered over and picked up the campaign outline.

"It's pretty impressive, all right," she agreed. "These houses are beautiful," Audrey added, glancing at the elevations and blueprints. She saw the initials "K.W." at the lower right-hand corner of each and shook her head in amazement.

"Wouldn't you just love to own one of those?" Nancy peered over Audrey's shoulder and sighed wistfully. "I wonder what it's like to be rich?"

"According to this," Audrey was reading the specifications, "these houses could not only revolutionize the housing industry, they will be surprisingly affordable."

"There's affordable, and there's affordable!" laughed Nancy. "Barney's been literally floating on air since he got that call from Harkness."

"He may look like a balloon," Audrey giggled wickedly, "but it is hard to imagine all that bulk floating through the air."

"Bumblebees do it," snickered Nancy, at which they dissolved into gales of disrespectful laughter that the familiar roar of Barney's huge, luxury gas guzzler immediately banished. "Get to work," Nancy warned as she raced back to her desk.

Barney came in with Jack, who must have arrived at the same time. The two men went immediately over the advertising outline Harkness and Walker had supplied.

"Did you see this, honey?" Barney tapped Audrey on the shoulder. "This is what every ad man dreams of. And it just fell into my lap!" He spread his arms in an expansive gesture. "The gods are merciful. Merciful!" he beamed, clasping his cowboy hat to his breast. "I guess word of ol' Barney's ability to deliver must be gettin' around," he chuckled. "Just look at all of this!"

He thumbed through the material, periodically moistening his spatulate fingers with a quick swipe at his tongue.

"Mmm! Ol' Barney's gonna make a bundle. A bundle! Come on, little lady, you can sit in with Jack an' me. This campaign is gonna be so big," he shook his head and spread his beefy hands again, "So-o-o-o big! We're gonna need any and all ideas."

He waddled into his office with Jack in quick pursuit.

"You heard the man." Jack ordered Audrey as he hustled past her drafting table, and to her surprise, she did not trip him.

Audrey entered the large office that was furnished with an excess of leather and mesquite and cow skulls. Barney was enthroned behind an enormous desk, its top surface a huge slab of redwood encased in acrylic; poised and suspended above his bald pate, as if in imminent coronation, was a pair of longhorns. "The Royal Order of the Bum Steer" was one of Audrey's more charitable descriptions of its silent pronouncement, and she always had difficulty concentrating on anything in this room, not the least of all, her ludicrous employer.

But, she reprimanded herself in an attempt to maintain her sobriety, Barney did know his business, and his hokey mannerisms did not interfere with his uncanny ability to present his clients to their most profitable, if corny, advantages. The world was indeed roomy enough for the Barneys who inhabited it. Certainly, they always managed to make room for themselves.

Jack was standing at Barney's side, bending over his shoulder to study the elevations.

"I think we ought to play up these fancy models and the fact that that ritzy Phoenix country club is nearby. You know, appeal to the wealthy, status-conscious sector. The doctors and the new money. The 'I want to be first with the best' crowd," Jack suggested.

Barney rubbed one of his chins while he studied the drawings. "Maybe, play up the fact that the senator's wife's family finds it high-classy enough?" he mused aloud.

"Yeah. Go for the snob approach."

"Excuse me," interjected Audrey, "but isn't the main thrust of this project supposed to be that solar energy is an accessible, readily attainable alternative for the average man?"

"Does that look like the sort of crackerbox the average man would expect?" Jack contemptuously sneered, holding up a drawing of an elegant structure nestled comfortably into its desert environment.

It was the one Audrey had been studying earlier, but she leaned forward slightly as though seeing it for the first time. She was not sure how Barney would take the knowledge that she had glimpsed this material before he had, but she could not allow him to go off on that ridiculous tack.

"From everything I've read," she slipped a sheet of paper from Barney's desk and scanned it quickly, "this isn't just any subdivision. It is one of the most creatively designed solar communities ever conceived. It incorporates active and passive solar energy systems to their maximum. Surely that would be the angle to stress." Her eyes had found the information she sought and she made a point of handing the sheet of paper back to Barney. "That," she indicated the elevation Jack was holding, "is one of the most moderately priced houses offered."

Barney glanced at the fact sheet and nodded in agreement.

"Excellent point, missy." He glanced at Jack. "I knew she was smart as well as beautiful the minute she walked in here. How come you know so much about this solar stuff?" he asked Audrey.

"My brother has always been interested in this. He works for the senator and personally handled the funding for the demonstration model and helped write the tax credit legislation for solar equipment," Audrey answered, none too modestly, as she did whenever discussing her brother.

Barney idly drummed his fingers on the blotter while he considered Audrey, then the sullen young man at his left, and a calculating twinkle glimmered in his beady little eyes.

"Tell you what," he mused, "there's a sizable bonus for whichever one of you comes up with the campaign Harkness and Walker go for. Let's get those creative juices flowing," he chortled. "Nancy," he bellowed, "make copies of all this written material and see that the little lady gets a copy. And hang up all these purty pictures in the art room for inspiration."

He thrust all the material at the diminutive blonde, overloading her arms, and when she maneuvered out the door, he turned to Jack and Audrey.

"Well? Get a move on, you two. Time is money, and it could be yours!"

Chapter Two

When Audrey sat down at her desk, Jack paused alongside.

"That's one of the cheapest shots I've ever seen," he hissed at her.

"What?" Audrey asked in all innocence.

"Come off it! If you think for one minute you're gonna pull off that 'my brother's got connections' angle, you're stupid as well as brassy," he snarled menacingly. His cold, blue eyes were narrow slits and his jaw was twitching in anger.

"I've never used anyone to further myself and I am not about to start now, so you can just retire your ugly little suspicions. If you come up with the successful campaign, you can have it with my blessings. But don't think I don't intend to work damned hard to get it!" Audrey retorted, her decision to ignore anything connected with Ken Walker negated in the time it took to transfer her indignation to Jack.

"You lousy women who just play at these jobs in between snaring some poor sucker make me sick. Some of us have to work our tails off to support families," he growled.

"Yes, *I* know," Audrey stated.

"Hey," he jeered, spreading his hands in an empty gesture, "just 'cause you couldn't hang onto your man, don't come cryin' to me. You probably took the poor slob for every cent he had. Now you're out prowlin' for another victim."

Audrey stood up to go to the drafting table and at

5'9", she was eye-level with Jack. She glared at the weasel-like wretch of a human being before her, and her temper slowly subsided. He was just a scared, insecure, obnoxious little man, struggling to survive in a high-pressure business he really was not that well-equipped to handle. With a sigh and almost imperceptible shake of her head, Audrey turned her attention to the day's work.

She handed Jack the drawings for the lighting account at eleven and quickly prepared the used-car ads for insertion in the weekend edition of the newspaper, working through her lunch hour. The day was over before she had a chance to put pencil to paper on the solar project, but she had studied the various plans and drawings throughout the day. When she left that night, she took the information Nancy had duplicated with her.

She stayed up until well after two in the morning reading the Congressional Research Service reports Mike had sent her, familiarizing herself with the theories and rationales behind the various solar energy systems, and it was only when she had hit upon a direction for the campaign that she went to bed. She awoke early, called Nancy, and met her in the parking lot, waiting close to twenty minutes. True to her word, Nancy kept a watch for Jack and warned Audrey when he arrived. She barely had time to remove her layouts and stow them behind the table before he entered the room, and she did not have another opportunity to work on the solar project, for Jack kept her busy all day with revisions and petty corrections on every ad she attempted to complete.

"Walker'll be in at ten Friday." Barney's booming voice disturbed the relative tranquillity of the art room when he poked his head in before leaving for the day. "I surely do hope you two will have something I can be right proud of to show him." He grinned amiably, but there was a hard, unamused cast to his eyes, and Audrey knew he expected an extraordinary effort from them—in fact, would settle for nothing less. "I want to see something from each of you, first thing in the morning."

Fortunately for Audrey, a sallow-faced young woman, hiding behind a mask of makeup that was caked in the roots of her stringy blond hair, arrived almost immediately after Barney's departure and planted herself on the edge of Jack's desk.

"C'mon, Jackie," she whined in a nasal tone, "you promised."

"All right," he grumbled, standing up to take her arm.

The phone rang as he put on his jacket.

"Yeah?" he snarled into the instrument. "So? How d'ya expect me to tell him over the phone, for cryin' out loud?" he complained. "When I get there," he growled, hanging up the phone with a bang.

"Li'l woman checkin' up on you, Jackie?" cooed the blonde as she slithered her arm around his waist.

"She knows better'n that," he gloated. "Got to find another doctor for my kid, though," he added, opening the door, and Audrey was surprised to detect a shred of concern in his voice.

"Can you believe that guy? Him? With a 'chickie' on the side?" asked an incredulous Nancy. "His wife is real nice, too. And the way he yells at her about his deaf son," she added in disgust. "Like it was her fault. What a worm!"

Audrey was not even mildly interested in Jack's personal life and she shrugged indifferently.

"Watch out for him," Nancy warned, helping Audrey pack up the hairline rule and T-square she would need to work at home. "He's had his slimy eye on you from the beginning, but he figures you're out of his class, which only makes him resent you that much more."

"He doesn't bother me," laughed Audrey.

"Wait 'til he sees what you've come up with," said an awestruck Nancy as she looked at the preliminary sketches Audrey had worked up that morning. "These ought to impress the hell out of Barney!"

Audrey had kept the format simple and direct, playing up the "pioneering" aspect of the concept that she sensed would appeal to southwesterners and newcomers to the state. She was anxious to get home to finalize the major drawing that would serve as the basis and identifying factor in the series of ads, brochures, and press releases that would comprise the total campaign.

"Just as long as they impress Mr. Walker," she said as she rolled up the papers and slipped them under her arm.

"Mr. Walker!" she repeated to herself, formally enunciating the syllables. It sounded strange to her ears. She had always thought of him as "good ol' Ken," or "Ken, the clown," or "Walker the Marauder." But "Mr. Walker?" Never!

If she lived to be one hundred, Audrey would never forget that high school incident with the statue. She and Mike and Ken had all been in the high school art room one afternoon, the two boys egging Audrey to "get a move on" so they could go out to lunch. While they waited for her to finish a poster, Ken sculpted a humongous clay orangutan. In a fit of evil spontaneity, the incorrigible boys had christened it "Almendaro" after an obese, oppressive Greek pedant of a chemistry teacher. In a moment of weakness (insanity?) brought on by the flattery of having two seniors include a lowly freshman in one of their preposterous pranks, Audrey had gleefully helped carry it through the halls, thoroughly enjoying the cheers and encouragement of their fellow students. When they arrived at the chemistry lab, the plan called for the three of them to present it to Mr. Almendaro with great fanfare. But as soon as Audrey stepped into the room bearing the insulting statue, Ken slammed the door shut behind her, locking the horrified thirteen-year-old in with the fearsome man whose volatile Mediterranean temper exploded.

Audrey Samuels, straight-A honor student, became the sole target of the teacher's self-righteous wrath, and she vowed all manner of revenge against the two delinquents who were doubled over in hilarity in plain view of the traumatized girl who pulled and beat on the heavy wooden door, her entreaties clearly evident to the howling youths on the other side of the window. Alan Mathieson, class president and basketball captain, had come to Audrey's aid, rescuing her from the vituperative, if well-deserved, tongue-lashing. With a guile born of a conceit the naive teenager could not begin to comprehend, her knight placated the blustering teacher. From that moment Audrey had become one of Alan's most ardent hero-worshippers, and nothing Ken or Mike said about him could dissuade or curb her adulation. Especially nothing Ken could say.

The fact that Ken had been right in his assessment of Alan as a self-centered egomaniac whose only concern was his own immediate gratification did not endear Ken to Audrey now, any more than it had then. Ken had always been an officious busybody, Audrey did not need to disturb too many cobwebs to remember. Unaccountably irritated, Audrey parked her ancient vehicle in front of Mrs. Haskell's home, amazed that, independent of her meandering thoughts, her arms and legs had guided the automobile to its proper destination.

There must really be such creatures as guardian angels, she mused a half hour later when she arrived at her own home, for once again Ken had intruded on her thoughts. That in itself surprised her, for he had always been her brother's friend, not hers. The incident with the chemistry teacher had been relatively innocent and extremely funny, she had finally conceded, although she had taken every opportunity to make her partners in crime suffer over the ensuing weeks, but she was not looking forward to seeing Ken again. Protective scar tissue had begun to form over the wounds from her miserable failure of a marriage, and she needed no reminders of the folly of her action.

"You're worrying over nothing," she scolded herself as she hoisted Bonnie out of the carseat. "It was none of Ken's business eight years ago. Why after all these years would he give it a thought or a comment now?"

"Because he's Ken," she answered herself.

No, Audrey concluded while she prepared Bonnie's dinner, she was not looking forward to seeing him. She fed the baby and bathed her, and only after she had cleaned the kitchen and read her daughter a bedtime story, did Audrey tackle the layouts.

"A bonus is a bonus," she muttered to herself in an attempt to rationalize her interest in the project, wondering at the same time why she felt compelled to justify her attitude.

She reread the cover information and knew that she could not in good conscience sit back and allow that dolt Jack, nor Barney with his heavy-handed approach, to ruin the opportunity to handle such a tremendous contract. Her trained eye studied the elevations, and the initials "K.W." stood out with undue prominence, considering their small size and modest placement.

She owed it to... "herself," she hastily interjected, growing excessively agitated that Ken, of all people, should be occupying so much of her thoughts.

Audrey worked most of the night, and the next morning her diligence paid off. Nancy had correctly surmised Barney's reaction. Sufficiently impressed with Audrey's ideas, he verbally promised her the bonus and the contract if it met with Walker's approval.

Friday morning Audrey cleared off her table and arranged the campaign proposals in what she deemed the most logical progression, placing her most spectacular layout on top and the mock-ups for the brochures to one side.

"Barney wants you to run down and get some of those walnut pastries he likes to go with the coffee," said Jack.

"Why can't Nancy go?"

"She's taking dictation." Jack glanced up at the clock. "Walker'll be here in ten minutes and Barney's expecting you to be in that meeting, Miss Hotshot," he sneered, "so, you'd better hurry."

There was a bakery across the street and Audrey reluctantly went out. She was annoyed to be used as an errand girl, but it would only take a few minutes, she consoled herself. She had forgotten, however, that Friday was "bargain day" and there was a long line at the bakery. Audrey watched the minute hand of the big old clock jerk ever closer to ten and eventually, ten past.

"Damn Barney and his sweet tooth," she muttered. With any luck Ken would be late. He was always late, she reminded herself in an effort to cheer her sagging spirits. He had made a career of being late in high school, had even boasted of his unbroken record for tardiness! No one could change that much.

At a quarter past Audrey entered the art room to find a tall, dark-haired man bending over Jack's drafting table. His back was partially turned and his suit exhibited a western influence in the cut and subtle topstitching of the lapels and two back seams that descended from the meticulously defined yoke, yet it was conservatively tailored and colored, the expensive, lightweight wool fabric neither brown nor gray, but the soft hue of the desert mourning dove. The open jacket was casually shoved back by a sun-bronzed hand in one angled pocket, revealing a pale blue shirt that was tucked neatly into a trim waistband as he stood, one leg flexed, the length of both long limbs exaggerated by the topstitching that traced the outer seams of his slacks.

The stance, the lock of hair that curled boyishly over his forehead, the pensive frown, the straight, patrician nose, the wide, slightly crooked mouth, Audrey knew well, yet she found the familiarity disturbing rather than reassuring, and she was seized by an inexplicable shyness.

"This is more like it," a deep, rich voice was saying with increasing enthusiasm.

He turned and looked up when Audrey approached. She had never thought Ken particularly good looking... had never given him a thought, actually... but this tall, darkly tanned man with the penetrating, almost black eyes was extremely attractive. Upon seeing her, though, his handsome face was immediately suffused with distaste and Audrey found herself unreasonably dismayed.

"I can't believe anyone with any training would attempt something so trite." He spat out his disgust with a precursory nod of his head toward Audrey's drafting table.

Crushed by that scathing denunciation of what she fully considered a respectable effort, Audrey numbly looked where he indicated and saw Jack's proposal on her table. Too stunned by the art director's incredible gall in substituting his worthless layouts for hers, and in the face of Ken's undeserved contempt, Audrey could not summon the words that would point out Jack's duplicity.

"Do you have any idea what we are trying to do at Nava del Sol?" he snarled.

"I have an excellent idea," snapped Audrey, finding her voice at last. "I've read all the newspaper articles and the CSR reports Mike sent me."

Ken raised his eyebrow in sarcastic dismissal.

"Still working for Brownie points I see." He glowered at Audrey and shook his head. "Unlike your brother, I see you haven't figured out yet that all those little 'A's' had nothing to do with real smarts. I expected at least a decent effort from a Samuels though." His eyes narrowed and his features settled into a dark, disdainful scowl. "But you are a Mathieson now, so I should have known what I would get." Without another glance he went into Barney's office.

"Brains don't necessarily run in families," Jack ventured as he touched up one of Audrey's sketches.

Audrey was livid and she snatched the mechanical pencil out of Jack's hand. "Don't you dare touch that," she warned him, her eyes flashing dangerously.

Before she could continue, Nancy anxiously instructed her to pick up the phone right away. While Audrey tried to decode the frantic call from Mrs. Haskell, Barney called them into his office.

"They're waiting for you," said Nancy when Audrey

hung up. "What's the matter?" she asked, concerned by Audrey's pale face.

"Bonnie's burning up with a fever," she answered. "I have to go get her."

"What about Walker? Barney will blow his stack!"

"It can't be helped," Audrey said with a shrug, although she did not relish the prospect of telling him.

Nancy raised her left hand, displaying her crossed fingers and flashed an encouraging smile when Audrey put her hand on the doorknob.

"Thanks," she mouthed and taking a deep breath, went in.

"It's about time you showed up, young lady," said Barney, the irritation exaggerating his florid complexion.

"I've warned her about personal calls," volunteered the obsequious art director.

"I...I have to leave," Audrey began. "It's an emergency."

Barney trained his hard, brittle eyes on Audrey and they bored through her with an almost inhuman intensity.

"Now, see here..." he harrumphed.

"It doesn't matter," Ken dismissed the interruption. "I don't have anything to discuss with her."

Audrey stared at him in total disbelief. He had not even given her an opportunity to defend herself, and she stood in the doorway with her mouth agape.

"You did say it was an emergency, didn't you?" He turned a look of complete boredom to her. "My time is valuable, even if yours is not," he said succinctly.

"Run along, gal," Barney waved her away. "But before you start making a habit of this, you'd better think about how important this job is to you. Nancy," he bellowed, "come in here and take notes."

Bonnie had been running a fever of 104° for the past two hours, and Audrey paced the floor with the child, waiting for the aspirins and the sponge bath to take effect. She had been home for twenty minutes. Why didn't the doctor call back?

The phone rang and Audrey pounced on it. It was Nancy.

"Get over here, right away. There's a pile of work that has to go out tomorrow morning, and Jack's looking for a goat."

"I can't," Audrey said as she rubbed the hot little back.

"If you don't, you won't have a job," Nancy warned before hanging up.

Audrey called the doctor's office again, but he was still out.

"Take her to the emergency room," suggested the nurse, so Audrey bundled up the child.

She stopped at her office on the way to the hospital and carried the listless little girl while she made a list of the ads that had to be handled immediately. Bonnie felt cooler, but she was still feverish, and Audrey made nearly illegible notes in her haste.

"You can't be a nursemaid and do your work at the same time," scowled Jack.

"I'm going to take this home with me," Audrey replied as she gathered up the copy, orders, and several layout pads and illustration boards.

"Get Nancy to give you a key so you can get in later in case you forget anything," he grudgingly offered, but it did not diminish Audrey's fury at the way he had falsified the proposals.

Bonnie began to cry and Barney came blustering out of his office to see what was going on.

"What's that kid doing here?" he demanded. Audrey bent down to pick up her purse and he spotted Jack's layouts on her table. "What's Jack's stuff doing all over your place?" frowned the large man.

Audrey bit her tongue to keep from answering Barney while she was still so livid. A display of temper would gain her nothing and convince these overbearing men that she was an emotional female incapable of maintaining a professional demeanor under pressure.

"I came by to pick up the work that had to go out without delay," was all she said, exercising phenomenal control.

Ken chose that moment to walk in, and Audrey's temper ignited. She did not trust herself to look at him, and to her complete frustration, it required an unusual effort. Her resolve to remain aloofly superior to the three chauvinists crumbled under an attack of righteous indignation.

"As for that," she spat out the word and pointed to Jack's layouts, "I can't swear to it, of course, but I could certainly come up with a good guess!" She turned her back to the lot of them and felt Ken's eyes on her. "Why don't you ask Jack?" she snapped, but that was as far as she would go toward drawing Ken a map of what had happened. If he was half as smart as he thought he was, he could figure it out for himself.

"Watch your mouth, little lady," warned Barney. His eyes darted from Audrey to Jack, but Bonnie's crying subsided into a pitiful moan and he was momentarily distracted. "What's the matter with the kid?" he asked.

"She's burning up!" cried Ken when he put his hand on the child's brow while Audrey stared at the table, not wanting to confront those perpetually disapproving eyes. "Are you crazy, dragging her around in that condition?"

"I'm on my way to the hospital," Audrey defensively retorted. "I only stopped by to pick up my work."

"You have a fine sense of the importance of things," he sneered in a cold voice dripping with scorn.

Audrey felt like some loathsome, subspecies of life under Ken's wrathful gaze, and she wanted to rip that smug, insolent sneer off his face. She snatched the office key from Nancy and awkwardly maneuvered the pads and folders under her arm. Only Nancy made any move to assist her to the door.

With an effort Audrey placed everything on the hood of her car and secured Bonnie in the carseat.

When she turned to retrieve the materials from the front of the station wagon, she discovered that Ken had already removed them and was carrying them around to the driver's side. He placed them in the back and held the door open for her.

"Get that child properly taken care of first," he ordered as he shut the door firmly.

How dare he? Audrey had raised Bonnie single-handedly, without any help from anyone. Who did this sanctimonious busybody, this "bachelor"—her brain shouted the word like an epithet—think he was? Too many caustic rejoinders came to mind for Audrey to sort out, and knowing she would sound like a blithering idiot if she did not take the time—time she could ill afford—to organize her rage, Audrey roared off, blinking back tears of anger and humiliation, her arm still warm from the gentle pressure of Ken's fingers when he guided her into the seat. But no amount of blinking would erase the sight of those piercing black eyes that continued to burn through her, searing her soul in their unrelenting wrath.

At the hospital, Bonnie was seen immediately by the pediatrician on duty, and he ordered numerous blood tests, the two for meningitis and encephalitis filling Audrey with dread. The tests and examination took well over three hours, during which time Bonnie's fever rapidly subsided. When the preliminary results were negative, mother and child were sent home with a list of instructions and guidelines to be strictly followed.

Audrey took Bonnie's temperature the minute she got home, and again an hour later. By then it had returned to an anxiety-relieving 99°, although Audrey continued to check the slumbering baby every fifteen minutes for the next two hours. Satisfied at last that Bonnie was resting peacefully, Audrey went through her mail, remaining by the crib while she read the letter from Elaine Mathieson, Alan's mother.

Despite the messiness of the divorce, Audrey maintained a regular contact with Elaine, and that kind, generous, although addled woman sorely missed her little granddaughter. In every missive she offered Audrey motherly advice on raising her and always closed with the fervent hope that Alan would come to his senses.

"Poor Elaine," sighed Audrey. She had such a tenuous hold on reality, and while there was no bitterness left, Audrey had no desire to patch things up with Alan. She reread the last paragraph. Elaine had inquired about the state of Bonnie's health, as usual, but she wanted to know specifically about her teeth. Apparently Alan had run abnormally high temperatures with the onset of his molars, and those fevers had mysteriously disappeared with the eruption of each tooth. Audrey patted the baby and felt her forehead. Bonnie was definitely much cooler, and come to think of it, her gums had been swollen and she had drooled excessively the past few days. Once the upper and lower front teeth had emerged, Audrey had refrained from probing around in the little mouth at the risk of losing her fingers. She would have to discuss this with the pediatrician. He got paid to have his fingers chomped.

When she mentioned it to him on the phone that afternoon, the learned man dismissed it as nonsense.

"That's an old wives' tale," he scoffed. "A little discomfort and a temperature of a degree or two, perhaps. But not 104°."

But he could offer no satisfactory explanation for the fever, as all the tests had proven conclusively negative. Audrey was so relieved to learn that Bonnie was not suffering from anything dire or contagious that she was willing to temporarily shelve her questions until she met with the physician.

"Watch her closely for the next day or so, and bring her in tomorrow afternoon," he instructed. "Just feed her lightly. And give her lots of fluids," he added before he hung up.

Bonnie slept through what was left of the afternoon and Audrey was able to complete the dull TV cards. They were the singularly most uninspiring aspect of the advertising business, for no creativity was warranted or desirable. The time-consuming cards required the tedious alignment of dry transfer lettering onto a colored board to spell out the phone number and address of the client featured in the commercial without frills or flourishes that would distract from the pertinent information. The only graphic consideration was that the contrast be strong enough to be legible in black and white as well as color.

After stacking the cards neatly, Audrey inserted a sheet of beeswax into a flat, wide machine, plugged it in, and turned it on so that it would be ready to coat the copy when it was time to do the final pasteup for the newspaper ads. While the waxer heated, she did the drawings for the furniture account.

She had angrily crumpled and flung aside her preliminary plans for Nava del Sol, and every minute spent on the routine accounts brought her closer to the boiling point.

"Damn it!" she cried in exasperation. "I won't even get the bonus!"

Bonnie awoke and demonstrated her improved health by bellowing for attention. Audrey answered the summons, changed the child, and prepared her dinner while she tried to formulate a way to get the credit due her.

"I'll have to go to Barney," she muttered, enraged to think she would have to beg for what she had earned. He knew Jack had stolen her idea, so he couldn't possibly give him the bonus. Still, the penny-pinching tightwad would probably use the confusion to weasel out of giving it to either of them.

"Damn it!" she repeated, seething anew at the way Ken had cavalierly dismissed her. Pompous, egotistical beast! He hadn't changed at all. "Not even worth discussing it with, am I?" she sputtered, slamming a pot onto the stove. "Well, I don't want your stupid account. I wouldn't work with, or for you, Ken Walker, if you were the only client in the world!"

There was a knock on the door.
"Damn it!" she shouted to herself.
In no mood to chat with one of her gabby neighbors, Audrey went out of the kitchen to the French doors in the dining room that also opened onto the front porch. The object of her anger stood there calmly.

Chapter Three

"What the devil are you doing here?" Audrey ungraciously asked, not daring to look into those piercing black eyes.

"Such language," Ken tutted with a teasing grin. "Is that any example to set for your child?"

Audrey turned back into the dining room and Ken followed.

"Thank you, don't mind if I do," he smiled, as he invited himself in. "Hi, baby," he said, bending down to Bonnie and rubbing the curly head. The little traitor rewarded him with a beaming smile and he sat down opposite her. "Feeling better?" he grinned at Bonnie, who burbled cheerfully.

Audrey came back with a bowl of mashed fruit and sat down next to Bonnie to feed her.

"I have a lot of work to do," she snapped, "so, state your business and go."

Ken sniffed the air.

"Something's burning."

"Oh, the waxer!" cried Audrey. She ran through her bedroom to the back porch, which had been converted to a studio, pulled the plug, and turned to confront Ken who had followed her.

"This is so terribly important?" he asked, pointing to the Color King TV ads.

"It is if I want to keep a roof over my head," she snapped.

"You almost burnt this one right off," he dryly commented, observing the pile of crumpled layouts next to the waxer. He absently started to shove them into the wastebasket when he noticed the receptacle's contents. Ken pulled out Audrey's sketches and smoothed them on the drafting table.

"I owe you an apology," he said quietly.

"Yes, you do." Audrey snatched the drawings from him and hurled them back into the trash basket.

Ken studied her, his penetrating gaze making her extremely uncomfortable. Or was it the fact that she was so painfully aware of his overpowering physical presence? Audrey had never noticed that Ken's shoulders were so broad.

"You don't want the account?"

"It's a little late, isn't it?" she snapped, glad to have something besides his masculinity to concentrate on. She would love to have two minutes alone and unrestrained with Jack.

"Not necessarily," Ken calmly stated.

"I don't need you or anyone else doing me any favors!" she retorted with an aloof toss of her thick golden-red hair.

Ken grabbed her arm as she flounced past him and spun her around.

"I don't have any reason to do you any favors, little Miss High and Mighty. It's this project I'm concerned about. If that work on your table represents Jack's finest efforts, I don't want him to have anything to do with this. I've worked too hard to have the whole thing destroyed by a bunch of incompetents. Now you and I will meet with Barney Monday morning, or I'll take my account elsewhere, but don't go flattering yourself that I'm doing you any favors!"

Ken's face was inches from Audrey's and she found herself focusing on his wide, sensitive mouth, overcome by the most absurd inclination to kiss him.

"Perish the thought," she snapped when he abruptly released her.

She resumed feeding Bonnie in the dining room and looked up in surprise when Ken deposited the wastebasket in front of her.

"You rummage through that thing," he commanded, taking the dish from her hand, "while I finish feeding the baby."

Incensed almost beyond endurance, Audrey had to severely curtail the urge to kick the wastebasket across the room.

"I can get copies of everything at the office tomorrow, when I drop off all that other work," she said between clenched teeth.

Ken consulted his watch without glancing at her.

"I can spare an hour. You made some glaring errors and we can correct some of them now," he said as he spooned the fruit into Bonnie's cherubic little face. "I have a deadline to meet."

Audrey felt fifteen again, to be dutifully following Ken's directives, but she knew he was right. There was no point in putting off the project. Six months was not that long, and it was going to be almost impossible to coordinate the entire campaign... especially to the extent his firm seemed willing to go. Each day's delay would lead to costly amendments.

Ken mopped up Bonnie's face, making a gentle pass over her tiny features that set up a giggling response in the little girl, then he carried her into the bedroom and put her into the crib while Audrey took the information back into the studio. The laughter died down when Ken settled Bonnie with her favorite toy, and soon he stood by the French doors that led from Audrey's bedroom to the studio, studying the ceiling in her room. He wandered over to the window and ran his hand along the sill, then went back into the hallway. When he returned, he again studied the point where the curved edge of the rough plaster walls became the ceiling.

"Looking for cobwebs?" Audrey asked, unable to contain her curiosity.

"No," he grinned, and Audrey noted how it lighted up his dark face, "but you've got quite a few."

She glanced quickly away from the glare of that dazzling white smile that threatened to reduce her to a mass of jangled nerves. Placing her heel against the horizontal support beam of her drafting table, she slid her stool in and did her best to concentrate on her task.

"This is an interesting house," said Ken. He came down the two steps into the studio. "Ribbon-grain mahogany everywhere." He tested the floor. "Oak?"

"Yes," she mumbled, wishing he would go stand somewhere else. The fresh, clean scent of his aftershave was making her woozy.

"How old is this house?"

"About sixty years, I think."

Ken strolled over to the long drafting table that occupied almost the entire length of the wall and stood behind Audrey. She could feel his lean, hard, muscular warmth and she was careful to maintain the two-to-three inches that separated them.

"That's not wide enough," he said, bending over her shoulder to indicate the overhang of the house she was sketching.

He did not touch her, but the meager distance that separated them was tangible, and Audrey had to force herself to look at the area he was pointing to. Ken moved away while she made the correction and picked up the information he had sent to the agency.

"What do you think of these?" he asked, holding up several elevations.

"They're beautiful."

Ken came back to stand beside her, as close as before. "You still haven't got that right." He handed her the kneaded eraser and picked up the mechanical pencil. "More like this."

His face was alongside hers, but his eyes were on the sketch. When he had finished, he turned his head slightly and his dark eyes filled her entire vision.

"You didn't think I was capable of anything like this, did you?" he asked, his eyes bright and teasing. "I was just a big zero, as far as you were concerned," he laughed, standing up. "Just shows to go," he chuckled, using her own mixed up cliché. He handed back the pencil and watched her closely, the teasing glow still in his eyes. "Think you've got it, now?"

Audrey began to rework the drawing, confident that Ken could read, and was indeed enjoying, her discomfort.

"How do they pay you at the agency?" he asked when she had made the corrections to his satisfaction.

"By the hour. Why?"

Ken checked his watch and marked one and a quarter hours on her calendar.

"Just want to make sure you get paid properly for your time," he said as he initialed the notation.

Audrey walked with him to the front door but he stood with his hands characteristically in his pockets, lingering at the door as though reluctant to leave.

"How's Mike?" he asked.

"Fine. He loves Washington. I thought you'd been in touch with him about this project."

"Some," Ken answered with an indifferent shrug. "Your mom still in Laredo?"

"Yes. You knew she remarried three years ago, didn't you?" He nodded. "How do your folks like Hawaii?"

"Love it."

The stilted conversation served to fill time while Ken surveyed Audrey from head to toe.

"You don't seem to be too much the worse for wear," was his assessment. "How's Alan?"

"Married, I think."

Ken raised his eyebrow and his dark eyes probed her soft green ones. "We tried to warn you," he said softly.

"You have to make your own mistakes," Audrey shrugged.

"You don't have to," Ken countered, the corners of his mouth turning up in a wry grin. "Some people just insist on doing so!" He opened the door. "Good night, Audrey."

Audrey remained in the doorway and waved to him, feeling a twinge of fondness for her brother's old friend. Ken had never been such a bad guy. Obstinate and opinionated and an incorrigible clown, true, but not such a bad guy. How come she had never noticed before how virile he was? He must have changed over the years.

The next morning at breakfast Audrey examined Bonnie's mouth. Sure enough, a large molar had appeared. No matter what the doctor said, her instincts told her Elaine had been right and she decided to cancel the doctor's appointment. Bonnie was in perfect spirits and Audrey prevailed upon elderly Mrs. Hudson, next door, to watch her for two hours while she went over to the agency.

On Monday, Bonnie was back with Mrs. Haskell and Audrey headed for a full day at the agency. Barney summoned Jack and Audrey into his office.

"Nice try," he winked at the art director. "Though, I wouldn't try that in the future," he warned, fixing his cold, beady, blue gaze on Jack. Any satisfaction Audrey received from that pat on the wrist was negated by Barney's next remark. "'Fraid you're no match for the little lady here. Seems she's wangled that project back from you without any intervention on my part." He grinned rather unpleasantly at Audrey. "Never underestimate the power of a determined female."

"It was my proposal that did it," Audrey quickly answered, resenting his insulting implication.

"Sure," sneered Jack. "That 'proposal' is the oldest game in town."

"Now, see here—"

"That's enough," Barney cut off the bickering. "I don't care what you had to do to get that contract, darlin', just see that you keep our customers happy. As for that bonus, I've decided to split that between you. Seems to me, Jack deserves something for initiative."

"And, if he had gotten the contract based on his proposal, would you have offered to split it with me?" she bitterly asked.

"No way, sweetie." Barney leaned forward menacingly. "You'd better not let this one success go to your head, missy. I don't want to see you gettin' pushy and greedy. You women have all sorts of little tricks at your disposal to—shall we say—improve your advantage.

We men have got to stick together. Jack here, after all, has a family to support."

"So do I," Audrey calmly reminded him.

"And whose fault is that?" Barney shook his head at the injustice of it all. "The world has gotten so full of pushy broads who want everything and think we men're goin' to just hand it to 'em."

"Is that all?" Audrey asked in as pleasant a tone as she could muster.

"You got that stuff ready for the printer?" asked Jack when she started for the door.

"Yes."

"Well, there's a pile of junk on your table that has to go out today."

"Oh, that reminds me." Audrey handed Barney a sheet of paper. "My hours for Friday."

"What's this?" he asked suspiciously. "I'm not paying you for your extracurricular activities."

"All that work from Friday went out on time," Audrey calmly stated.

"Well, how do I know you're not padding your time?"

"I guess you will just have to trust me. I haven't put down any more time that I would have spent here."

"Maybe," his bushy brows converged above his bulbous nose in a disgruntled scowl, "but I can't be too careful. Everyone's out for what he can get. The only one who looks out for ol' Barney is me!"

Audrey swallowed her response and went out to collect the supplies she would need for the day's work.

"Did you see this article about Walker?" asked Nancy, as she handed Audrey the society page of the newspaper. There was a picture of Ken and Janet Collins, the Channel 8 Weather Girl. "Don't they make a gorgeous couple?"

"Yes," agreed Audrey, experiencing a sharp pang in the pit of her stomach. She skimmed the article and the pang grew into a gnawing pain. "What nonsense!" she reprimanded herself. He was nothing to her. And she was nothing to him. This last was a surprisingly depressing thought to acknowledge.

She had little time to assign that clearly definable reaction to its proper insignificance, for Ken came in to take Barney and Audrey to lunch, and she was reminded of how very attractive he was. He, however, was unmistakably irritated to find her working on a series of supermarket ads. Before long Audrey was summoned, along with Jack, to Barney's office. The outcome of that meeting was that Audrey was to work exclusively on Nava del Sol until completion, much to Jack's ill-disguised annoyance.

"Sorry I couldn't make it this morning," Ken apologized to Audrey while he waited for her to collect her purse. "Barney did tell you I called about the assignment?"

"Yes."

Barney lumbered over to them and the conversation remained on the project. During lunch Ken gave Audrey a detailed itinerary, which included numerous excursions to Phoenix for meetings with state and federal officials, and to her delight, a week-long trip to Mazatlán for a major international solar energy convention. In addition, Tom Harkness, the senior partner in the architectural firm, was scheduled to attend a fundraising dinner for the Tucson Art Center that evening, and Ken conveyed Tom's message that he was looking forward to discussing the campaign direction with Audrey.

"It's rather formal," he discreetly mentioned to Audrey when Barney had returned to his office. "If you need an advance..."

"Really, Ken," Audrey barely contained the peevishness in her voice, "I do know how to dress."

"I only meant..." With a small shrug he dropped the topic and left with no more than a brief wave.

A car was sent to pick up Audrey at seven, and as she luxuriated in the silvery recesses of the sleek, black limousine, Audrey absently ran her hand over her jade-green skirt, ostensibly smoothing the fabric, secretly relishing the waxy coolness of the panne. Audrey had overridden her tendency to fiscal conservatism when she purchased her "investment," but she knew she would never have set foot in Cele Peterson's had she not made up her mind to treat herself to an extravagance.

There were any number of useful things she could have done with the bonus (which, until the end of the month, was not a reality): get that old clunker tuned, for one, nagged her conscience... but, the moment Audrey had tried on the striking, off-shoulder garment, she had known exactly how she would spend the well-earned money. Blatantly sexy, yet almost prim in its modesty, hinting suggestively at the feminine lusciousness it demurely concealed, the exquisitely fashioned dress enticed and tantalized while revealing nothing.

It had been the first time Audrey had ever used her credit card for a vanity purchase, but she did not doubt that she would pay it off, in full, on payday. "A sound business decision," she repeated to herself as she was chauffeured to the Tack Room, high in the Catalina Foothills. She harbored certain misgivings about this project, and if she was not totally convinced she had merited the huge contract solely on ability, she was not about to compound Ken's patronization by presenting a shabby appearance.

When she arrived at the banquet, Ken introduced her to Tom Harkness, and she relished the admiration those dark eyes could not conceal when they fell on her. Old friend of her brother or not, Ken was a man, and the appreciation was flattering... as was the attention from Tom, a distinguished gentleman in his late forties with an attractive dusting of silver at his temples. The charming man seemed genuinely entranced by Audrey, and he introduced her to a number of colleagues, all of whom expressed a desire to become clients of the "beautiful redhead," as Tom persisted in referring to her.

At dinner Ken was seated at Audrey's left and Tom, her right. Throughout, Audrey tried not to notice how devastatingly handsome Ken was in his white jacket, nor how extraordinarily perfect Janet Collins looked at his side. The ravishingly beautiful brunette with the wide, dark-blue eyes hung on Ken's every word, and while Ken devoted most of his attention to Janet, Audrey was keenly aware of him at all times. No matter how she adjusted her position, she always seemed to be mere inches from contact with him, although, again, he never actually touched her.

She bent forward to answer a question from Janet about the campaign and felt Ken's dark eyes on her as she looked across him to his companion. When she turned to Tom in answer to an inquiry from him, she was startled to detect a mischievous glimmer in his gray eyes and caught him glancing with amusement from Ken to her on more than one occasion. Surely she wasn't that transparent, Audrey thought in a panic!

"May I see you safely home?" Tom asked when the event drew to a close.

"I would be honored," Audrey smiled.

Tom was a gracious, considerate man with a sparkling wit, and Audrey had so thoroughly enjoyed his company, she welcomed his offer to escort her home.

"How long have you been divorced?" he inquired in a kind, interested manner when the limousine began its southerly descent to the city.

"A little over a year," she replied.

Tom nodded pensively. "I've been widowed three," he said. "I understand Mike Samuels is your brother," he changed the subject. "He's one of the finest men I've ever had the opportunity to meet in Washington."

"I would certainly have to agree."

"I am sure you would," he grinned. Tom patted her hand. "He and Ken go way back, don't they?"

"Forever!" laughed Audrey. Her smile turned quizzical under his steady scrutiny.

"I wondered why Ken had selected the Longworth Agency," he answered her puzzled expression with a twinkle. "I should have known there was a beautiful woman involved."

Audrey's obvious bewilderment increased and Tom laughed heartily.

"I really don't understand..."

"No, I am sure you don't," he chuckled. "You and your brother are very close?"

"Are you implying that my brother talked Ken into this?" Audrey tried to keep the irritation masked.

"I doubt that anyone had to do too much persuading." Tom took Audrey's hand and shook his head. "I, for one, am delighted with the selection. And with your proposal, I might add." He sat back and grinned mischievously at Audrey. "Janet Collins is quite spectacular, don't you think?"

"Yes," she said levelly. "They make a perfect couple."

"Indeed they do." Tom continued to study Audrey as she sat beside him, and she was beginning to feel decidedly uncomfortable. She did not want to think about Ken and Janet, much less talk about them. "Of course, there was that blond model in Phoenix," he went on, wearing that same expression of benign amusement. "She presented quite a striking contrast to his dark, good looks. An equally 'perfect' couple. That man does lead a varied social life," he laughed lightly.

Audrey grinned impishly at Tom and deftly steered the conversation away from Ken.

"I imagine you have more than your share of attractive feminine companionship."

"Why, of course, my dear," he said, gallantly kissing her hand. "Look at me right now!"

Audrey blushed becomingly at the compliment, but she was relaxed and comfortable. Although the distinguished man exuded an undercurrent of masculine attraction, the difference in their ages removed any sexual overtones, and Tom radiated a paternal security that Audrey found extremely, if platonically, appealing.

Tom admired her modest, Spanish-style house from an architectural standpoint when they pulled up in front of it.

"One of the early, classical examples of the Territorial influence," he noted. "Very charming." He walked her to the door. "You are scheduled to be in Phoenix next week?"

"Friday, for the groundbreaking I believe."

"Good." He kissed her forehead and returned to the car.

Tuesday morning Ken called the office and requested that Audrey have dinner with him to discuss some ideas Tom had suggested. Chiding herself for being so inexcusably excited over something so trivial, Audrey nevertheless frantically called every teenager in the neighborhood to find a babysitter when Mrs. Haskell was busy, all to no avail. She tried to reach Ken at his hotel, but he was not there. The number she was given turned out to be for Channel 8, but Ken could not be reached and Audrey was reluctant to leave a message. But then, she reasoned, he would probably prefer to dine with Janet, and she asked the receptionist to inform him that she would be unable to keep her commitment this evening.

Ken was waiting in front of Audrey's house when she pulled into the driveway, and her heart skipped a beat when he absently brushed that thick, glossy hair out of his brow. His movements were casual, yet deliberate, and incredibly sensual. While not handsome in the classic movie-star sense, Ken exuded a lean, rugged magnetism that stemmed from pure physical strength... a virility and power and wiry resistance demanded by the often harsh, primordial southwestern desert as a tenet for survival.

"What's this all about?" he asked, handing Audrey the phone message when she got out of the car.

"I couldn't get a sitter," she shrugged, valiantly preserving her calm exterior as she shifted Bonnie onto one hip.

"So?"

"I... well, I just thought... that is, if... you might prefer to go... to see..." Why did Ken always seem to be looking right through her?

"Did you think this was a date?" he coldly asked.

"Of course not!" she snapped, brushing past him to unlock the door. As soon as she opened it, she put Bonnie down, and when she turned to close the door, she found herself staring at Ken's chin.

"Of course not," he hissed through gritted teeth, tipping her face up with a brusque, yet surprisingly gentle, motion. His eyes were like two dark coals, burning with a deep, inner light, and as they glowed brighter, they grew until they obscured all else from her vision. His mouth crushed her lips as his hand clasped a handful of her hair and pressed against the back of her neck, pulling her head closer.

Audrey had not expected this. Nor was she prepared for the effect his yearning mouth was having on her as she put her arms around his neck and returned the embrace. Her lips parted and he kissed her hungrily, sliding his other hand around her waist. Very slowly, his hand traveled back up along her side and across to cup and caress her breasts. With a soft moan, Audrey swayed against him and he slid his arm around her back to hug her tightly.

She was overcome by a euphoric calm, an ecstatic longing underlaid with a peace and security she had never experienced, and she wanted it to last forever. Too quickly the kiss was ended and Ken placed his face beside her head while he gently massaged the back of her neck and breathed deeply. After several moments he pushed her away and held her at arm's length.

"It's been a long time, hasn't it?" he asked with a crooked, skeptical grin as he peered into her glassy eyes.

"Yes," she breathed, lowering her long lashes to protect herself from his penetrating gaze.

Ken shrugged and released her.

"Time's wasting," he sighed, checking his watch. "Get a notebook and I'll take you both out for hamburgers." He picked up Bonnie and settled her comfortably in the crook of his arm. "You like hamburgers?" he asked her.

"She can eat french fries," laughed Audrey, and I'll

take a few jars of her food with me. I'd better change her first, though," she said as she walked over to Ken and Bonnie. She took the baby from him, letting her fingers brush his arm, but he did not acknowledge her touch in any way. She went out of the room, grateful for the opportunity to compose herself.

On the way to the bedroom, she stopped to brush her hair and studied her reflection. Her normally green eyes were wide, almost black, and her lips were nearly red and still hungered for his kiss. Yes, it had been a long, long time.

Chapter Four

At the restaurant Ken took the notebook from Audrey, recorded the date and time at the top of the page, and initialed it. He handed it back to her and fed Bonnie while he went over the list of suggestions he had removed from his pocket. They included a timetable for publicity releases, the type of information to be released at each phase of the development, and the numbers of pages required for each of the series of pamphlets to be inserted in the packets for the delegates to the International Solar Conference.

"Have you got all that?" he asked.

"Yes."

"Can you have something mocked up by tomorrow?"

"No problem." Audrey looked up from her notes and could read nothing in those black depths.

Ken's manner was brusque and impersonal, and she found it hard to believe this was the same man who, only an hour earlier, had kissed her with such thinly veiled passion. Bonnie was the one who held his attention, and Ken doodled animals on the paper napkins while he made up stories to go with them. There was not a trace of condescension in his tone when he spoke to the toddler, and to a casual observer, they appeared to be engaged in conversation in an obscure foreign language, for Bonnie's babbling assumed the phrasing and inflection of intelligent discourse.

"I'd like to have something to show Tom when I go

up to Phoenix tomorrow," he said, adding a flourish to a benign wolf and not bothering to look up at Audrey.

"I'm sure I can have a sample ready. What time will you be leaving?"

"Four thirty. If there are no major revisions, Tom will expect a complete set of mock-ups for the brochures when he sees you in two weeks."

Ken's eyes finally rose and he studied Audrey for a long moment before his gaze wavered.

"If you work evenings or over the weekend, you will keep track of your time?"

"I know how to handle my business," she said, somewhat annoyed that Ken's sole interest was like that of a worried older brother.

"I know you need the money," he softly answered, his voice low and full of concern.

"I manage!"

"Don't get so defensive with me. I'm not the one who left you in this predicament. Alan's the one you should be ticked off at!" he snapped irritably.

The indifference Audrey felt she could deal with, but she definitely did not want Ken's pity. "Here," she handed him the open notebook, "you can initial the time."

"Are you going to work on it tonight?"

"Maybe. It depends on how tired I am."

That was not exactly what she meant, and when a smile appeared briefly at the corners of his mouth, she knew precisely what sarcastic remark Ken was thinking.

He laughed good-naturedly at Audrey's angry countenance and scooped up Bonnie for the short walk to his rental car, but Audrey made a point of carrying the baby when they reached the house. The child was getting entirely too chummy with her mother's lifelong nemesis, and Audrey's agitation increased with each minute she spent in the company of the maddeningly inscrutable man.

"What are you doing?" she asked after she had put

Bonnie to bed and discovered Ken seated before her television set.

"Are you going to work on those revisions now?" he asked, leaning forward to flip the stations.

"Why?"

"If you are, I'll watch television 'til you're through," he shrugged indifferently.

"Then what?"

"Then, I'll initial your time and go home." His dark eyes glinted. "What did you think?"

"I told you I know how to keep track of my hours!"

Infuriated, Audrey turned to leave the room. She had never gotten along with Ken.

"You forget, I know Barney. He'll charge me double for everything, then find some excuse to worm out of paying you what he owes you."

"What is that to you?"

Audrey could not believe she had asked that. She certainly did not want to know the answer to that question.

"If I have to pay through the nose for something, I like to make sure I'm getting what I pay for." He stopped flipping the dial when he reached Channel 8, and Audrey left the room before Janet came on to do her spiel.

She knew she had not wanted an answer to that question. But now, there was no way around it. Kiss or no, as far as Ken was concerned, she was an employee, nothing more, and she had better never forget it if she did not want to court disaster. As a boy, Ken had always taken a perverse delight in disconcerting Audrey. Now that he was a man, his methods, if not his motives, were all that had improved. The effect this newly discovered proficiency had on Audrey, however, was debilitating and complete.

Shoving everything out of her mind but the task at hand, Audrey worked for two hours until her eyes began to bother her. Confident she would have no trouble completing the work by four thirty the following afternoon, she turned out the lights and went back into the living room, dutifully toting the notebook which she held out to Ken. He initialed the time and turned off the set.

"We'll be doing some publicity work on Friday, and Channel 8 will have a crew up there. Have you made arrangements for Bonnie so you can be there?"

"During the day. I thought I'd drive up early and get back that evening, so I don't see any problem."

"You may have to spend the night. The senator is coming out on Saturday, and so is the governor."

"I know. I called Mike so he could include it on the senator's schedule."

"Well, what arrangements have you made?" he repeated icily, his voice laced with sarcasm. "You are going to be there for the actual groundbreaking?"

"Why should *I* be there?"

Ken scowled at Audrey's blank expression. "Because I'm telling you to be there."

"I'll take care of all the publicity preparations on Friday, so you won't need me."

"Truer words were never spoken," he muttered angrily. "When are you going to grow up, Audrey?"

"What are you talking about?" she practically shouted in frustration.

"You've never seen the area, you have no feel for the layout of the terrain. Not to mention the fact that there are going to be an awful lot of people who could be potential clients, Audrey. Are you going to spend the rest of your life slaving for some slob like Barney, waiting for projects like Nava del Sol to be dropped in your lap? Or are you going to start thinking and acting like a professional?"

"I can take care of myself!" she retorted, throwing her head back and sending her thick, shimmering hair behind her shoulder. She did not have to take this abuse from him.

"You've got a great track record," he sneered, making a sweeping gesture.

Now he had gone too far.

"You've got your nerve," she cried, raising her hand to strike his contemptible face.

Ken caught her wrist in midair and spun her around when she attempted to kick him, grabbing her waist to steady her.

"Grow up, Audrey," he sighed, letting himself out.

She had never liked Ken. Never. What had Mike seen in him? He was good for a laugh, that was all. And frankly she had never found him all that amusing. How dare he tell her what to do, how to act. She didn't need him or his advice. And she didn't need to go to Phoenix. He would have Channel 8 and Janet.

The thought of Janet brought tears to her eyes and she angrily brushed them away. It had simply been a long time, that was all there was to it. After nearly two years any man would look good to her. She thought of Barney and Jack. And Alan. Well, not any man, maybe. She laughed hollowly, and the laugh caught in her throat very much like a sob.

Morning brought a renewed optimism. At the very least the Nava del Sol project filled her workday with the opportunity to test those skills for which she had been trained, and Ken Walker notwithstanding, it was an exciting and challenging assignment. If only Audrey could find some way to separate herself from the complicated emotional involvement that was intertwined with her brother and his interests; her own predilection toward solar energy innovations; and—there was no way around it—Ken, the annoying pest she had known and endured all her life and this alluring stranger who had, with the obstinacy of his youth, imposed himself upon her life—the job would be perfect.

Diligent work and a restrictive time frame successfully precluded dwelling on those things about which Audrey did not care to speculate, and in the middle of a layout design, she absently reached out to silence the jangling phone.

"Hi, Sis," Mike cheerily greeted her. "I just found

out I am going to be in Phoenix with the senator on Saturday. Can you bring Bonnie up with you? It's been ages since I've seen you guys," he added in a pleading tone.

"I'd love to, Mike, but what would I do with her? I have to go up on Friday, and I wasn't planning to stay for the actual shooting."

"Why not? Everyone'd rather look at you than ugly ol' Ken," he laughed, and Audrey checked herself before she disputed her brother's assessment of Ken's looks. "Come up early on Friday and I'll babysit. I'm getting in at noon, and Kathy, in our Phoenix office, has volunteered to watch Bonnie on Saturday. So what do you say?"

"I don't know, Mike," Audrey hesitated. It was a tempting offer; she didn't get to see her brother that often. "Where will I stay? Hotels are so expensive during the winter season."

"You're on an expense account, dummy. Run up a tab on ol' Ken. We can even have an expensive dinner on him. How about it?"

The idea of taking advantage of her generous expense account had not occurred to her. Why not? Ken could well afford it. Still...

"Let me think about it, Mike."

"Okay. I'll call you tomorrow. Bye."

But Audrey had little time to think about anything but the sample she was preparing for Ken, and the wretched clock inexorably and inexhaustibly ticked on. Promptly at four thirty, Ken arrived to pick up the items Tom had requested.

"These are final drafts," he said in amazement as he stared at the mock-ups.

"No, just roughs."

"If these are roughs, I can't wait to see the finished editions."

"You don't have any choice," Audrey stated the obvious.

Barney came out to speak to Ken.

"Not bad for an amateur," he grinned in approbation. "Smartest move I ever made was hirin' that little gal." He winked at Ken. "'Course, everythin' ol' Barney does is first class. First class! You keep that in mind, boy, when you're talkin' to all your fancy friends about where to put their advertising dollars."

"You'll be in Phoenix, this weekend?" asked Ken.

"Yessir! We'll be stayin' at the Camelback Inn."

"We?" Ken raised his eyebrow.

"Me 'n' Jack, of course. Didn't mean to imply I was takin' the little woman," he hastened to explain.

"What about Audrey?"

"She's got that baby to take care of, so's I thought it'd be better for us men to go. Women don't understand all that technical stuff anyway." He winked and poked Ken in the ribs with his elbow, but the younger man was not amused.

"I thought I made it very clear about who was to handle this account."

Ken had not looked at Audrey once during this exchange, and while she appreciated his taking her side, she resented being ignored.

"I'll be there," she said, gazing steadily at Barney and noting the flicker of interest in his eyes and the quick, knowing glance he gave her.

"You got your reservations, honey?" he asked in a not particularly solicitous tone. "I thought they told me the Inn was pretty full, what with all the snowbirds this time of year."

"I'll make the necessary arrangements."

Audrey was not sure how, but she had no intention of staying at the expensive resort; in fact Barney's blatant disregard for his client's best interests shocked her. Perhaps Mike could make a suggestion. He was well acquainted with the Phoenix accommodations.

"She can have Jack's room," Ken announced, at which Barney's face contorted into an apologetic grimace.

"Why, of course, she can. Of course, she can. If she hasn't anyplace else to stay," he pointedly added. "I was just about to suggest that very thing."

"That isn't necessary," Audrey quietly declined the offer when Barney had departed. "I can stay downtown, near Mike."

"Mike is staying with me," Ken informed her.

"But," Audrey frowned in confusion, "he was going to take care of Bonnie for me."

"So? He still can."

"What's going on around here?" Audrey muttered, more to herself than to Ken.

"If you hadn't spent all those years as a little parrot, working so hard for all those damned 'A's,' maybe you'd have learned how to think by now."

"Nobody asked you!" she snapped.

"That's very true. Don't forget to put gas in the tank before you leave," he said as he turned to leave.

"How did I ever survive without you?" she sarcastically asked.

"Beats me." With that, he left.

Ken's unsolicited advice resounded in her ears when she pulled off at Picacho Peak and coasted into the service station on fumes. If Ken had not mentioned it, she seethed, she would never have forgotten!

She arrived at Sky Harbor Airport with Bonnie and spotted Mike out front, his bright red hair shining like a beacon.

"Hi, girls," he greeted them, kissing both. "Would you look at you," he laughed, tossing Bonnie into the air. "What a heartbreaker you're going to be," he teased the laughing child. "She's got my hair," he proudly informed Audrey as he climbed into the car, folding his long legs under the dashboard.

"You noticed? How's Susan?"

"Great. Furious with me for getting an extra chance to see you guys. She's taken up horseback riding with the boys. It's costing me an arm and a leg," he groaned, "but, they're having fun."

"I hope you brought pictures."

"Have you ever known me not to be the 'bore' of the party?"

"No." Audrey steered sharply to the right to avoid a van with out of state plates that pulled out in front of her. "Where to?" She eased out onto the main highway. "I have to be at Nava del Sol by two o'clock. Do you want to go out to Camelback and play the rich tourist or go to Ken's?" she casually asked.

"Ken's. He's got a pool and I can get cleaned up for dinner. I need to call Kathy to get directions to her place so we can drop off Bonnie tonight."

He turned his head and inspected his sister.

"You look good, Audrey," he concluded. "Ken's not giving you a rough time about this, is he? You two never got along."

"No, not at all." It wasn't the project that was responsible for her discomfort, nor Ken's criticism of her work. "Barney's being a pain, but he always is."

"Have you heard from Alan?" he asked after a long interval.

"No. I got a letter from his mom last week."

"She still hoping you two will get back together?"

Audrey glanced at her brother. The hostility in his voice was unmistakable.

"Yes," she answered truthfully. "But that's more for her sake and Bonnie's. She would hate to lose touch with her only grandchild. I could never do that to her," she quietly added.

"Don't let that keep you from making a new life, Sis. She's a little flaky, and even if she is Bonnie's grandmother, a lot of men might not be as tolerant of your ex's mother."

"Oh, there are so many men in my life I have to be worried about," Audrey laughed breezily.

"I honestly can't understand that. What are you doing, Audrey—wearing sackcloth and ashes? Walking around with a bag over your head?"

"I guess I just don't appeal," Audrey shrugged. "Right, here?" she pointed out the windshield, then made the turn when Mike nodded.

"Who are you kidding? Everywhere you go, guys are suffering whiplash from swinging around to see you. I saw at least six pitiful cases back at the airport!"

"Liar. Besides, you're prejudiced," she laughed.

"Not so. All my friends only hung around with me so they could be near you."

"Not all," she rebutted him, thinking of Ken.

"All!"

Audrey flashed a puzzled frown. "You're such a terrible fibber!" she teased. "No wonder you went into politics."

"Cheap shot," he grinned, punching her lightly in the arm. "Just for that, I won't tell you who had the worst case. Besides, it would make you even more impossible to live with," he chuckled. "You'd never believe me anyway."

He couldn't possibly mean Ken? Audrey stole a quick glance at him. No, of course, he didn't mean Ken. He must be referring to Todd. But, she had known about Todd, all along. Poor, shy, awkward, clumsy Todd. He had been such a dear. He was happily married and living in Monterey, and every year Audrey got a Christmas card from him.

She negotiated the heavy tourist traffic in downtown Scottsdale and turned into the entrance Mike indicated. Ken's residence was an elegant contemporary condominium in the Paradise Valley section, and the severe, modern structure was silhouetted in its angular whiteness against the miles of cloudless, azure, desert sky. Audrey declined Mike's invitation to come in, partly because she was running late, and partly because she did not want to enter Ken's home. She did not want to get that close to him or know that much about him.

She had to stop once for gas and directions, but Audrey turned onto the road to Nava del Sol at exactly two o'clock. Dotted with creosote bushes, cholla, and prickly pears, the 6000-acre parcel northeast of Scottsdale was nestled between the Salt River Indian Reservation and the Tonto National Forest. Ever jealous of guarding its treasures, the centuries-old desert stubbornly presented a formidable appearance to the human intruders. To easterners familiar with verdant pastures, babbling brooks, and meadow flowers, the first impression was of a barren wasteland impressive for its hostile ugliness. To those it did not discourage but who set down roots as deep and tenacious as the determined mesquite, enduring generation after generation, it was a land of awesome beauty.

True, the scrub grass with its wiry runners, the bane of all gardeners foolhardy enough to think they might civilize the barbarous terrain, was coarse when compared to the hybrid bluegrass that carpeted eastern lawns; and yes, there was nothing graceful about the scraggly, haphazard, stringy, black tangles that comprised the branches of the creosote and Russian thistle, best known in its dry, transient form as tumbleweed; and no, the silent monolithic giant saquaro that forested the thermal belt would never rival the spectacular sequoias of California. But to the wary observer, there was an immeasurable wealth to be found in the quiet, understated beauty.

Spring and fall were drab affairs when held up to the azalea riot that besieged the South and the blazing oak that heralded the bleakness of winter—an unwelcome visitor anywhere, which rarely tarried in the Southwest—but, with an unpredictability that scoffed at the scholars who tried in vain to assign a precise timetable to the cycles, dainty blue lupine sprouted from the miserable soil to blanket the sloping foothills; fragile, delicate flowers of vibrant pinks and reds perched precariously atop the most lethal of thorns; spires shot toward the heavens by spiny plants that had lain dormant for decades became columns of silky white ruffles; tongues of fire blazed from the tips of thorn-covered wands; golden yellow fronds decked the green branches of the palo verdes; and waxy white blooms adorned the leafless giants.

Audrey, who loved this land of rugged splendor and endless sky, momentarily neglected her driving to marvel at the pristine wonder that was rapidly being displaced by a shortsighted expediency that masqueraded as civilization. On this patch of virgin growth, the unpaved road was the only sign of human encroachment, and judging from the looks—"feel"—of it, Audrey groaned when the rear end of her long vehicle pounded into a shallow ravine. The bulldozer that had demarcated this scar had made only one indifferent pass, and that, with its blade up. Fortunately Audrey did not need to concern herself about any cosmetic damage her aged, discolored station wagon might suffer. What all this pitching and heaving on the battered springs was doing to the brittle, most likely rusted underside, however, was another worry. Every scrape of the metallic belly triggered a nervous glance in the rearview mirror, but so far, none of the vital organs appeared to have been dislodged.

On a rise she spotted several vehicles and, when she neared them, saw that the Channel 8 crew had already arrived. There was no sign of Janet in the entourage. Feeling nonsensically elated, Audrey parked next to a black-and-gray four-wheel drive automobile that bore the Harkness & Walker logo.

"Idiot!" she scolded herself. What would the Tucson Weather Girl be doing at the groundbreaking in Phoenix? Several possibilities and reasons came to mind, none of them reassuring, for she knew that whatever her job, if her fiancé were in charge of Nava del Sol, she would find an excuse to be here.

"Hello, Tom," she smiled at the distinguished architect as she walked over to him. "Will you be joining us for dinner? My brother just arrived from Washington, and I know he would love to see you again."

"Sorry, my dear. I have to fly out to California the minute this nonsense is over with, and I have a great deal to do."

"Nonsense? Now, is that any way to describe my backbreaking efforts?" grinned Audrey.

"Oh?" one gray-flecked eyebrow arched attractively. "Is all this your doing?"

"Not really." She spotted Ken and pointed to him. "He's responsible for securing the television crew."

"Ken or Janet?" laughed Tom with a wink that Ken acknowledged by a broad grin that cut deeply and savagely and, quite unreasonably, through Audrey.

Ken spoke briefly to Barney, who then ambled over to the camera crew and began issuing orders as he strutted about self-importantly.

"How do you endure that man?" murmured Tom.

"It's a job," Audrey shrugged. "Besides, you get me in the bargain," she laughed. In a spontaneous surge of commiseration, Audrey impulsively squeezed his arm and briefly rested her head against his shoulder.

"So I do." Tom patted Audrey's hand and his smile was kind, almost beatific... a gentle profession of affection by a trusted relative.

Ken directed the cameramen where to set up for the next day's shooting and after a few minutes motioned Tom and Audrey over. The technical questions ironed out, both men walked around the site with Audrey, pointing out where the townhouses would be, the community center, and the single-family homes, explaining the decisions behind each section and emphasizing how little of the desert they intended to disturb.

Audrey was fascinated, and since Barney had declined to join them, Tom and Ken were more garrulous than usual. She found it difficult to concentrate, however, for her attention was constantly drawn to the man at her side and she felt tongue-tied. She caught herself inanely muttering "I see" at any and every pause, but it was a habit that, once started, was hard to break. In addition, she had to pick her way carefully around the spiny vegetation, and when she stepped into a depression that threw her off balance, Ken slipped his arm around her waist. To Audrey's chagrin as much as her delight, he kept it there, loosening his hold until the pressure his arm exerted was barely perceptible, tightening it whenever she appeared likely to stumble as he guided her back to the waiting cars, and it was all Audrey could do not to dissolve completely into the warmth and security his arm provided.

"Can I catch a ride with you?" asked Ken. "I came up with Tom, but he's heading off in the opposite direction."

"What if I said no?" she asked, studying him with the same, practiced indifference she had used so often with Mike's friends. Only now it was totally feigned.

"I'd have to walk," he shrugged.

Audrey looked deeply into his dark eyes but could not detect any hidden spark of interest. It must have been one of Mike's other friends. Still, he had said all.

"Get in," was all she said, and Ken slid into the passenger side. She drove automatically, unaware of anything or anyone on the roads as she tried to jar her memory for any latent hint Ken might have given her over the years, but not one instance came to mind. Mike was her brother, after all, and his constant teasing aside, he was genuinely fond of her, so she concluded his perception of her attraction had been faulty, at best.

Ken intruded on Audrey's thoughts when she pulled up in front of his condominium. "Care to come in?"

Chapter Five

Audrey had always thought of Ken as an indifferent slob, a carefree youth totally ignorant of his domestic surroundings...as likely to sit on a book as read it. It was an erroneous impression of Mike and Ken she based on a dim recollection of adolescent arms and legs sprawled in awkward disarray by bodies too long and too charged with energy to be confined to the prim, fragile antiques favored by her mother. Left to his own devices, Ken had erected a lush, chocolate-brown environment that was as inviting as it was exciting...beckoning with soft textures, surprising with a solidity that bent and curved in an uncompromising concession to rigidity that deprived it of its aggression without sapping it of its strength.

The Camelback Mountains provided the backdrop for the earth tones of modern furniture highlighted by accessories of polished chrome and oak. A large landscape that was exquisite in its simplicity, two oils by Jimmie Abeita, a Navajo painter, and a small, delicately painted desert scene tied all the furnishings together through the use of color and form that was repeated in a Navajo rug hung over the bed and the intricately patterned woven bedspread.

In the midst of those objects of genuine value and artistic merit, there were numerous, unabashed glimpses of the man who inhabited these rooms: the slightly out-of-focus wedding photo of his parents, simply framed and tucked into a corner of the bookcase in the study, prominent in the modesty of its placement;

the bronze sculpture displayed by the stereo in the living room...a clumsy first effort by a high-school friend who had been killed before graduation in an automobile accident; and, to Audrey's complete amazement, a small pen-and-ink drawing she had done of Ken's hands for a class assignment, inconspicuously hung in the hallway. That flattering discovery aside, these touches of personal taste and preference lent warmth and humanity to all the angular, hard-edged sterility, and Audrey felt she knew and liked the Ken who had created this environment.

"Ready?" asked her brother, looking up at the two of them when they reentered the living room, the tour complete.

"Yes," Audrey answered, wishing her brother would not look as though he could read her mind. "Is Bonnie?"

"Sure." Mike held up the gaily clad child he had been dressing.

The little carrot-top sported a red-and-white polka-dot cotton pajama top, blue-flowered flannel bottoms, one pink and one blue sock, and yellow, fuzzy-bunny slippers.

"What have you done to her?" cried a horrified Audrey, taking the little gypsy from him. "Nothing matches!"

"I just put on whatever I came to first," he shrugged. "She helped with the socks."

"The blind leading the blind," she muttered, perching Bonnie on her knee while she rummaged through the disorganized suitcase.

"What's wrong?" laughed Mike. "She's only going to bed. Aren't those pajamas?"

"I can't take her out looking like...Oh, what's the use?" Audrey whipped off the slippers and put white socks on the tiny feet, then changed the pajama tops.

"Now, honestly," she demanded when she was through, "even you have to admit she looks better."

"I guess," grinned Mike. "I thought she looked fine

before." He took Bonnie from her and hugged the child.

"How could I have ended up with such a dodo for a brother!" Audrey muttered, closing the suitcase with a sharp click.

"Same way he got such a pigheaded mule for a sister," commented Ken, and he and Mike roared.

Audrey snatched Bonnie from her brother and picked up the suitcase.

"You two can stay here and entertain each other," she snapped. "Bonnie and I will go out for dinner."

"Now, Audrey," laughed Mike, taking the bag from her, "you'd just have to dress her all over again." He turned to Ken. "You coming? Dinner's going to be on you, so you might as well."

"Why not?" he shrugged. "I can drive you back here later. Where are you going?"

"I don't know," Audrey hesitated when Mike looked to her for an answer. "I guess, the Inn."

"Why don't I pick you up there, and I'll choose a place," said Ken. "Since it is my treat," he added with a mock-serious grin.

"Suit yourself," snapped Audrey, miffed that he was accompanying them solely because he had nothing better to do.

"What is the matter with you?" Mike asked when they were seated in her station wagon. "Why are you always so nasty to Ken?"

"I don't know," she sighed. "I honestly don't." But she was beginning to have her suspicions.

Mike didn't say anything more on the subject, although Audrey knew he was continuing to study her.

"I'm not a bug!" she retorted.

"What?"

"Everyone's always looking at me like I was under a microscope or something!"

"Now there's conceit for you," he laughed. "What makes you think you're that interesting?"

"Oh, shut up!"

"You missed your turn," he mildly informed her,

clutching the dashboard when she made an abrupt U-turn. "You really must try to do something about that lovely, gracious personality of yours."

"Shut up!" she repeated.

Not having reached the "terrible twos" and accustomed to babysitters, Bonnie reacted favorably to Kathy, her sitter, and immediately settled in with her three-year-old daughter. Fifteen minutes later Audrey passed the pillared gates of the Camelback Inn and followed the palm-lined drive to the imposing stuccoed structure. The buff-colored geniculated facade glowed pale cerise, its shadows a deep mauve, in the setting sun, and the starkness of its simplicity was softened by a harmonious integration of the soaring arches indigenous to the Spanish style that influenced so much of the regional architecture.

Mike accused Audrey of "soaking" Ken for expenses when he saw her lavish suite and, laughing at the hornet's nest of indignant wrath he had stirred up, hastily retreated to the Terrace Lounge to wait for Ken.

There was a knock at the door as Audrey finished dressing. Giving herself one last appraising glance, she opened it to a grinning Mike and Ken. Audrey wished that Ken would stop doing that. It was hard enough to maintain her equilibrium in his presence. That brilliant smile made it impossible.

"I told Ken you had taken the entire east wing of this place for yourself, and he had to see," said Mike, indicating the huge, plush sitting room with a broad gesture.

"God!" Ken rolled his eyes. "This must be costing me a fortune!"

"I didn't select this, Jack did," Audrey hastened to set him straight. "Or at least Barney."

"I can just imagine what he's got for himself," Ken grimaced. "The Presidential Suite!" He turned those black, mesmerizing eyes on Audrey. "You look like you belong though."

"Audrey always looks good," beamed Mike.

A playful twinkle glimmered in Ken's eyes. "Not always," he smiled. "Remember that time she got her hair all frizzed?"

The permanent! She had been thirteen and the result had been a disaster. Ken would remember that! Audrey glared at him and made an angry grab for her purse.

"Come to think of it though," Ken continued, watching Audrey with a great deal of amusement, "she didn't look half bad." His eyes were warm and teasing. "You'd have to do a lot worse to make that hair look bad," he said softly, and Audrey blushed becomingly under his affectionate gaze.

"Come on," he grinned, offering her his arm. "Let's go to a fast-food joint. That's about all I can afford!"

She slipped her hand through his arm and made a vain effort to ignore the firm, muscular warmth so evident within the light fabric of his light-blue suit and the seductive memory that sensation evoked.

"I'm overdressed," she laughed lightly to cover her inexplicable nervousness.

"We won't tell," laughed Mike, taking her other arm.

"You don't have to do this," Audrey protested when they were shown to a private room in an elaborately appointed French restaurant on the outskirts of Scottsdale.

"I know that," Ken amiably agreed. When he seated her she was disappointingly cognizant of the fact that he did not touch her.

"Try not to spill anything or use the wrong fork, Sis," admonished her brother.

"Would you know?" she laughed, happy that Mike was here. She could always depend on Mike.

"I am a suave easterner, I'll have you know, dear little sister. Not some western bumpkin, like some folks I could mention," he nodded toward Ken.

"Don't tell me Susan has finally discouraged you from tucking your napkin under your chin?" teased Ken.

Mike gave him a blank look. "You mean it doesn't belong there?" he deadpanned.

"Not unless you tie it behind your neck," snickered Ken.

"You two!" Audrey rolled her eyes. "You can dress you up, but you can't take you anywhere!"

Ken and Mike began to reminisce about their graduating class and Audrey finally had all she could stand.

"If you think I am going to sit here in this beautiful restaurant and listen to you two discuss 'Benny the Belcher' and 'Lardo Almendaro'..."

"You can go sit in the ladies' room, but you'll be awfully hungry," grinned Ken.

"Come on, Sis," laughed Mike. His bright blue eyes were trained on her face, "you know you are going to drop that stuffy facade any second now."

"That's just how she looked in Almendaro's lab," Ken mischievously provoked, and in spite of herself, Audrey began to laugh.

"I can't stand either of you," she gasped, wiping her eyes on the corner of her napkin when she had recovered to a degree.

"Here, Sis," Mike handed her a package of photographs, "you look at these, and Ken and I'll get back to 'old times.'"

"Later," said Ken, bending toward Audrey. "Let me see those. We've got all night to bore each other."

He and Audrey went through the pictures of Mike and Susan and their three boys, heads against each other, the way they had so many years ago. Except tonight the scant distance between them was charged with a powerful electricity and Audrey was petrified that she would disgrace herself by melting against Ken. Her eyes began to mist and when her hands started to tremble, Ken quietly took hold of the snap-shots. Mike glanced at her, once, but did not comment.

The arrival of the waitress gave Audrey an opportunity to return to the safety of her little space and she remained there for the rest of the meal. When they arose to leave, Audrey positioned herself on the outside, with Mike in the middle. They had sat three across in the front of Audrey's station wagon on the way over, but the magnetism that drew Audrey to Ken had been tempered by a fraternity that was no longer valid, and she sat stiffly, not daring to lean with the car at any turn. Mike insisted upon seeing her to her room while Ken backed his sports car out of her space, but Audrey firmly dissuaded him. She was in no mood to hear the lecture written all over his face.

Nor was she any more receptive the next morning. Mike had called from the lobby and offered to buy her breakfast, so she had no alternative. She had spent a restless night contemplating the two old friends idling away the hours, analyzing, scrutinizing, and no doubt laughing at, the dilemma they had with minimal effort maneuvered the naively transparent "kid" into once more.

Sparks of static electricity flashed from the red-gold hair, ignited by the brush Audrey energetically wielded.

"Well, I'm no kid anymore!" she fumed.

The hairbrush clattered onto the bathroom counter where it had been flung by the impatient hand that gave the broad bow of her ruffled white blouse a sharp yank. Audrey snatched her navy blazer from the bed and further irritated herself by indulging in the feminine conceit of glancing in the mirror. In retaliation she took little satisfaction in the approbation she registered when she glimpsed the tall, striking redhead in the efficient, tailored suit.

"Who cares?" she muttered to herself, closing the door with unnecessary force, but when she spotted Mike under the sea of orange umbrellas that shielded the white tables lining the turquoise pool from the glare of the morning sun, she was sorely disappointed to see he was alone.

"Where's Ken?" she asked, displaying as little interest as possible when the question popped out before she could prevent it.

"He went over to the construction site." Mike ordered another cup of coffee and waited for Audrey to speak.

"It was like old times for you two, wasn't it?" she

asked gaily, as though there were no other reason she might inquire as to Ken's whereabouts.

Mike gave her a lopsided grin. "Almost."

"Oh?" She buttered a muffin, sorry she had asked. She did not want any verification of what appeared different to Mike.

"Audrey," he gently began.

"There you are, little darlin'," Barney's booming voice rolled across the desert air. He pulled out a chair and joined them. "You get everything over to Harkness and Walker like they asked?"

"Yes," she replied. "Barney, this is my brother, Mike Samuels."

"Oh, the Washington connection," he chortled. He extended one large hand after wiping it off on his jacket. "That all you're havin'?" he asked, pointing to Audrey's half-eaten muffin and coffee. "You got to learn how to live. This is the big time. The big time!" he sighed contentedly, ordering a sizable breakfast. "After all, if you don't get your share, the gov'ment's just goin' to take it. Ain't that so, sonny?" He winked at Mike. "When's the senator due in, boy? It surely was nice of you to help out your little sis by gettin' him scheduled for this. 'Course, it'll be a mighty nice free plug for him."

"He doesn't need any 'free plugs,'" Mike said in a tightly controlled voice. "It was his legislation that made most of this possible."

"Now, now, that's all fine 'n' dandy, sonny, but just between you 'n' me, you know it can't hurt. Long as they spell his name right," he chuckled. He rubbed his meaty hands together. "Can't wait 'til we get to Mazatlán." He winked at Audrey again. "You gettin' your own room. For show?" he added with a leer. "No point in not takin' advantage," he grinned, enunciating each syllable, emphasizing the last one. "If you're not goin' to be needin' yours, darlin', maybe we could work us out a little deal?" he winked conspiratorially.

"Why wouldn't I be needing mine?" she asked, her voice dripping with acid.

Barney grinned lasciviously and his beady little eyes danced nastily as he looked her up and down. "Keepin' up the prim appearance for big brother? Fine with me. Fine with me!" he chortled. "'Course you know he knows how these things work, him bein' in Washington 'n' all, so you ain't foolin' no one. 'Cept maybe yourself," he added.

"It's time to go, Audrey." Mike rose and extended his hand to his sister. "The senator's waiting."

As soon as they were out of earshot, Mike hissed at her in total annoyance, "Why do you put up with that?"

"It's a job," she sighed with a shrug. "I don't pay any attention to him."

"You could have done a lot better than that!" he chided her.

"Could I?" Audrey walked quietly out to the parking lot. "Everyone wanted his bill paid and two of my best contracts dried up for lack of funding. While I was working on theirs, I lost two others I couldn't handle. I had to take what I could get." She unlocked the station wagon.

"Well, after Nava del Sol," he asserted, "you can write your own ticket."

Audrey thoughtfully considered her brother.

"Did you talk Ken into this?" she quietly asked.

"Not exactly." He looked away from her and made a point of fiddling with the tangled seatbelt he never wore. "I may have mentioned that you were working for Longworth," he warily admitted. "But if you hadn't been any good, he wouldn't have pursued it," he stated in defense of his interference. "This project means a lot to Ken."

"I suppose you know that he thought my ideas were no good?" She watched him closely.

"I know he was furious about the first proposals he saw." Mike grinned sheepishly. "He called to tell me what a mushbrain you had become and I told him there had to be some mistake."

"There was. Yours!" She glared at her brother. "Did

you send him over to talk to me that evening?" Her green eyes were bristling with fury, but she was satisfied with Mike's blank visage.

"What?"

"Forget it." Audrey started the engine.

"Ken's not so bad," Mike said after they had driven several miles in silence. "He just wants to help."

"I'm not a charity case," Audrey pouted.

"I didn't say you were. And Ken doesn't see it that way, either," he added, scrutinizing her for any change in expression. "His birthday is on the twelfth, Audrey. Why don't you try to be nice to him, for once in your life?"

"I am nice. If Ken doesn't think so, that's tough!" Audrey knew that was not an accurate declaration of her feelings, but it was none of Mike's business.

"What don't you like about Ken?"

"Everything," she lied convincingly and Mike heaved a resigned sigh.

To Audrey's dismay, Janet Collins was at the site when they arrived, but Audrey did her best to graciously introduce her to Mike.

"Weather Girl?" he asked, raising his eyebrow.

"What have I got to do with this project?" Janet laughed.

"Wait, don't tell me. You've got an inside track on the sun."

"What else? This project couldn't begin to succeed without my intervention. It's the least I can do for the biggest thing this state has ever seen!" she laughed brightly. "Actually, I'm here as a favor to Ken. He needed a media rep to negotiate with PG Productions, and since my meeting with the 'powers that be' over at the station was rescheduled, I decided to swing by to see how things were going. Too bad I missed Tom," she added with a sigh that went unnoticed by Audrey, whose ears had perked up at mention of the prestigious Phoenix advertising firm.

She knew PG was handling the television aspects of

the campaign, as well as the construction of the model and the compilation of all the government-required documents for the experimental project, but Audrey resented the fact that Ken had chosen Janet to be his negotiator. That her anger was irrational and unfounded... for Janet was the logical choice and Audrey, as an employee of the Longworth Agency, was not in a position to enter any of those discussions... did not make the situation any more palatable.

Janet smiled at Mike and nodded to his sister. "Audrey is doing a fabulous job, so Ken tells me." The compliment was accompanied by a tantalizing glow that sparkled from her lapis lazuli-colored eyes. "I believe you are supposed to be in that publicity shot," she said, pointing to where Ken and several gentlemen were standing. "You three go way back, I hear."

"To the dark ages," Audrey had the good grace not to say.

"I hope this gets you launched, Audrey," Janet added. "You have a lot of talent."

The stunning brunette flashed a brilliant smile full of warmth and sincerity, and Audrey hated her. She managed a dazzling smile of her own, though, and walked over to Ken.

So, Ken was just doing a favor for an old friend? She should feel honored, Audrey scolded herself. Instead she felt like a poor relation. Still, she scintillated and teased and made clever responses to the often-absurd questions she was asked. She knew the senator and governor on a first-name basis, through her brother, and she relished the slight edge it gave her over Janet. When it was all over, Janet strolled over to Ken's sleek, silver sports car and waited patiently while he bade farewell to Mike and Audrey.

"Give everyone a big hug and a kiss for me," he instructed Mike. "See you in Tucson on Tuesday," he waved to Audrey as he went back to his car. And Janet.

Audrey and Mike picked up Bonnie, and after more hugs and kisses and promises to get together more often, Audrey left Sky Harbor Airport and made the

135-mile trip back to Tucson in record time. She retired early, but all her dreams were filled with Ken, and the taste of his lips was as strong as if he had just kissed her.

On Sunday she made up her mind to actively pursue him. Sunday night, she saw Janet Collins on the evening news and gave up the whole idea as hopeless.

Chapter Six

Expecting the printer to call back with a quote for the brochures, Audrey called out to Nancy and answered the phone herself on Tuesday morning.

"Are you free to have dinner with me tonight?" Ken asked once the pleasantries were out of the way.

"I'm not sure." Audrey hesitated for a moment. "Should I try to get a sitter?"

"No." Her spirits sank. "Trying isn't good enough. Get one!"

"Is that an executive order?" she asked, not sure where this conversation was going.

"No," he said gently. "It's a request. Will it be a problem?"

"I don't think so," she replied, her pulse racing at the change in his tone.

"Good," and she could see the smile in his voice. "I'll pick you up at seven."

This time Audrey's efforts were rewarded, and she tried on at least eight different outfits before she was satisfied with her appearance. "This is ridiculous," she kept telling herself, not that she once listened.

The babysitter had already arrived by the time Ken got there. "What time will we be back?" Audrey asked Ken.

"About midnight I would imagine. Is that permissible on a school night?" he asked the chubby, yet pretty, sixteen-year-old.

"Fine with me," the teenager answered, blushing profusely and doing a very poor job of masking her infatuation when Ken flashed that disarming grin.

It was an appropriate reaction, Audrey concurred as she walked beside the tall, handsome man to the dark-green rental car he had parked out front.

"Where are we going?" she asked when he slid under the steering wheel.

"Rustler Dan's."

"Where is that?" Audrey frowned. "I've never heard of it. Is it new?"

"Nope," was all he would say and Audrey ceased asking questions that went unanswered.

He drove northeast and to Audrey's utter astonishment pulled into the Northside Airport, a small airport used by private planes.

"Trust me," was the only answer he would give to the startled woman as he led her to a red-and-white twin-engine plane. "All set, Gregg?" he greeted the lanky blond pilot.

Audrey climbed up into one of the seats behind the pilot's chair and turned in expectation for Ken and Gregg to enter. When they did not, she looked out the window and was horrified to see how thin a shell separated her from the outside. Gregg and Ken were examining the underside of the wings with a flashlight, but she could not hear what they were saying. Much to her alarm, each grabbed a brace under a wing and the flimsy apparatus began to roll away from the fence, guided by the two men. Minutes later, they bolted into the plane. Ken buckled his safety belt while Gregg started the engines and requested tower clearance.

"What were you doing down there?" Audrey asked Ken.

"Looking," he shrugged, testing the slack on her belt.

"For what?" When he did not reply, she repeated the question to Gregg as they became airborne.

"Loose bolts," said the pilot, flipping a succession of switches and exhibiting no emotion.

"What?"

"Loose bolts. Sometimes kids loosen them. They get

their kicks watching the wings fall off when you try to take off."

"What?" gasped Audrey. "You're joking!"

"Nope," he calmly insisted.

"What kind of fiends..." Audrey was pale and could not finish the question.

"All kinds loose in the world," he shrugged indifferently.

Audrey thought about Bonnie, alone with the sitter. Nothing to be gained by being maudlin, she blinked away the idea. It certainly didn't seem to affect either of the two men.

"Nice night," commented Ken. He leaned across Audrey to look out the window. So casually that she was not aware of his doing so, he slipped his arm around her shoulder and pointed out the areas they were crossing.

"Where are we going?" she asked again, feeling herself being drawn into the black, fathomless depths of his eyes.

"Phoenix." His lips brushed against hers when he said it.

Gregg asked him a question about the return flight and Ken leaned forward to consult with the pilot. He sat back while Gregg filed the flight plan with the Tucson and Phoenix airports.

"Worried?" grinned Ken, hugging Audrey to his side and kissing the top of her head.

"No," she whispered. Not anymore. It felt natural and comfortable to be with Ken and she patted the hand on her shoulder.

"Mike'd have my head if I scared you."

Audrey frowned. "Doing Mike a favor?" she asked with an archness she did not conceal well.

Ken shrugged and removed his arm, and Audrey stared silently out the window. Why couldn't Mike mind his own business?

"Sky Harbor Airport," Gregg broke the long silence. He received clearance for landing and made his approach.

"What's that?" asked Audrey. She pointed to the white and green lights to their left and slightly above them.

"Oh, hell!" gasped Gregg. "It's a jet!" He radioed the tower but they continued to give him clearance.

"But, it's on top of us!" hissed the pilot, pressing his face against the window.

"Negative. They're coming in on runway 3, but you're overshooting 4, and we can't clear you for another pass."

"Okay," muttered Gregg. "You're the boss." He headed the small plane into a nosedive. What appeared to be seconds later, they were safely on the ground, although their stomachs and hearts had not landed with them.

Gregg taxied to the private plane/commuter terminal and watched the jumbo jet lumber onto an adjacent runway shortly after.

"Boy, those things are big!" exclaimed the ashen pilot. "Next time, Ken, do me a favor and pick a restaurant in Scottsdale. Landing between those things gives me the willies!"

"I needed to hear that," groaned an equally pale Ken.

"It wasn't all that close," Gregg managed a tentative smile for Audrey as he helped her down from the cockpit, and she could not be certain whom he was trying to reassure.

"Sorry about that landing," he grinned sheepishly. "Rental car's over there," he pointed out the burgundy sedan to Ken. "If you still feel like eating."

Once they were seated in the car and a bit more relaxed, Ken drove out along a narrow road for several miles until they came to a large, barnlike structure.

"Best steaks in the state," he said, leading Audrey to a quiet corner table. He ordered a bottle of wine before they were seated. "By the second or third bottle, my insides may have caught up with me," he grimaced.

"I guess I shouldn't have mentioned that jet," giggled Audrey.

"No, you shouldn't have," he grinned. "Troublemaker."

Audrey reached out and impulsively patted his hand.

"Mike'd never forgive me if I frightened you," she grinned impishly.

"No, he wouldn't," Ken agreed, trying unsuccessfully to look stern. He squeezed her hand before she could remove it. His eyes glinted in the flickering light from the kerosene lantern on the table and he raised his eyebrow teasingly. "Doing Mike a favor?"

"No." Audrey put her hand in her lap and he raised his wineglass to her.

"To a more relaxing return flight," he winked.

"There was nothing wrong with the flight," she saucily disputed his allusion. "It was the elevator ride at the end that scared me."

The waitress placed a sizzling platter on a wooden board before each of them.

"Well?" he asked when she had tasted her steak.

"Good. But not as good as Pinnacle Peak's," she loyally defended the famous Tucson restaurant.

"I've still got my tie," he grimaced, referring to that establishment's infamous policy of cutting off patrons' ties and adding them to the collection that lined the open beams of the ceiling. "Not that I can stand the damned things," he added, giving the annoying garment a loosening tug. "Still think I'm a traitor for leaving Tucson?"

"No." Audrey smiled fondly. "But going to ASU? How could you?" She shook her head in dismay.

"Old rivalries die hard," he laughed.

"They don't die at all!"

"How true." An enigmatic smile flitted across his face and Audrey looked away from him.

His eyes were wide and playful and Audrey always had the dread suspicion Ken could see through her and read her mind. And what he saw did not necessarily please him. She had never been comfortable with him but had only recently come to the realization that she had always wanted desperately for him to like her, or at least approve of her. But, he never had. In retaliation, she had erected a protective barrier of indifference between them.

Relying on that familiar tool, Audrey steered the conversation to the project and she had little difficulty persuading Ken to discuss Nava del Sol throughout dinner.

He disclosed that he had selected the site ten years ago, while still in college. Extensive research had revealed, and subsequent interviews had confirmed, that the owner, Tom Harkness, was an architect whose philosophy was compatible with Ken's. Amused, but also intrigued by the idealistic student's grandiose plans for his land, Tom had consented to preserve the parcel for five years while Ken refined his ideas. During that time, solar technology improved, albeit at an excruciatingly slow pace, until a severe energy crisis prompted a flurry of activity that resulted in harebrained, at times outright-fraudulent schemes, that confused, obscured, and discouraged many sound, practical solutions. Hampered by the lethargy of government, financial institutions, and the industry itself, which resisted innovation less out of indifference than a clumsy bureaucracy that favored the status quo by default, valid breakthroughs surfaced to be skimmed from the morass of hyperbole and the unworkable by shrewd members of the public and private sectors. A needed boost occurred when the utilities and petroleum companies jumped on the bandwagon.

Through their correspondence, Mike and Ken knew that the very real demand that already existed for energy-efficient homes could be translated into a feasible program. Armed with his published theories, architectural plans and the pertinent funding data Mike had been eager to share, Ken laid out Nava del Sol to a delighted Tom who then prepared the proposals that took another four years to win congressional approval.

"These past two years, waiting to hear, making rush revisions, have been the most frustrating of my life," Ken confessed as he signaled for the check. "Tom is cautious by nature. He hasn't amassed a sizable fortune, not to mention reputation, by plunging into anything with his eyes shut. As it is, we are going to develop only 3200 acres first to see how the public reacts.''

The dim light in the room reflected off the silky blond curls that framed Audrey's face in a golden aureole and Ken's eyes wandered slowly over her finely chiseled features as he spoke, but when she raised the green eyes he looked quickly away from the disconcerting frankness in them.

"I would have come back sooner," he said softly, "but Tom wouldn't make any commitments until more of the details were final. I had a pretty good job in the Islands that allowed me to work on it," he added with a shrug.

"It worked out better this way, didn't it?" Audrey asked, a hint of confusion in her voice at the flicker in Ken's eyebrow when she offered that opinion. "What more could you ask?" she asked with a shake of her head that sent her shimmering hair bouncing jauntily behind her shoulder. "You're just thirty and a full partner in one of the most respected architectural firms in the state. The country," she amended that statement, "if this project is as successful as I am sure it will be."

Ken's lopsided grin put in an appearance that wryly punctuated the unintentional, implied gibe.

"Who would've figured?" he asked, holding out his hand to Audrey, mildly amused at her embarrassment.

"I didn't mean... I'm not surprised that you have succeeded," she quietly asserted when she slipped her hand into his. Ken's only response was a subtle tightening of his grasp as they walked to the parked car.

"It's early," he said, opening the passenger door for her. Very little light came from the lamp post outside the front entrance of the restaurant, but he did not miss the slight frown that creased her forehead. "Worried about Bonnie?"

"Not really. It's just that," Audrey tossed her hair

back over her shoulder, "I've never been this far away from her. The sitter would have no way of reaching me in an emergency."

Ken was bending toward her and his dark eyes traveled slowly along her hair where it spilled over her shoulder and down her back.

"Let's go," he sighed with a small, indulgent smile.

He pulled out onto the narrow pavement and stared quietly ahead for several minutes.

"I won't bite," he said softly, not looking at her.

"What?" Audrey turned to look at his strong profile and she felt nervous and silly as she tried to quiet the butterflies fluttering foolishly in her stomach.

Ken put his hand on the back of the seat and absently twisted a lock of her hair.

"I'm pretty good at one-handed driving," he said, and Audrey was surprised by the shyness in the grin he flashed her.

"Is that so?" she said, studying her hands.

"That's so." He waited a moment. "Want me to demonstrate?" As he spoke, his hand slid onto her right shoulder and he gently increased the pressure.

"Okay," she said very quietly.

"Okay?" he grumbled, but as she moved over he adjusted his arm to cradle her against his side.

"I'm not doing Mike a favor," he whispered, placing a soft kiss on her forehead.

"No?"

"Nope. I'm doing one for myself," he grinned, squeezing her tightly.

"You were saying something about the contour lines," she said, settling comfortably against him. She had never been anywhere that felt as safe and natural as in his arms.

"Are you a workaholic?" he laughed.

"No...I just..." Audrey could not explain why she wanted to keep the conversation on a safe, neutral level when she had an even stronger desire for this cozy arrangement to become more so.

"Never mind." Ken patted her arm. "I don't mind

mixing business with pleasure." His thumb stroked her upper arm and he kissed the top of her head. "It takes some getting used to," he said quietly.

"What does?" But she was not sure she wanted to get into that. "Dividing along contour lines?" she asked in an effort to keep the discussion on a less personal footing.

"That too," he sighed. He patted the top of her head. "Your penchant for earning your keep is going to come home to roost someday. Soon, I hope," he added.

"I make more sense than that," giggled Audrey.

"Not much," he teased.

"I don't get it," she informed him, making no move to adjust her position.

"You never do, Audrey," he laughed good-naturedly. "Comfy?"

"Very."

"Good. Pay attention. I certainly have no intention of going over any of this but once tonight. We are after maximum efficiency, not profit, per square inch," he began to explain the rationale behind the subdivision of Nava del Sol. "Not that we don't expect to make money on this," he added with a disarming grin. "Rather than imposing an arbitrary grid over the parcel, the homes will follow the natural slopes to make them part of their environment, not a clumsy adjunct to it. What we're trying to do, in effect, is design each house to fit each lot. The townhouses are the easiest because they are blocks of six to eight units, each. The individual homes were trickier because we have to allow for easy access without impinging upon privacy or function. And we didn't want any of the entrances facing a rear view, especially since to qualify for the federal grants, we have to strictly monitor the efficiency. All those meters are an eyesore, no matter how you try to disguise them. The collectors are not particularly attractive, either, so we've incorporated them into the natural lines of the homes. We wanted to preserve a semblance of familiarity with the designs."

He glanced at Audrey to see if she was getting bored, but her attention was rapt and complete.

"The average home buyer," he continued, "isn't ready for a 'Star Wars' environment, and frankly, there is no reason why he should have to sacrifice aesthetics for economics."

"I agree. I had a spat with a traffic engineer and a city councilman over that," laughed Audrey. "I asked why they had put up that hideous gunmetal tunnel of lights along Sixth Street, and they said it would have been prohibitive to make them more attractive. My answer to that spurious argument was that someone had to design them to be ugly. They didn't just magically appear."

"Bet that caused a donnybrook," laughed Ken.

"It livened up a dull party," Audrey replied as they pulled up next to the fence at the airport.

"You always were a troublemaker," Ken murmured, bending forward to place a gentle kiss on her smiling lips before he helped her out of the car.

When the plane was once more safely in the air, Ken put his arm around her again. The small, high-backed seats made it uncomfortable for her to curl up against him though, and eventually he settled for holding her hand.

The return flight was smooth and uneventful and they arrived at Audrey's house before eleven. Ken paid the babysitter before Audrey realized what he was doing and gently waved away her attempt to reimburse him.

"Do you need a ride?" he asked the teenager who flushed and declined, sorely tempted Audrey knew to have the handsome man see her home.

"She lives across the street," Audrey paused to inform him on her way to check on the sleeping baby.

"I'll watch until you get in," he offered, inducing a beaming smile.

"Would you like some coffee or anything?" Audrey asked, meeting Ken in the hall when she came out of Bonnie's room.

"Or anything," he said quietly, drawing Audrey into his arms.

With a gentle urgency his tongue separated her lips and began to probe and taste her soft, yielding mouth, whetting her appetite until Audrey hungrily responded. His hand supported her chin while his long fingers caressed her neck, his thumb extended, tracing the delicate skin covering her vocal chords, descending lower with each stroke until it reached her breastbone. His lips moved to her chin, then traveled slowly along her throat, following the line of his hand that inched lower, his thumb leading the way through the deep cleavage while his fingers spread to traverse the full, sloping curve that swelled to fill the cup of his palm. In slow, sensuous circles, his hand moved over her breast, uncovering only that much that could be caressed by his mouth and tongue, and the excited flesh strained against the annoying fabric that prevented full enjoyment.

In a display of abandonment that was alien to the normally shy woman, Audrey arched her hips, allowing the persistent hand that was fondling the firm curve of her derriere to press her closer, and the strength of his desire jarred her wanton, lust-dimmed senses. All doubts and questions had fled, all qualms as to propriety had vanished the instant Ken's mouth possessed hers, and when he held her in his strong, protective embrace, Audrey longed to remain forever in the haven of his arms. But she was afraid.

"Ken..."

She hesitated, lowering her eyes self-consciously. She had never engaged in casual sex, and although there was nothing casual about her feelings for Ken, she was troubled.

"I...I don't think..."

Tears welled up inexplicably in her eyes and began to roll slowly down her cheeks. She trusted Ken completely, with a confidence rooted in years of camaraderie, but she was no longer a silly schoolgirl, and Ken was no longer just her big brother's best friend. He was a warm, vital, sensual man with needs she longed to satisfy, and he had enkindled in Audrey a desire that threatened to consume her.

She buried her face in Ken's shoulder, not trusting herself to give him a rational explanation for her vacillating spirit. She did not understand it herself. She only knew that she had never wanted anyone to the extent she wanted Ken, and she could not reconcile the Ken she knew with this stranger.

"It's too soon," he sighed. He kissed her forehead and turned to leave.

"Will you be in the office tomorrow?" she asked, heartened that he held her hand as she walked him to the door.

"There's no need, is there? Everything is going as planned?"

"Yes."

"The less I have to see of Barney and Jack, the happier I'll be. I have a lot of other things that require my attention besides this advertising campaign," he grinned at Audrey. "That is what you are getting paid to do, which reminds me," he turned Audrey back toward the hall and gave her a little shove, "go get your notebook."

She returned shortly with it and was appalled when he wrote down the date and checked his watch before making the second entry.

"What's the going rate for a good night kiss?" she snapped, her face florid with wounded indignation.

Ken glared at her angry, hurt face while he held the book open. "One hour and forty-five minutes," he said tersely. "I believe that covers the time in the restaurant and the drive back to the airport?"

"Oh."

"Oh," he repeated. He frowned uncertainly, then bent to kiss her forehead. "Be a good girl. I'll be at Channel 8 all day tomorrow if you need me. But," he sternly added, "only in an emergency."

He held the door ajar after he had stepped through it, his reluctance to leave apparent.

"I'll send a car for you Thursday. We'll fly up for that meeting with Tom. No more elevator rides," he promised with a wide grin.

For a moment Audrey thought he was going to kiss her again, but he only patted her cheek lightly.

"Don't forget those brochures," he said in a strangely husky voice.

Chapter Seven

No, she would not forget the brochures.

Audrey shut the door, feeling vaguely disturbed, yet not exactly depressed. She listened to Ken's car drive off and locked the door. She would have preferred that he not mention Channel 8. There was always the possibility she would have to get in touch with him. Still...

The way he had touched and held her came vividly to mind. Surely it had not been casual for him? True, nothing had come of it, but that in itself was significant. Or was it? A cold fear gripped Audrey. What if, out of loneliness and desire, she were making more of Ken's involvement than was warranted? Was she so desperately in need of physical and emotional comfort she was willing to take things for granted? She had known Ken for years and he had never once deceived her. Angered and teased and deliberately confused her, but never deceived.

But that had been a century ago. Everything about him seemed new, and she realized with a wrenching pang that she did not really know him at all.

The society page of the newspaper was lying atop her desk the next morning, one item boldly circled in red.

Can that be orange blossoms we smell for our very own Channel 8 Weather Girl and a certain dashing, prominent Phoenix architect? Wedding plans do seem to be in the works, according to a reliable source. Watch this spot!

It couldn't be true. Not after last night. The article had obviously been written several days ago, Audrey tried to console herself. She did not like to think of herself in the role of stealing someone else's fiancé. And was she anyway? The nagging doubts gripped her anew when Jack pointed to the article.

"Kind of cramps your style, huh?" he smirked.

"What are you babbling about?" snapped Audrey, flinging the paper onto the pile of drawings and layouts. "It has nothing to do with me!"

"That's just the problem, isn't it," sneered the offensive man. The truth ripped through Audrey with a vengeance. He sauntered back to his desk where he made a very vulgar, insultingly personal remark that Audrey did her best to ignore.

Determined not to let Jack get to her nor to think about the article, she went through her mail and checked the answering service for messages.

"I have to go to the printer to proof the brown lines," she informed Nancy at eleven. "After that I'll be at the photographer's studio making the final selections of those slides. I should be back by four."

"Okay. I made the reservation for you at the Desert Oasis Thursday night. It won't be nearly as nice as the Inn," she shrugged, but Audrey had insisted.

"I know, but that was outrageous, considering the circumstances. Besides, it's only for two nights. How did you do with the Mazatlán reservations?"

"Barney insisted upon handling them," said Nancy. "Don't worry. Harkness made it very clear he wanted both of you at the Playa, so you haven't got any choice."

"Are you sure Bonnie will not be a problem for two nights?"

"Not a bit. Hal will be out of town until next weekend and I'm looking forward to the company."

Audrey stayed up late that night doing laundry, packing for herself and Bonnie, and thinking of the day just past and those ahead. The brown lines had looked sensational and she was sure Tom would be pleased. Three women were scheduled to be interviewed Sunday afternoon and Audrey was confident she would find a suitable sitter for the time she would be in Mazatlán.

The society blurb in the paper resurfaced as she was preparing for bed. Once more Audrey tried to disregard its importance. It could always be someone else, she tried with minimal success to reassure herself. No names had been mentioned after all. But she feared she was deluding herself. It did not seem likely that after all these years Ken could develop an interest in her. Not when he knew all her idiosyncrasies and foibles.

She clicked off the light.

"It is probably useless to even consider the possibility," she thought with a weary sigh.

When Audrey arrived with Gregg at the Northside Airport, Janet Collins was waiting with Ken, and the tall, exquisite brunette was lovelier than ever.

"Hi," Janet warmly greeted Audrey. "All set?"

"Yes," said Audrey, who was determined to be at least as charming as the weather girl.

The two women sat behind Gregg and Ken, who rode in the copilot's seat. To her amazement Audrey found Janet friendly and sincere, and she developed a grudging respect for the sharp-witted woman. It was only when Ken smiled or winked at Janet that Audrey found it difficult to contend. That, she knew, was neither Ken's nor Janet's fault.

Ken dropped her off at the Desert Oasis and continued on with Janet. He had given no indication that anything had ever transpired between himself and Audrey. Except for the way his eyes seemed to glow whenever he looked at Audrey, which had been often, it was as if the previous night had never occurred. And, Audrey knew she could not rely on the accuracy of her perception as far as the "glow" was concerned. His relationship to Janet had struck her as peculiarly reserved, in light of the passion she knew he was capable of exhibiting, but she had steadfastly refrained from inquiring where Janet was staying.

The limousine arrived at eight and Tom escorted Audrey to it. Ken and Janet were already comfortably ensconced in the commodious interior, and Audrey immediately registered the fact that his arm was draped casually on the back of the seat, his hand resting lightly on Janet's shoulder. They drove to a private club in northeast Phoenix where Tom made a great to-do about introducing Audrey to the members, lavishly praising her abilities and the progress of the campaign. There was a small orchestra and Tom led Audrey onto the dance floor. She saw Ken and Janet waltz by, Ken's head bent low to murmur into Janet's ear and, involuntarily, Audrey emitted a soft sigh.

"Lovely couple," said Tom, looking down at Audrey with a twinkle in his gray eyes. "I'll have to keep my eye on those two."

Audrey stared at Tom's shoulder and he drew her closer. "We're turning a few heads ourselves," he whispered.

But Audrey could not relax. Her tension caused her to misstep and she muttered an apology.

"How about a breath of fresh air?" Tom asked, slipping his arm through hers and guiding her out to the terrace.

"Well, you seem to be establishing quite a reputation for yourself, young lady," he said, turning her toward him. "Most of these fine people seem well acquainted with your work."

Audrey gazed out at the dark purple mounds of Squaw Peak, barely discernible in the deep, velvety-blue distance.

"May I ask you something?" she asked, turning after a long moment to look steadily into his eyes. "Why are you doing this?"

"Doing what?" Tom leaned casually against the railing that bordered the terrace and studied Audrey with a quizzical look of amusement.

"Am I someone's 'pet charity'?"

Tom laughed in good humor. "What makes you think that?"

"Why me? Why Longworth Advertising? We're strictly small potatoes. Was this part of some deal my brother worked out as part of your funding package?"

"You, my dear, have a very bloated opinion of your brother's influence!" he laughed pleasantly. "But, yes, I believe your name did come up when I spoke with Mike. You had already signed on with Longworth, so there was no way to approach you on this without going through Barney. A most distasteful proposition, I might add," he grimaced. "If you had not been any good, however, I can assure you we would not have chosen to work with you. It's standard procedure to consider a number of agencies prior to making such a momentous decision." He raised his eyebrow sardonically. "Surely you are aware of that?" Without expecting any reply, he went on, "Those things with which you are not experienced, the television work, for instance, we have another agency handling." He tipped Audrey's chin up and peered into her face. "So you see, I had no ulterior motives in this selection. With the possible exception that, having had to break into a competitive field myself not so very long ago, I am willing to give an assist to a talented newcomer."

"Like Ken?" she asked with a gentle smile.

"Exactly. That is how this creative business works, and don't you ever forget it." He grinned broadly and kissed the tip of Audrey's nose. "If I ever hear of your riding roughshod over another talent, I will personally skin you alive!"

"What's going on out here?" trilled Janet. "You two look awfully cozy."

"We are," laughed Audrey, hugging Tom's arm. "Tom has been explaining which end is up when who's on first."

"Please," groaned Ken. "How can you do that to the language?"

"She's in advertising," chuckled Tom, patting Audrey's hand before gently removing it. "She has no respect for the spoken word!" He walked over to Janet. "May I have this dance?"

"I thought you'd never ask," she smiled, taking his arm.

Ken shrugged and bent his elbow toward Audrey while he watched the tall, attractive couple walk back in.

"I don't know when I've had such a charming invitation," muttered Audrey, seriously flirting with the idea of refusing. It was only weakness on her part that made her acquiesce. She knew it might well be the only opportunity to feel his arms around her again and cursed her inability to ignore Ken.

"Audrey," he hissed into her ear when they were on the dance floor, "what is the matter with you?"

"I don't know what you are talking about!" she sniffed with an aloof lift of her head.

He pulled her closer with a jerk and bent his head alongside hers. "You've already got the account," he snapped. "Why do you feel compelled to butter up Tom?" He pinched her waist. "Janet is a very nice girl and you ought to try to be more like her, instead of such a brat!"

Audrey made a quick, angry wrench to get free but Ken had anticipated it.

"Don't make a scene," he warned, his eyes dark and foreboding. He held her tightly, but his anger and annoyance overshadowed the seductive warmth of his body, implanting a hardness to the embrace that gnawed at any pleasure she might have experienced.

"Since you prefer her company, why did you insist on dragging me along?" she asked in an infuriated whisper.

"I didn't, Tom did. You've got a job to do, remember?" He released her enough to allow her to move freely and he was still scowling, but there was a faint glimmer back in his eyes. "For someone with so much artistic ability, you are not very perceptive," he grinned.

His manner was suddenly soft and warm and enveloping, but Audrey was too annoyed to succumb.

"Private joke?" she retorted.

"Yes," he said, brushing his lips against her hair and subtly adjusting his hold to a tender caress.

"Am I the butt of it?" she asked, so distracted by the familiar teasing that always seemed designed to keep her in the dark she did not notice what he was doing.

"Aren't you always?" he laughed.

Audrey stalked over to the table and he strolled slowly after her. "Staying up late always made you irritable," he said, clucking disapprovingly at her.

Janet and Tom rejoined them then, both smiling radiantly, but Audrey did not notice—she was still scowling at Ken.

"Tom has been wondering what you think of his houses, Audrey," Janet asked. "Don't you like them?"

"They're spectacular! And from what little I understand of the technology, they are excellent. I was a little surprised to see so much Spanish-Territorial influence in the designs," she smiled, glancing at Ken, "considering who the main architect is."

"What do you mean?" asked a perplexed Ken.

"You always made fun of 'territorials.' " I can't think when you ever had a kind word for them," laughed Audrey.

"Only the fakes," he stated defensively. "The shoe boxes with the pasted-on arches. Those idiots see arches as so much gingerbread. They have no idea of the concepts, so I suppose it is useless to expect them to use them properly."

"My, my!" laughed Janet.

"Don't stop him now," teased Audrey. "He's just getting warmed up."

Ken grinned sheepishly. "Audrey has a knack for pushing the wrong buttons. But to get back to your original comment," he turned to Audrey, "the Spanish utilized the most efficient system of passive heating and cooling, working with the materials they had. The high ceilings, thick walls, and atriums all served a purpose: ventilation and heat circulation. The arches were actually a series of graduating sunscreens and light barriers. They were never just decorative. They were deep, to shield the windows from the desert glare. And the structures were never placed in nice, neat, self-defeating rows!"

"Did you know he was so opinionated?" Audrey sweetly asked Tom.

"Actually, yes. That's why I formed this partnership." He winked at Audrey.

"At least, I didn't mention Arcosanti," she responded to Ken with a mischievous grin, knowing how strongly he despised Paolo Soleri's supposedly progressive architectural experiment in the desert outside Phoenix. "A festering sore on the face of the earth" had been one of his more repeatable descriptions when he and Mike had driven her out to the site to complete a high school assignment on the philosopher-futurist's plans, and Ken glared at Audrey for daring to bring it up.

"What about Arcosanti?" asked Tom, greatly amused by the bantering between the two stubborn principals.

"Difference of opinion," Audrey twinkled coquettishly.

"An easy feat when one of us hasn't an intelligent opinion," Ken remarked, decidedly out of sorts.

"Which one?" teased Janet. She flashed a lovely smile at Ken, and Audrey suppressed the unreasonable urge to kick him.

Okay, Ken had asked for this. She was not the only one who could be made the butt of some stupid, private joke. Audrey turned to Tom and favored him with an ingenuous smile.

"Mr. Soleri has an unique approach," she began.

"Uniquely ridiculous!" interrupted Ken.

"He professes to have a great love for the desert," she continued, ignoring Ken, yet obviously baiting him.

"That's why he has plunked all those arbitrary, hideous shapes all over the landscape with no regard for the terrain or the environment," was Ken's scathing dismissal of that assumption. "Those pompous, spaced-out inhabitants of that eyesore, in their bloated self-esteem keep poking and prodding, heaping so much incompetence upon decadence they don't allow the desert the opportunity to scar over that blight with the far nobler greasewood or other hardy vegetation!" he seethed.

They glared at each other for a long moment, and Audrey conceded that the game had gone on long enough.

"Nava del Sol is a perfect blend of architecture and environment," she said quietly in an effort to be conciliatory.

"Maybe not perfect," Ken smilingly acknowledged the ceasefire, his tone proud, yet devoid of conceit.

"You are both to be commended," Audrey complimented Tom and Ken with great sincerity.

"I think," Tom arose and smiling broadly took Audrey's arm, "we should call it a night. While we are enjoying a momentary lapse of civility," he added with a wink as they went out to the waiting limo.

Audrey bade them all good night in the car and waved as they drove off. They were scheduled to tour the solar plant near Picacho in the morning, and she decided to go over some of the background information Mike had sent her so that she would not be woefully ignorant. They did not expect her to fully understand the complicated technology, but she felt she should have a working knowledge of the basics, if only to be certain she did not inadvertently contradict herself in one of the ads.

She realized there was so much to absorb when she began to tackle the stack of papers she had tossed into her suitcase, and it was well after midnight when she ceased poring over the data, her mind a jumble of kilowatts, megawatts, therms, heliostats, solar trajectories, and countless other jargon peculiar to the solar sciences and, at the moment, totally incomprehensible to her exhausted brain. Audrey took a shower, set her hair, and climbed into bed, no nearer to deciphering anything she had read. Clinging to the dim hope that seeing and hearing the actual processes in operation would instill a modicum of understanding, she turned out the lights.

Of what joke was she the butt, she wondered as she drifted off to sleep?

Audrey overslept the next morning, so she had to forgo breakfast. She had just finished dressing when the black-and-silver Bronco pulled up before her room. To her carefully concealed delight, Audrey saw that Janet was riding in front with Tom.

It was an hour-and-a-half drive to the Ocotillo Power Plant...an hour and a half next to Ken who kept up a running dialogue with Tom about the beginning of construction at Nava del Sol. He sat close to Audrey...so close she could well have interpreted it as a conscious act had he not been so thoroughly absorbed in the project to his complete ignorance of her existence.

The utility spokesman explained in great, lucid detail how the heliostats, mirrors mounted on axes which rotated to track the angle of the sun, reflected heat to the central tower, from which the heated liquid was directed to a turbine, thus using the energy of the sun to generate the steam required to power the turbines. The beauty of the system was that, in addition to the fuel savings, conversion from one source of energy to the other was simple and inexpensive.

The tour complete, they drove to Ken's condominium to pick up his car, then on to lunch in Old Scottsdale. When they were ready to depart, Tom and Ken lingered to confer while Janet and Audrey window-shopped along the main avenue of the renovated area of arty shops. They strolled back to the restaurant and Tom took Janet with him in the Bronco while Ken conducted Audrey to his car.

"Janet has to be in Tucson this afternoon, so she's flying back with Tom," Ken explained. "We've got the afternoon free. Any ideas?" he asked, sliding into the driver's seat.

"I see. When there's nothing to do and there are no

better offers, gosh, let's entertain little Audrey," she pouted.

Ken grabbed her shoulders and gave her an abrupt shake. "Come off it, Audrey!" he snapped. "Grow up!" He shoved her away in disgust. "Oh, sit there and sulk. I don't know why I bother. As for 'seeing,' I doubt that you will ever 'see' anything!"

He started the engine, threw it into reverse, then sped out onto the road. They stopped at a light and Audrey looked up penitently.

"I'm sorry, Ken." She sat back and sighed, resolved to accept the inevitable. "You're right, I am being very childish. It's time I grew up. Truce?"

"Truce," he grinned, wrapping a lock of her hair around his index finger and giving it a gentle, playful tug. "Where to?"

"Arcosanti," she wickedly suggested.

"Just for that, you are going on a hike!"

"I don't have the proper shoes," Audrey protested.

"Serves you right!"

He drove southeast to the Superstition Mountains and parked at the base of one of the ridges.

"Be nice," he warned, "or I'll leave you out here to wander around with the ghost of the 'Lost Dutchman'!"

Audrey obstinately refused to take his hand and trudged along behind him for a distance of about three miles.

"Come on," he called to her when he realized she had stopped and perched on a large boulder. She refused to budge.

"It hasn't been that far," he rebutted her complaint. "What a cream puff you've become in your old age." Audrey screwed up her face in annoyance and he grinned as he sat down. "Still as charming as ever."

He glanced at his watch. "I have an interview at seven."

"Good for you!"

Audrey did not want him sitting so close to her. She had unwillingly come to like Janet and was not in the habit of pursuing men who had been spoken for. She was not in the habit of pursuing men. Why did Ken always have to make everything so difficult?

"Tired?" he asked, leaning toward her.

"No," she said decisively, standing up.

Ken grabbed her arm and pulled her back down. "You're a terrible liar," he said, putting his hand on the back of her head and pulling her to him.

Audrey found him impossible to resist and her longing for him was too great to conceal. She kissed him eagerly and he moved closer, pressing his lean, strong body against hers.

"No, Ken," she softly pleaded and he buried his face in her hair as he clasped her to him.

"What's the matter?" he asked, gently stroking her face which she succeeded in keeping averted.

She tried to blink back the tears but they escaped and rolled down her cheeks.

"Audrey..." He kissed her tear-streaked cheek and made vain attempts to raise her face. With a sigh of defeat, he hugged her tightly. "What's wrong, Audrey?" he whispered, but she could not answer him.

She was convinced it was only kindness on his part. Ken was a better friend than she had realized. All along he had been trying to boost her self-respect and confidence, and he had sensed how badly she needed him. It was not his fault that she was not in better control of her emotions.

Eventually she pulled away and wiped her face with the back of her hand. They walked silently back to the car and Audrey stared forlornly out of the window until she gradually regained her composure. By the time they reached the television station where Ken's interview with the Maricopa County Chairman was to be taped for later release, Audrey was in a much improved state of mind.

She sat in the monitoring room and watched the filming. Later, over dinner at a small, Mexican restaurant, she and Ken joked about the shallowness of the questions.

"It infuriates me when the reporters don't do their homework!" said Ken.

"You? Upset about someone not doing his homework?" Audrey stared at him, eyes wide in exaggerated amazement. "My, my, how time does change things!"

"Two points," he laughed, raising his glass to her.

"My favor?"

"I've lost track over the years." He gazed steadily at Audrey. "Seems to me," he said softly, "it was always in your favor."

Audrey made a face and laughed self-consciously. "Was I always such a terrible little 'Brownie'?"

"Yes."

She looked at his face and was vaguely disturbed. Ken's expression was affectionate and amused, but there was something else, and she did not trust the accuracy of her discernment.

He drove her back to her motel, attempting, unsuccessfully, to draw Audrey out of her pensive shell.

"You don't have to economize," he scowled, inspecting the pleasant but uninspired courtyard of the Desert Oasis complex.

"I know. But, frankly, I'd rather stick you with the cost of all that blank embossing than a huge hotel bill," she referred to the expensive process of making an inkless impression in heavy stock that she had chosen for the covers of the information packets.

"Good point. Tom loved the sample you made up. You're very good," he added.

"You sound surprised," Audrey retorted with a toss of her head.

"No."

He stood awkwardly outside her door, hands in his pockets, rocking on his heels. "I take it you're not going to invite me in?" he asked with more than a trace of hopefulness in his voice that he might be wrong.

"Considering... everything, I don't think that would be a very good idea," she said softly.

"Considering what?" he asked, bending toward her.

Janet, she could not bring herself to say aloud. It required every ounce of her willpower to resist. All she had to do was open the door, she had already opened her heart. Audrey gave a soft, shuddering sigh. Where had that gotten her?

Ken's face broke into a broad grin and he hugged her tightly. "You are such a stuffy, dense creature," he chuckled, and Audrey automatically snuggled closer. She immediately resumed a proper distance with a shrug of her shoulders, and Ken kissed her lightly, bending forward to brush his lips against her set mouth.

"What am I going to do with you?" he laughed softly. "Be ready at nine, and we'll have breakfast together, okay?" The back of his fingers glanced her cheek when he raised his hand in a brief wave, and still sporting that affectionate half-smile, Ken folded his long frame into the low sports car.

But the next morning Ken was forced to renege on his offer, for something had come up at the site that required his immediate attention.

"I won't be going back to Tucson with you after all," he apologized.

"Oh." Audrey tried to keep the disappointment out of her voice, and there was a slight pause before Ken spoke again.

"I'll be tied up here for three weeks. I don't want to leave any loose ends when I go to Mazatlán, and there is so much that needs to be done to prepare for that convention," he groaned.

"Anything I can do to help?" Audrey volunteered.

"You have more than enough to keep you busy," he laughed. "But thanks for the offer. Audrey..."

"Yes?" She heard him give a soft, hesitant cough.

"Nothing. Gregg will pick you up at ten thirty. See you Thursday morning."

"Okay. Ken..." There was so much Audrey wanted, needed, to say to Ken, but perhaps it was better this way. "Thank you. For everything," she softly added, meaning his friendship, his kindness, his reliability, his confidence in her...hoping he would not recognize and subsequently resent the depth of her dependence on him.

"My pleasure," he answered, and the gentleness in his inflection partially assuaged Audrey's fears.

At least he appeared to genuinely value her friendship, but while that filled her with a warm glow of satisfaction, it fell far short of what she ached for and had been deprived of for so long.

The plane ride, alone, without Ken's companionship, was no more than a lapse in time... an hour's void during which Audrey neither thought nor hoped, but merely existed... as she had until Nava del Sol and Ken.

Gregg drove her home to pick up her station wagon and departed with a friendly reminder that he would be at her service whenever Tom or Ken deemed it justifiable. The congenial pilot had been politely reticent, so the long drive to Nancy's house, north of the Casas Adobes area, afforded Audrey her first opportunity to mull over the sudden turn her life had taken.

For the first time in more months than Audrey cared to remember—since long before the divorce when Audrey had had to give up her fun assignments and accept a job of stability and tedium—she felt intellectually and artistically challenged. Nava del Sol, in all its fascinating complexity, was the product of intensive research, elaborate attention to detail, and often frustrating encounters with a profit-oriented mindset so thoroughly entrenched that it had required near-Herculean efforts to mobilize. But of greater interest to Audrey, it was the brainchild of a very creative, extremely likable man whose genius she had, through years of complacency, failed to recognize. With the assistance of his lifelong friend, Mike, Ken's dream was becoming a reality, and in the way of their youth, the two had included Audrey. She had come to accept her inclusion almost as much as she accepted the absolute correctness and naturalness of Ken's success that she saw as a vindication of his idealism.

Ken had always been firm in his convictions... opinionated, Audrey had in her own obstinacy adjudged him, although she was beginning to recognize that assessment as a reflection of her own hardheadedness. Their arguments had essentially been the inevitable result of two inflexible wills locking horns, and the source of their ire had been the methods by which each had arrived at identical conclusions, for neither could, nor would, understand how the other's illogical reasoning could lead to sound judgment. In fact Audrey could not recall one instance where they had philosophically differed... except, over Alan, and Audrey knew well the value of the position she had taken on him. The bitterness of a situation that defied compromise had severed all ties, but until Ken had blundered back into her life, Audrey had not been aware that she missed his stubborn, unasked-for advice and guidance.

Until Nava del Sol Audrey's one ray of sunshine had been Bonnie and she looked forward with eager anticipation to her reunion with the bright, loving child. Necessity had forced the daily separations that Audrey tried to keep to a minimum, and Ken, she knew instinctively, understood and approved. She and Bonnie were a unit she thought fondly. A formidable one that Alan in his insecurity had found threatening. He had resented the bond between mother and child and had been afraid—rather than reluctant, Audrey had slowly come to recognize with the wisdom of hindsight and distance—to establish any attachment to his own offspring. Oddly Ken had, without theatrics or sanctimony, accepted the child as readily as he condoned her mother, and ironically his intrusion on their lives was destined to cause numerous, longer separations.

Audrey pulled into Nancy's driveway and her heart leaped at sight of the angelically beaming face pressed flat against the living room window.

"Poor lonely Alan," she thought with a twinge of sympathy but no remorse. He never knew what he had missed.

Chapter Eight

Audrey was kept busy almost around the clock for the next few weeks, working on the campaign and preparing for Mazatlán. On a Wednesday evening after picking up Bonnie and enduring another disagreeable encounter with surly Mr. Haskell, Audrey pulled into her carport. An unfamiliar car was parked in front, but no one was around. She wondered if Ken had gotten in earlier than he had anticipated. If so, where was he? She let herself in the front door and stopped dead in her tracks when she entered the kitchen. Alan waved to her from the side window and came around to the kitchen door.

"What...?" Against her better judgment, Audrey opened the door.

"Hi, beautiful," he grinned, walking past her. "Where's my little girl?" He strolled into the dining room and swooped up Bonnie. "Mommy treating you good?" he laughed, kissing the little moppet.

"Alan! What do you think you are doing?" Audrey frostily inquired.

"Hugging my baby." He tickled the toddler until she writhed in hilarity.

"Legally she is not yours," Audrey stated in a deceptively calm voice.

"I know that." Alan gave Audrey a peck on the cheek. "Don't get in a huff. I'm not going to take her away." Alan held up the giggling baby and looked her all over. "You've done a passable job. That hair though." He shook his head and scowled at the bright orange mop of curls that capped the blue-eyed, pink-cheeked face. "She had to take after your side of the family, didn't she?"

Less than two minutes to obnoxious, Audrey thought with a weary, irritated sigh. "What do you want, Alan?" she asked as she sat down at the dining room table.

"I got lonesome for the old place." He sat down opposite Audrey. "You're getting haggard-looking," he observed after critically appraising her. "I heard you got a hefty contract workin' for ol' Walker." He laughed derisively. "Who'd have thought he'd ever amount to anything?"

Audrey debated a moment. Alan was not there to see Bonnie, on that she would have bet her last dime. He wanted something and, true to his infuriatingly self-centered nature, would tell her in his own good time. She should never have allowed him to enter the house. Had she not been too tired to engage in an ugly scene, she would have ordered him off the premises. Then, too, she knew what an adverse effect such an encounter would have on Bonnie. The terrible memories of Bonnie's infant body tensed into rigidity by Alan's harsh voice raised in anger still haunted Audrey, and she would never, under any circumstances, subject the trusting little girl to a repetition of such a dreadful ordeal.

Unfortunately one miscalculation at the onset could not be easily corrected.

"Why are you here, Alan?" she asked. "How long are you planning to stay?"

"Few days," he shrugged. "Quit worrying. I'm not planning to stay in this dump any longer than I have to." He looked around the small, neat house. "Why did I ever let you talk me into buying this hovel?"

"It hasn't cost you anything, Alan. I've made all the payments," she quietly reminded him.

"That's right, Audrey. Keep putting the old needle in," he sneered. "Look at me, baby. I'm making a bundle. Me an' Carla've got a huge house, swimming pool... the works."

"I thought you married Maura?" Audrey frowned, sorry she had asked for she had less than no interest.

"That was ages ago. Women are like cars. They get rusty and cranky, then the only sane thing to do is dump them. 'Specially when something better comes along," he added with a pointed wink.

"I have to feed Bonnie, and I have a lot of work to do tonight, so I'd appreciate it if you'd leave now."

Her tone was cold and impersonal and made absolutely no impression on the inconsiderate man.

"I'll leave when I'm ready. You trot on out to your playpen and I'll feed my little girl. Get the stuff ready while I get something out of the car."

If he referred to Bonnie as "his" one more time, Audrey feared she would smack him. She opened a jar of vegetables and combined it with a jar of meat, which she heated to lukewarm. She was setting the dish of dinner and a jar of fruit on the table when Alan returned with an enormous purple hippo and a six-pack of beer.

"Don't give her that!" snapped Audrey, espying Alan pop open a beer and put it to Bonnie's lips.

"It won't hurt her. It's the good stuff." He made a grotesque face at the vegetables that Bonnie had smashed between her fingers. "She'll need something to wash that garbage down."

Granted the sight of the mashed food often made her gag, Audrey knew it was nutritious and was not about to let Alan give her daughter anything harmful.

"If you can't feed her properly, you are not going to feed her at all," she snapped, snatching the child from him.

"Some mother you are," he snarled when Bonnie cried at the unaccustomed rough treatment, "hurting the kid like that!"

Audrey ignored him and settled Bonnie in the high chair, then she fed her while Alan finished one beer and started another.

"All right. You're done. Now let me have her for a while," he insisted. "Go do your work. I can manage."

In all fairness to the impossible man, Audrey could

not see where any harm would come of letting him play with Bonnie...so long as she kept a close watch on him. With any luck Alan would bore quickly and depart just as fast. She did have a great deal of work to do, and she silently fumed at the inconvenience Alan's very existence seemed to wreak on her life as she carried the baby into her bedroom and placed her in the center of the bed, where she could be seen from the studio. Alan followed and sprawled across the spread to play with Bonnie.

The bell rang and Audrey put aside the layout she had barely started to answer it.

"Ken! I wasn't expecting you," she said, admitting him, relieved by his timely arrival.

"So I see." He nodded toward the car parked in front and glanced toward the back of the house and the commotion coming from her bedroom.

"Alan," she sighed.

Ken glowered at her and turned to leave.

"Please, Ken," she pleaded, "don't go."

Ken frowned for a long moment. "Okay," he sighed and followed her to her room. "Hello, Alan," he said in a cool voice.

"Hey, Walker! What're you doing here?" Alan made no attempt to smooth his disheveled hair or shirt. He sat up and bounced Bonnie on his knee. "Oh, that's right. Little Audrey, here, works for you now," he snickered. Bonnie crawled off his lap and wrestled the hippo while Alan stood up and walked over to Ken, holding out his hand. "Congrats, Walker. Never thought I'd see the day," he sneered, and Audrey glared at him with undisguised loathing.

"Want a beer?" he offered, walking past them and into the kitchen.

"No, thanks. What's new with you, Alan?"

"I'm sitting on top of the world, what else?" he laughed. "Wheeling and dealing in real estate down in Patagonia."

"You've moved back to the state?" Audrey asked, totally unprepared for that item of information. She studied the expensively dressed, handsomely dissipated young man in front of her. Why hadn't he stayed in California?

"Yeah," he grinned at Ken in answer to Audrey's question. "Everything's coming up roses. I've got everything a man could ask for. Only thing missing's a kid."

Bonnie's babyish giggle rippled from the bedroom and a cold, nameless fear gripped Audrey's heart in an icy claw when Alan's glance momentarily wandered toward the sound.

"Things've gone up, up, up, since I shed the little albatross," he gloated to Ken, indicating Audrey with a jerk of his head. "Say that's some gorgeous chick you're about to lasso for yourself," he went on, impervious to Audrey. "Janet What's-Her-Name." He insolently surveyed Ken and shook his head. "Never thought you had it in you," he leered, "to hook a dame as classy as that. Remember the old days?" he continued when Ken did not comment. "I took every girl you ever had," he laughed, slopping his beer. "And everyone you ever wanted."

He sat down at the dining room table and straddled a chair he had reversed with a flick of his wrist, and folding his arms across the back rung, rested his chin on them.

"Even Audrey, not that you ever wanted her," he sneered. "Even you had better taste. But I did rescue her from your little prank with Almendaro." He took a long swallow of his beer while he studied Audrey. "Earned her undying gratitude. 'Course, once she snared me, she turned it all off."

"I am glad your life has taken a change for the better," Audrey calmly stated. She couldn't bring herself to look at Ken and stared at the oaf to whom she had been married, blushing, not for what Alan said, but at the blatant stupidity she had manifested in her choice. With a sinking feeling she knew she could never win Ken's respect. Not when she was capable of such a gross error in judgment.

"Sure you are," sneered Alan. He turned to Ken and his mouth spread into a broad, conceited smile. "Bet I could get that Janet broad eating right out of my hand," he challenged. "You can have Audrey," he laughed generously. "She's been saving up for years, and I'm sure that Weather Girl's more woman than you can handle." He made a leering wink. "That cold fish is more your speed."

A split-second later, the words barely out of his mouth, Alan was sprawled on the floor where Ken's right cross had landed him. The enraged architect towered over the obnoxious boor who was gingerly rubbing his jaw, Ken's eyes black with hatred, his strong, angular jaw clenched tight. Without a word Ken yanked Alan to his feet and, with one hand on Alan's biceps and the other clasping the collar of his shirt, escorted Audrey's ex-husband to the front door.

"Sorry you have to be leaving so suddenly," he uttered through grimly set teeth as he shoved Alan out the door and slammed it shut.

Ken immediately returned to the dining room and placed his hands firmly, yet gently, on Audrey's shoulders.

"Are you all right?" he asked the ashen-faced woman.

Audrey nodded but could not raise her face. He folded her into his arms, holding her until the sobbing was no more than a series of intermittent hiccups. Bonnie had toddled out and clung to both their legs; Ken absently rubbed the curly little head while Audrey nestled deeper into the protective web of his embrace.

"Come on," he whispered, leading Audrey to the bedroom. He flipped off the lights. "Lie down. I'll put Bonnie to bed."

Unable to rest comfortably, Audrey pulled herself together after a while and walked slowly back to Bonnie's room. She watched as Ken tucked the child and a teddy bear in for the night.

"I think everything matches," he grinned, pointing

to the mismatched parts of Bonnie's pajamas. "At least, they are the same color."

He looked so tenderly vulnerable standing there with that lopsided grin, proudly showing her his handiwork, Audrey could not bear it.

"Oh, Ken," she laughed, walking into his open arms. She placed her arms around his waist and reached up along his back to hug his shoulders, marveling that such a strong, self-assured man could be so sensitively, appealingly awkward.

"Feeling better?" he murmured against her hair.

"Yes." Always with you, she wanted to add.

The bell rang and he put his arm around her waist. "That must be the pizza," he said, walking her back to the dining room.

"Do you think of everything?" she asked when he seated her.

"Of course," he answered with a straight face. "Haven't you figured that out yet?"

"I'm learning." She blushed, averting her eyes lest he see the naked love she felt for him.

"All those straight 'A's,'" he shook his head ruefully, "and such a slow brain."

"What if I'd fallen asleep?" she asked when he opened the pizza and she saw the size.

"What?" Ken stared at her for a second until he understood what she meant. "Oh, then I wouldn't have had to share," he teased.

"Pepperoni! My favorite," she laughed. "You'll be sorry you did."

"I am rarely sorry for what I do," he replied with a smug grin that faltered when his dark eyes beheld hers. He did not say anything more until the pizza was finished.

"What did Alan want?" he casually asked. "And when did he get here?"

"Just before you did, I think, and I don't know. Not in that order," she replied, meaning the sequence of her answers. She ignored Ken's confused stare and continued. "But I sure am glad you showed up when you did," Audrey shyly confided. "He's gotten sort of weird."

"He's on drugs, Audrey."

Audrey looked up in amazement. "How do you know?"

Ken studied her and slowly shook his head at her naiveté. "He was on them in college. That's why he was kicked out of school. You never knew?"

"I knew he smoked pot, but I thought it was just a fad," she shrugged. "He always wanted to be the life of the party." She heaved a small, sad sigh. "It's kind of pathetic actually."

Ken patted her hand. "It is. But he's unpredictable."

"Maybe," Audrey stared wistfully out the French doors to the darkened street, "things are really working out for him this time."

"Maybe." She arose to remove the leftover crusts from the pizza, Ken watching closely. "Do you still care?"

"Only in that I hate to see anyone ruin his life." Audrey gazed steadily at Ken. "I guess I'm not a very nice person. I don't care what happens to Alan, and if I never saw him again, it would be too soon," she said evenly.

"Do you mean that?" Those black eyes searched the honest green.

Audrey's gaze wavered then regained its unswerving focus. "I've felt that way for several years. He scares me when he's around Bonnie. He never wanted her," she softly added before taking a slow, measured breath. "He's never mean to her, but he doesn't have any sense of responsibility and I'm afraid he might hurt her."

"Can he come and see her whenever he pleases?" Ken's voice was strangely controlled.

"No," Audrey hastened to explain, although she could not tell what it was that prompted her. "He never made any of the support payments and he has no legal claim on her whatsoever. When he first arrived though," she mused aloud, "he seemed happy to see her." A worried frown creased her brow and she gave up trying to apply reason to anything Alan did. "Who can figure Alan?" she sighed.

"Not even Alan," said Ken. "Will his arrival interfere with the trip to Mazatlán? If it will, take Bonnie with you."

"Oh, I don't think that will be necessary." The efficient lady gendarme she had hired came to mind and she smiled. "Mrs. Potter seems quite capable of dealing with a half-dozen Alans," she giggled, "and he'll probably be gone by tomorrow. He wears thin in a hurry!"

"That he does," Ken agreed.

"I'm... I'm sorry for what he said about Janet," Audrey said in a quiet voice.

An angry scowl settled on Ken's attractive features. "He did a nasty number on you, too."

"I'm used to it," she shrugged, and his frown darkened. "You must think I'm the world's biggest idiot," she said, lowering her eyes in embarrassment.

"Not the biggest maybe. But you're definitely a contender." He heaved a deep sigh and squeezed her hand. "Sometimes," he said softly, "not doing anything is stupider."

"What?"

"Never mind." He patted her cheek and stood up. "I almost forgot. I came over here to undo all your hard work," he laughed. "We had to change the specs on three of the models, so you'll have to redo the elevations."

"Oh, no you don't!" Audrey threatened. "That's the only thing completed. You can't do this to me!"

"Yes I can, and I have."

Ken went out to his car and returned bearing a stack of blueprints, which he carried to Audrey's studio. He spread out the elevation for the Piedra Solana model, the largest of the individual homes to be offered. It was a beige, slump-block building, hence its name, "Sun Stone." In the initial concept, the long, single-story dwelling meandered across its lot, one wing protruding first to accommodate the living room, then again for the garage; the other wing, first receding the width of the den before advancing to define one bedroom, then jutting forward with dramatic emphasis to encase the master bedroom suite and its companion, a privacy-screened patio and garden. Crowned by a peaked roof of curved, red, Mexican clay tiles, a trio of arches united both sections with stately elegance, the two narrower arches supporting the angled walls that formed the half-octagon of the covered portion of the nearly square low-walled front porch.

Ken had expanded the covered portion to the full width of the porch, opened the angled sections to a flat wall, and added a fourth arch so that the house now resembled the Solanay Sombra model. The striking sun-and-shade aspects that inspired the name for the least expensive home in the subdivision were more pronounced in the imposing size and proportions of the Piedra Solana, and the classic simplicity of the carefully delineated masonry that framed each of the tall, arched windows, clearly distinguished it from its modest relative.

It had not only been the spectacular original elevation that had entranced Audrey. The floor plan was a masterpiece of design with its sunken master bedroom suite, gardens in the two largest baths, formal entertainment areas, casual, comfortable living rooms, an easily accessible kitchen that bowed out into the rear patio, a bright, roomy breakfast nook, a conveniently located laundry, and a full pantry. To Audrey's relief not a feature had been altered, but she dreaded correcting all those layouts.

"That was my favorite," she protested. "Now I hate it."

"It's still going to be available. But because of the change in the size of the solar collectors we are going to use, we won't be able to feature it as often in that elevation. Do you really hate it?" he asked, and Audrey was surprised by the extent of his disappointment.

"If you had to redo two weeks' worth of work, you'd hate it, too," she grinned.

"I did, and I don't, and it was three years' worth, not to mention a vast improvement!" he declared, pinning the corrected drawings onto the drafting table for her.

"And you say my sentences don't make any sense," laughed Audrey, looking longingly into those dark-brown depths.

"I've been hanging around you too much!" He blinked twice and forced a stern expression. "Get to work before I forget myself and you end up having to start on this thing after midnight."

"Why would I do that?" she asked, eyes wide and playful in mock innocence, her best intentions to steer clear of any further physical involvement gone in the time it took to focus on those mesmerizing brown eyes. His face came closer and she raised her chin to meet his wide, sensual mouth. He kissed her soundly and released her quickly, although he seemed to be having the same difficulty clearing his vision Audrey did.

"Because," he gruffly answered her question, "no matter what else goes on around here, those things have to be in Mazatlán on Friday. Now get busy."

Audrey made a face. "Slave driver!"

While she began to work, he picked up the newspaper she had brought home with the materials from the office and read the passage that had been circled in red.

"Is this what's been bothering you?" he asked, pointing to the article.

"Why should that bother me?" she asked, avoiding his eyes.

"No reason." He tossed it in the trash. "Funny you circled it though."

"I didn't. That's Jack's idea of subtlety."

"Oh."

He watched her quietly for several seconds, then began to study the plat map for the subdivision.

"Which of these did you like the best?"

"Which lot?" Audrey walked over to the end of the

table and carefully scanned the map. "This one that backs up to the National Forest boundary."

"Hmm." He frowned thoughtfully. "Why?"

"It's the highest, and there won't ever be anything around it. It's kind of isolated."

"Where would you put the house? It's not the best building site." His eyes were incredibly dark and warm. And inviting.

"In the back," Audrey replied, hastily focusing on the map. "Looking out over the National Forest."

"You can't put the Piedra Solana model on it though."

"Why not?"

"Angle of the sun. Hand me that blueprint." Ken turned it so that the compass points lined up. "You'd lose all the passive advantages. It wouldn't make any difference as far as the photovoltaic elements are concerned. They convert light directly to electricity, so the intensity and heat of the sun are not important. In fact, too much heat is detrimental. The possibility of a fire hazard is one of the reasons we've had to alter the specs. But you'd halve your efficiency and eliminate a valuable hot water source if you tried to build this house on that lot."

"So? Fix it."

"Just like that?" Ken pushed her hair back behind her ear. "Just for you?"

"Of course! You are going to make me so rich with this project, I'll have you custom design one for me," was her flippant reply.

"Do you realize what you are saying?" he teased. "You are asking me to give you that house!"

"Well, I am working for it, am I not?"

"You haven't begun to work that hard!" he laughed.

"Skinflint!" she sniffed.

"Ingrate!" Ken rolled up the map and his eyes slowly panned Audrey's beautiful, expressive face. "Get back to work," he said huskily. He proceeded to work on some of the blueprints while she redid the elevations for the display ad and the models.

It was almost two o'clock when Ken broke the silence.

"Want me to fix you some coffee?"

"No." Audrey stretched and yawned. "I'm quitting!"

"The project or for the night?" Ken reached out his hand to help her down from the high stool.

"Right now, I couldn't make that distinction. I'm asleep!" Audrey fell toward Ken, caught herself and straightened up. "Sorry," she mumbled.

Ken hesitated for a moment, but whatever thought crossed his mind, he shrugged it aside and took Audrey's arm. "Walk me to the door like a good little hostess."

His voice betrayed nothing and when he flashed that beguiling lopsided grin, Audrey felt a deep twinge of regret that grew and constricted into a painful spasm at the sight of the purple hippo lying on its side, its fat, stumpy legs extended from the enormous, fuzzy belly. The wide, day-glo pink swath that zigzagged across the end of the ridiculous snout in a moronic grin shrieked of Audrey's obstinacy, short-sightedness, dearth of elemental common sense, bad judgment... in short, her colossal stupidity, and she gripped Ken's arm.

"Don't go," she mumbled, her eyes on the raucous purple monstrosity. "Please," she begged in a whisper, raising her liquid green eyes to Ken, her plea little more than a tremulous exhalation.

"Audrey..."

The soft utterance brought a sudden realization of the audacity of what she had asked, and with an effort Audrey pulled herself together and stepped away.

"I'm sorry," she apologized. The tiny smile she summoned flitted uncertainly across her mouth. "We're not kids anymore," she shrugged, finding it nearly impossible to confront Ken with a direct gaze. "I can't expect you to hold my hand during all the scary parts..."

The light laugh failed, ending in a sob as the bittersweet memory of all those backyard "camping" trips came to mind. Ken and Mike had devoted all their energies to regaling Audrey with terrifying tales that resulted in the three of them sitting up all night, huddled together, hands tightly clasped, ears straining to detect the horrors that lurked in the dark. Without being aware of it, Audrey picked up the hideous toy and wrapped her arms as far around the unwieldy object as possible and hugged it to her chest while the tears rolled slowly down her face.

"I'm not the one who is frightening you this time."

Ken spoke softly, his voice unnaturally taut. The dark brown eyes wandered slowly over her lovely features, caressing her lips when they paused at her soft, pink mouth while his hand gently smoothed the silky hair from her face and tucked it behind her ear. The rich umber, so filled with tender understanding, rose to focus on the distressed verdancy that could not conceal the loneliness within. He removed the hippo, tossed it out into the hall, and in the next instant pulled Audrey into his arms.

"We're not kids anymore," he whispered thickly, but the words were absorbed in the gentleness of his kiss.

The yearning underlying the embrace, however, could not be denied nor contained by either, and when Audrey swayed forward, moving her lips in a wordless request, passion ignited, and Ken responded with a hunger that seemed insatiable—surpassed only by her own.

"Audrey," he gasped when they paused to breathe. Crushing her against him, he lifted and stroked her hair while he caressed her head and the back of her neck. His other hand exerted a steady pressure on the small of her back until he cradled her hips within his. Overwhelmed by the warmth and vitality he radiated, Audrey burrowed closer, the feminine curves of her body fitting naturally into Ken's masculine angularity. Softness molded to hardness as strength supported fragility and courage dispelled fear.

His mouth found hers again and his hand left her

neck to close over her breast, caressing, stroking, teasing, and finally releasing when he unbuttoned her blouse and slid aside the restrictive lace her aroused flesh strained against. Her hips began to move in rhythm with the circular motion of his fingers and palm, and Ken propelled her the few steps to the bed. He laid her back and his mouth continued the exploration his hand had begun, provoking a sharp inhalation as an incredible longing washed over Audrey... a profound emotion that prompted caution.

They were most assuredly not children anymore, and Audrey was seized with a terrible doubt and guilt. Her relationship with Alan had been so devoid of true affection that she had nothing by which to judge what was happening. If this was the purely physical reaction of two healthy adult bodies in too-close proximity, Ken would rightfully resent her, once passion was spent, for using her vulnerability to entangle him in a situation he neither wanted nor sought.

"Ken," she murmured while she ran her fingers through his thick, dark hair, pressing his face closer. "Why can't things stay the same?" she sobbed in her confusion.

"The same, how?" he asked, rising up enough to see her. His dark eyes studied her face in the moonlight. "Time doesn't stand still for anyone, Audrey. People grow up." A tiny frown furrowed his brow. "They don't necessarily change," he added with a sigh. But although there was a noticeable cooling in his attitude, he did not make any move to arise.

"It takes a while to see them for what they are though," Audrey hesitantly ventured the opinion.

"Alan?"

There was more to the question than the frigid utterance of the name and Audrey was puzzled.

"Him too," Audrey answered, apprehensive about how Ken would interpret that, surprised that she had dared to be so bold as to hint there was more to her feelings for him than she was ready to let on.

"Audrey..." The frown deepened and underwent a

subtle transformation from annoyance to confusion. "I won't hurt you," he promised. His eyes traveled down to the glow of moonlight on the full swell of her breasts that were exposed by the disarrayed blouse. "I'd never hurt you, Audrey," he mumbled thickly as his hand closed over one of the perfect curves.

But the void he would leave when he did not return the love she sought... ached for with all her heart... would cripple her. The pain wrought by the recognition, acceptance, and finally termination of a loveless marriage would be nothing compared to the desolation of sampling, but never attaining, something so precious and beautiful, and a flood of depression washed over Audrey.

"Audrey," Ken gently stroked her thick hair when she averted her face, "is it me you don't want?" His voice was soft, but unmistakably hurt.

"No." Audrey shook her head and reached up to touch his cheek. "No," she firmly repeated, and she was disturbed by the sadly skeptical expression that settled on Ken's face.

"No? After everything you've been through, even I seem desirable?" A small laugh accompanied the question. "Any port in a storm?"

"No," she stated emphatically, if weakly. "It's... it's not that..." Her eyes filled with tears as she struggled to find the words to explain and reassure him, but he removed her hand from his face and brought it to his lips.

"Don't lie to me, Audrey," he whispered, his eyes dark and troubled, his voice thick.

"I've never lied to you, Ken," Audrey quietly replied. "I never could."

"No, you never could," he sighed.

She slid her arms up to encircle his shoulders and when his eyes continued to probe hers, Audrey tightened her arms around his neck and buried her face in his shoulder.

"What is it you want from me?" he asked in a long, low groan.

"I... I don't want to be alone," she mumbled, fighting back her tears, not wanting to play on his sympathy.

"Audrey," he protested, "I can't stay here... not like this, and not..." A shudder racked her body and Ken hugged her close. "Okay," he sighed in a long, drawn-out exhalation. He kissed the side of her head and caressed her damp cheek. "Good ol' Ken to the rescue," he muttered as he rolled over beside her.

With a loud, unladylike snuffle, Audrey made a valiant effort to regain control of her emotions. If she had no right to expect his love, she had even less to expect him to put up with this nonsense.

"Maybe," she ran the back of her hand across her cheek in a childishly futile gesture and pulled away from Ken, "it would be better if you went."

"Look, I'll stay with you for as long as you need me, but you are going to have to fix your blouse," he insisted, pulling her back in place and nestling her head under his chin. "That reliable and trustworthy, I am not."

"Ken... I'm sorry."

"Do me a favor and shut up. Please," he gently added as he settled her comfortably in the crook of his arm. "The things I have done for you over the years," he grumbled. "But this one beats all!"

While she made herself presentable, Ken rubbed the nape of her neck and lifted a handful of the silky hair.

"You have the most beautiful hair," he murmured as it cascaded through his fingers. "It's the color of wild honey."

"You can't see it in the dark," Audrey laughingly discounted his compliment.

"Don't have to," he asserted, placing his face against her when he snuggled up to her. "I'd know it anywhere." He kissed her lightly. "Go to sleep."

Chapter Nine

They awoke to the sound of Bonnie throwing things out of her crib.

"I have to get up," Audrey sleepily mumbled, but she burrowed deeper into Ken's shoulder.

"Why?" he asked, placing a feathery kiss on her forehead.

"Because I have this huge, terribly important contract to work on, and my client is very demanding." This last she said with a giggle.

"Tell him to take a long walk off a short pier," Ken grumbled as he hugged Audrey to his side and prevented her from rising. "What kind of a beast would expect you to leave me to work?"

"A very opinionated, bossy fellow. With a rather warped sense of humor," chuckled Audrey.

"That I can believe." He tightened his grasp. "What if I won't let you go?"

"You'll have to answer to him."

"I can handle anyone," Ken confidently insisted.

"Such a tough, smug fellow you are." Audrey leaned up to rest her chin on Ken's chest as she teased him.

"And don't you forget it," he grinned, tweaking her nose.

"Ma-Ma-Ma-Ma-Ma-Ma!" demanded Bonnie.

"Domineering kid," Ken observed and a wry frown creased his brow. "Must take after her mother." He patted Audrey's shoulder and sighed. "Better go release the little tyrant."

Audrey sat up and Ken's dark brown eyes roamed slowly over her disheveled blouse and skirt.

"You're all wrinkled," he grinned.

"You should talk!" Audrey retorted with a laugh and a haughty toss of her head that sent the red-gold tresses bouncing behind her shoulders as she fumbled with the garments.

"Need some help?" Ken cheerfully offered.

"No, thanks. I have to take these off."

"Oh?" One black eyebrow soared quizzically and a broad leer adorned Ken's face. But Bonnie began to bang her crib against the wall in an angry demonstration of impatience.

"We're outflanked," he sighed. "I'll close my eyes."

"You won't peek?" Audrey bent her head to see Ken's face.

"I never cheat," he smugly asserted, scrunching his eyes tighter shut.

"Your loss."

Audrey jumped out of bed, snatched a robe off the hook on the closet door, and tied it closed around her waist as her skirt slithered to her feet. She changed and dressed Bonnie and Ken played with her while Audrey showered and dressed.

"Isn't that your babysitter?" he asked when he sat down to the breakfast she had prepared. He pointed out the French doors to the group of giggling teenagers who were passing the house on their way to school. "I think we've given her something to share with her friends."

"Oh, your car!" gasped Audrey. "I forgot it was out there."

"I didn't get an opportunity to hide it in the alley," Ken deadpanned, mildly amused by Audrey's crimson face.

"Oh, well," she said philosophically, "it's too late to cry over chickens before they've hatched."

Ken grimaced. "Must you do that to harmless clichés?"

"Nothing trite is harmless. You're the one who was always harping on that," Audrey saucily retorted.

"I don't harp. And I wouldn't have believed you ever listened to anything I said. Besides"—he placed his dish in the sink and picked up Bonnie—"I'm never ready for the linguistic contortions you engage in."

Audrey gathered up Bonnie's belongings and Ken carried the child out to the station wagon. He handed her to Audrey when she had stowed the large, navy-blue diaper bag in the rear seat.

"I wonder what your neighbors think of all this?" he mused, looking down the quiet street of modest houses.

"All what? Just what are you implying, sir?" asked Audrey, drawing herself up indignantly to her full five feet, nine inches, her eyes glittering mischievously.

"All these cars coming and going at all hours of the day and night."

"They all go. Eventually," she added, dissolving into giggles.

"Since they are rentals," Ken nodded toward the navy-blue sedan he had parked in front, "they're never the same. Folks are going to think you're running a business."

"I am. A most respectable business. It's called graphic consulting."

Ken burst out laughing and leaned back against the side of the station wagon for support.

"That's not what those girls were calling it!"

"Sh! Stop making such a commotion," scolded Audrey. She raised up on tiptoe to see over Ken's shoulder, and as she had suspected, Mrs. Hudson's gray head was visible through a crack in the drapes of the house on the other side of Audrey's driveway. "Too late," she groaned.

"All work makes Audrey a dull girl," Ken teased.

"Am I?"

Ken pulled her to him and bent her backward in a theatrically seductive pose. "Not dull, just stuffy," he grinned, giving her an exaggeratedly passionate kiss.

"Ken! What will people think?" Blushing scarlet,

Audrey pushed him away and straightened out her pale-blue primly tailored linen dress.

"They already think the worst," he laughed, holding the car door open for her. "I might as well move in."

Audrey glanced at him. Her green eyes shone, but she hastily concealed any emotion.

"I'd test your patience," she forced a light laugh as she slid behind the steering wheel. "I always have." She reached out to pat the hand on the window of her car and, suddenly shy, blushed again. "Thank you for last night," she whispered.

"Action above and beyond the call of duty." He grimaced, but at the hesitancy in those beautiful green eyes, he bent down and whispered, "Have I ever let you down?" His voice was as soft as the smile that kissed her cheek.

Ken's dark eyes were aglow with tenderness and a feeling of euphoria suffused Audrey's whole being. "No," she smiled.

Blinking rapidly, he stood up. "Go to work," he ordered, his tone of voice gruffly stern, yet reassuringly gentle. He strolled across the lawn to his car.

"Oh, wait," Audrey called out before he had gone too far. "Can I see you tonight? It won't take long."

Ken turned and a frown of irritation flitted across his brow. "Sure," he agreed with a shrug, whatever had annoyed him gone in the time it took to flash that dazzling smile.

"Great. Bye." She waved as she backed out of the carport.

She arrived at the office ten minutes late, having gotten stuck behind a school bus in Mrs. Haskell's neighborhood, and Jack made an elaborate point of consulting his watch, then the wall clock before telling her that Barney wanted to see her in his office immediately.

The heavyset man drummed on his desk in agitation for several moments while his beady eyes tracked her across the room to a stiff, uncomfortable chair.

"I've been hearin' some nasty rumors 'bout how

you're plannin' to go into business for yourself. Not only won't you be sharin' your new-found booty with ol' Barney, you might be thinkin' of helpin' yourself to some of my prime customers. Now, I just won't tolerate that kind of treachery. Won't tolerate it at all! Not for an instant! You put that nonsense out of your head. No one, I repeat, *no one* does ol' Barney out of what's rightfully his!"

"I can't imagine where you've gotten such an idea," said Audrey, exerting all her energies to modulate and control her voice. She knew exactly where he had gotten it: Jack. "The Nava del Sol account is yours, and I am your representative. That is the way I have presented myself at all times. I have never once tried to steal any client. As for going out on my own, you knew when I started that I was maintaining my free-lance clients on the side and that was perfectly agreeable to you, so long as it did not interfere with my work for you. In fact, I have not worked for anyone else in many months, and I do not have the capital nor the facilities to handle an account like Nava del Sol on my own, nor any other project of similar magnitude."

"But you've been approached," he growled. "Don't deny it.

"Yes," she freely admitted, "I've been approached. But at the risk of repeating myself, I am not prepared to take on any other projects at this time."

"Why didn't you send them bloodhounds to me? Where's your sense of loyalty, gal?"

"I informed everyone of them where I was employed. It's up to them to"—she wrinkled her nose distastefully—"'sniff' you out, as it were."

"You're one uppity little broad," snarled Barney, bringing his pudgy fingertips together and tapping them in a sequential rhythm. He gave her a nasty, warning grin. "If you were to play along with me," he said, looking her up and down in a pointedly suggestive manner, "we might both profit from your... hidden talents." A smarmy grin adorned his contemptible face as he sat back and patted his protruding belly.

Fury and loathing flooded Audrey's face at the reprehensible slur on her character, much to Barney's undisguised glee.

"First of all," Audrey spoke slowly, choosing her words with great care and enunciating precisely in an exercise of controlled temper, "Mr. Walker was impressed with my proposal from the start, despite the misrepresentation you did nothing to clarify. You know perfectly well that Jack could not have handled the campaign the way Harkness and Walker want, and either the truth would eventually have come out or the majority of the work would have fallen to me. In either case," her voice was beginning to rise, and with a conscious effort Audrey brought it back under control, "I owe no one an apology or an explanation."

"Maybe." Crafty blue glinted from beneath the flaccid flesh that draped from bushy eyebrows, while thick digits thumped in a slow cadence on the desktop, the rhythm and import not unlike the flickering tale of a cat poised to attack. "Still, Walker didn't discuss any of that here," Barney mused. "But you two are old friends, that much he let slip."

"Ken and my brother have been close since grade school," Audrey admitted, opting after a second's hesitation to drop the formality and use Ken's given name, a decision that prompted another knowing glance from the offensive man. "He and Janet Collins are practically engaged," she blurted in an attempt to close this topic of conversation. If her relationship with Ken was unclear to her, it was most definitely none of Barney's business.

"That's so. That's so," he promptly agreed. "Doesn't seem to have deterred you none," he persisted, like a dog with a bone on that obnoxious tack. Once more he insolently surveyed the well-rounded curves of her long, trim body. "So, what do you say? Is it a deal?"

"No, it is not!" Audrey rose to her feet, her height magnifying her insulted stance. "There is nothing between myself and Mr. Walker either," she blurted, hating herself for divulging anything to her dreadful boss.

"That a fact?" he snickered.

"That is a fact," she frostily stated, her glacial expression calculated to chill anyone possessed of a shred of decency.

"Well," he chuckled, obviously not falling into the category of a human being, with or without a soul, "the truth will out."

"Yes, it will." Holding her head at a regal angle, Audrey arched one perfect brow. "I have a great deal to do to prepare for Mazatlán, and I would like to get on about my business. May I leave?" she inquired in a voice dripping with acid.

"Any time, darlin'. The door is always open. And it opens both ways. Both ways," he chuckled.

Audrey closed the door behind her and took a deep, shuddering breath, then another, slower, steadier one.

"That bad?" Nancy commiserated. She flashed an encouraging smile and held out some papers. "Here are your plane tickets and your hotel reservations. Friday the thirteenth, ugh!" she shuddered. "What a day to fly!"

"I never knew you were superstitious," Audrey managed a wan smile for her friend.

"You're not?" Nancy gave an incredulous laugh.

"Well, I don't walk under ladders," Audrey sheepishly admitted. "But that's common sense," she defended it.

"Well, I'll knock on wood and throw some salt over my shoulder for you," grinned the blonde. "Oh, yes, I almost forgot," she called out before Audrey entered the art room, "There was a message from Walker." She waved a piece of paper. "Here's the number."

Audrey called the number and was put on hold for several minutes before she was disconnected. She tried again and the hotel operator asked if he could return her call. The remainder of the morning was spent collecting all the information for the solar convention. The printer who had solemnly promised to deliver the brochures by ten o'clock called and swore they would be ready by one. Not trusting him, Audrey swung by the plant after taking an unusually long lunch and waited impatiently for the covers to be cut, folded, and stapled to the printed matter. It was three when she returned to the agency.

She had missed Ken's call again, and she tried unsuccessfully to reach him. At a quarter to five, they finally connected.

"I've been trying to reach you all day," he complained.

"No, you haven't," Audrey disputed his claim. "I've been trying to reach you."

"Whatever," he sighed wearily.

"What's wrong?" Audrey gently asked.

"The usual last-minute runaround. Have you got your tickets?"

"Yes, I'm leaving at five."

"In the morning?"

"Oh, Lord! I hope not." Audrey rifled through the papers. "No," she breathed a sigh of relief, "in the afternoon. How about you?"

"Nine. In the morning," he clarified it.

"Oh." Well, that let out flying down together.

"Audrey, about tonight..."

"You can't make it," she said, trying to veil her disappointment.

"No, I can," he answered quickly. "But I can only drop by for a minute. I have to pick up Janet and fly to Phoenix tonight."

"Oh. Six okay?" she asked, maintaining a minimum of brightness in her tone after that depressing bit of information.

"Fine. What's up?"

"You'll see."

"I hate surprises, Audrey," he grumbled.

"Good!"

Ken heaved a resigned sigh. "See you at six."

Audrey recradled the phone and stared at it. "Try to be nice to Ken on his birthday," Mike had suggested, and on a whim Audrey had ordered a small cake decorated with a large, smiling sun the day she had spotted a signed print by Jimmie Abeita in a local gallery.

For the second time that month the little square of plastic had been called into service, but this latent streak of impetuous extravagance that Audrey had so recently discovered did not worry her in the slightest. Indirectly, Ken had paid for it himself, and if Audrey had not felt that she fully earned every penny of the generous account, that is what would have bothered her. It was a numbered edition of an oil portrait of an old Navajo. The strong, sensitive face was a three-quarter view and the sturdy chin of the indomitable old man rested on a hand gnarled with age. His pensive gaze was focused on the future and the knowing black eyes reflected the wisdom of the past. It had struck Audrey as a perfect depiction of the prudent optimism that characterized Nava del Sol. And Ken.

The gallery had promised to have it framed by noon, and on her lunch hour, Audrey had picked up the gift and the cake, then rushed home to wrap the print in gaily colored rainbow-festooned paper, and she placed in on the kitchen counter next to the pink box from the bakery.

It was a quarter past five when she finally left the office that evening, and when it took another half hour to get to Mrs. Haskell's, Audrey was glad she had taken the time to tend to her little surprise. A note on the door informed Audrey that Mrs. Haskell had taken Bonnie grocery shopping with her, and Audrey paced impatiently in front of the house.

"What a mob on Thursdays," puffed the cheerfully rotund woman as she walked up the street toting two huge bags of groceries.

"I hope you don't mind if I rush off," Audrey apologized for her rudeness in not staying to chat with the woman, "but I have an appointment at six, and I'm late."

She got caught in a traffic jam at Craycroft caused by a truck-car accident, and it was nearly half past six when she turned onto Seventh Street. Ken was just placing a note on her door as she pulled into the carport.

"I'm sorry," she mumbled, getting out of the car and extricating Bonnie from her carseat. She juggled her purse and the child as she fumbled for the door key.

Bonnie stretched her arms out to Ken and he took her. "What's this all about, Audrey?"

Without answering, she opened the door and ran into the kitchen, but the counter was empty. She opened the refrigerator and removed the pink box, certain she had left it on the counter. Still she had been in a hurry, and she opened the cabinet over the sink with one hand while she tried to remember what she had done with the gift. Simultaneously, her other hand opened the box, and her face fell.

"Oh, no!" she cried. As if in a daze, she slowly scoured the kitchen, looking on top of the refrigerator, under the counter, even in the oven. "Oh, no," she sobbed.

"What is it?" Ken, who had been watching her peculiar behavior with a bewildered look on his face, put Bonnie down then peered into the box.

It contained one thin slice of bright yellow frosted cake and a note scrawled on the back of a sales slip:

I left some for the kid. Aren't you a little old and more than a little shopworn for such tricks, Audrey? Still the hero-worshipper, I see. You haven't got the chance of a prayer in hell against Janet. Pretty classy print though. If you can afford presents like this, you must be rolling in dough, so I won't sweat paying you back.

                                                Alan

Ken turned over the sales slip. It was a receipt for "Reflections" by Jimmie Abeita. He put it back in the box and walked over to Audrey. She was standing very stiffly, looking out the French doors, and he put his arms around her.

"Audrey," he whispered.

"It doesn't matter," she shrugged, straightening her shoulders. "I wish you hadn't read that," she added, very, very quietly. She gave Ken a tiny smile. "You're going to be late."

"Audrey," he said, turning her toward him.

"No, please. I'd rather you go." Summoning up every ounce of self-control she possessed, Audrey smiled steadily at him.

"Are you going to be all right?"

"I'll be fine."

"Audrey..."

"Please, Ken."

He hugged her tightly and kissed the top of her bowed head. "Thank you, Audrey," he whispered. He placed his hands on either side of her face and brushed away the tears that spilled over her lashes despite her best efforts. "I'll see you in Mazatlán tomorrow night, okay?" he smiled tenderly.

"Okay," she agreed, gazing vacantly beyond him.

Bonnie came out dragging the enormous, wretched hippo, and the frowning glare Ken turned on the toy quickly vanished at the beaming smile Bonnie gave him.

"Lock everything," he said stiffly, bending to kiss Bonnie after he had hugged Audrey once more.

Audrey dutifully locked and bolted all the doors and windows and went to bed early, the ugly note still eating away at her confidence and self-respect. If only Ken had not read the note. What did it matter after all? He was engaged to Janet... was on his way to Phoenix with her now. It had been a stupid idea. Ken was right. It was high time she grew up. She had deluded herself into thinking she had done it as an act of friendship, but the minute she read Alan's note she knew she had been clumsily transparent. She was almost glad Ken had not seen the silly cake.

It had been one of those all-around, classic, bad days. A whole month of Mondays crammed into twenty-four miserable, wretched hours. They did not come often, but when they did, it was with a disgustingly unpredictable regularity, and they more than made up for their infrequency with their devastating impact. "Into each life an ill wind blows no good." That did not even sound right to Audrey, and thoroughly exhausted she pulled the sheet up to her chin.

Her bed seemed cold and large and terribly empty without Ken. She had not felt that way when Alan left. But Alan had not slept in their bed for so long and had slept there so infrequently, Audrey had gotten used to being alone, had even come to prefer it. Why had Alan ever married her? He had had a roving eye all along, but naive fool that she had been, Audrey had thought her love and adoration would magically change all that.

It had not been too difficult for Alan to place the blame on her. Deep down Audrey knew that she had come to resent Alan's demands, despise his touch. She had excused his liaisons during their engagement because she was "saving" herself for marriage. Maybe, as Alan had implied on more than one occasion, there hadn't been all that much worth saving. At any rate, the dalliances had continued unabated and the marriage had been dead for years... from the beginning, actually. Bonnie had been an accident. There had been no question that Audrey would ever neglect the child to cater to Alan's excessive, irresponsible whims, and once Bonnie arrived, every minute spent with the child affirmed that decision. She was going to miss Bonnie terribly this next week, and now that Ken knew and pitied her, there was nothing to look forward to but loneliness.

With Ken everything had seemed so different. Audrey was a private person by nature. Easily riled, but as quick to respond to the humor of a situation as she was to anger, she was almost painfully shy about allowing anyone too close to her innermost fears or dreams, and Alan's callous denigration of her ambitions and thoughts had made her doubly so. Yet Ken had held out a promise of a secure, safe haven, and Audrey had been ready to rush into it with an openness of spirit that astounded, and should have terrified, her. But there had only been warmth and gentle encouragement, and Audrey had felt welcome...and yes, loved.

Oddly, Audrey sensed a vulnerability in Ken despite the strength and comfort he exuded, and she wanted, ached with a yearning she could neither control nor stem, to provide that same solace for him...to cherish and nurture his dreams and aspirations. It was this realization that was the source of her desolation for she knew that she loved him completely, and, whether he returned her love or not, would continue to love him, and she did not know if she had the courage to relinquish the hopeless dream.

Her heart weary, Audrey fell into a deep sleep that did nothing to refresh her.

Chapter Ten

It took more bottles and jars than Audrey cared to enumerate to repair her face to a state this side of "death warmed over," but as she packed for Mexico, the prospect of the coming week cheered her. Friday the thirteenth or not, her knight in shining armor could always gallop up the beach and whisk her away. At any rate Tom would be there and he was more than passable company. He always seemed to be able to smooth over the rough, uncomfortable moments she experienced in the presence of Ken and Janet. Ken and Janet. Audrey did not like the sound of that. It sounded so terribly conclusively, perfectly correct.

At four a car came around to pick up Audrey, and she kissed Bonnie and quickly reconfirmed the accuracy of the information she was leaving with Mrs. Potter. When she was airborne, the stewardess came around with before-dinner drinks, and although Audrey declined, the stewardess opened the tray and pulled it down in front of her. After checking the passenger list and verbally confirming that she was indeed Audrey Mathieson, the stewardess placed a small vase containing one perfect, deep-pink rose on the tray and smiling, handed her the card.

> Audrey, I told you I hate surprises, but yours I would have loved, not that you've ever listened to me in your life! All of which is not to say that I have not planned one for you. See you soon.
> All my love, Ken

P.S. Does any of this make any sense to you? I have begun to write like you think. It is time to take drastic measures!

Audrey read the bizarre note twice and touched the delicate rose. Pink, not red. Yellow for friendship, she recited to herself, red for love. Did pink indicate a growing affection? Don't get your hopes up, she warned herself.

There was no one to meet Audrey at the airport and she took a cab to the Playa, passing tiny villages that could not begin to mask their abject poverty. En route they climbed a hill lined with expensive villas and luxurious hotels and arrived at last at an exquisite white building capped with orange curved tiles and flanked by gracefully arched porticoes.

Still carrying her rose, Audrey crossed the atrium to the front desk to register, then followed the bellboy to an elaborate suite, which even featured a sunken tub.

"Damn that Barney," she fumed at the needless expense.

"¿No le gusta, Señorita?" asked the worried attendant.

"No, no," she hastily assured him. "Me gusta mucho. Muy bien." She tipped him generously when he had placed her bags on the luggage stand in one of the two spacious walk-in closets.

First thing in the morning she would have to change this. Now she wanted only to take a bath. She started the water in the elegant bath, admiring the handpainted porcelain fixtures. There was a large shell of jasmine-scented bath oil beads beside the tub and she dumped a handful into the steamy water. While the tub filled, she placed a call to Tucson. Bonnie was playing happily in the backyard and Mrs. Potter seemed to have everything in hand. That worry temporarily laid to rest, Audrey wandered out to the balcony to look at the dazzling white beach. It curved and stretched into infinity, merging at the upper corners of the horizon with the deep turquoise ocean that sparkled and shimmered as it rolled out over the edge of the world.

Audrey remembered her three previous trips south of the border. Because of Tucson's proximity to Mexico, high school graduations and college recesses routinely culminated in a mass exodus of students to its pure white beaches, be they the luxurious resorts of Mazatlán and Puerto Vallarta on the Pacific ocean or, for those hardy enough to make the rigorous trek across the Sonoran desert in overcrowded cars loaded like pack mules with camping equipment essential to supplement the meager facilities available, to Puerto Penasco on the Gulf of California.

Audrey had been to all three in the company of Ken and Mike, and the nostalgic memories triggered a feeling of remorse that she had not paid any attention to Ken on any of those occasions. Instead she had resented his constant reminders to get out of the sun before she burned to a crisp and his insistence that weekend they had camped on the beach at Puerto Penasco that she not swim alone. Now all that was past. Opportunities lost that could never be regained.

The plaintive strains of mariachi music wafted on the ocean breeze and Audrey smiled sadly. Like so many southwesterners she had come to love this country, populated by proud, open, emotional people. She loved their music, their architecture, their spirit, their easy capacity to love. And, in many ways, she envied them.

As she turned back into the room, she removed her clothes and left them on the corner of the bed nearest the balcony, relishing the feel of the thick carpet under her bare feet. She luxuriated in the tub for nearly an hour, languidly climbing out only when the water had cooled significantly. She wrapped a thick bath towel around herself and stepped into the dressing room. Gradually, the steam evaporated from the mirror, and Audrey looked up, aghast. Ken and Janet had just stepped into the suite from the balcony.

"What in the world?" She spun around, clutching the towel tightly around her.

"I was about to ask you that same thing," said a wide-eyed, incredulous Ken.

"This is my room," sputtered Audrey.

Ken crossed his arms and stared at her. "This is my room."

Audrey blanched at that pronouncement and her steam-reddened cheeks glowed bright. "It... It can't be," she stammered, rummaging around on the dressing table for her key. "Here," she cried, tossing it across the nearer of the two beds.

Ken picked it up and glanced at it before he tossed it back on the bed. "So it is," he agreed, but he continued to stare at the towel-clad figure in the dressing area.

"Very interesting," giggled Janet. "I think I'll be toddling along." She slid the strap of her bag back up on her shoulder.

"Wait, Janet..." Audrey started forward, felt a draft on her bare legs and slid behind the long bench at the dressing table to hide as much of her nearly naked body as possible. "I can explain. There's been a terrible mistake!"

The brunette studied Audrey and her cobalt-blue eyes were bright and playful. "So there has," she laughed. She turned slightly and gave Ken a light kiss on his cheek. "Be gentle with her. She's in love with you."

"But, Janet..." wailed Audrey.

Her sandals made no sound on the carpet, and she quietly, yet firmly, closed the door behind her. Ken stretched out across the foot of the bed nearest Audrey and propped himself up on one elbow.

"This ought to be good," he grinned.

"This is the room they gave me," she cried in desperation. "You have to believe me."

"I believe you." He looked her over from head to foot. "That towel and that bench don't hide much," he candidly pointed out. "You might as well come out here."

Since there was no way Audrey could get to her clothes without passing him, she was trapped.

"It's not my fault!" she snapped.

"You made the arrangements, didn't you?" he asked as he got up and walked leisurely over to her.

"That's close enough," warned Audrey, but Ken ignored her. "I did not anyway. Barney did," she said, backing up against the dressing table. "Wait 'til I get my hands on that—"

"What a nasty temper you've got," he laughed, pulling her out from behind the bench. "Now what's this all about?"

"How should I know! No one ever tells me anything," she pouted. "I just get sent places."

"Tsk-tsk! Poor little Audrey." A wide grin curled crookedly across his mouth and his dark eyes fairly danced in amusement.

Trapped and defenseless, Audrey lashed out in the only way she knew how. Her temper took over.

"Oh, shut up! I'm getting out of here!"

"Dressed like that?" he grinned.

"If you had any decency, you would get out of here so I could get dressed."

"You are forgetting this is my room. And I reserve decency for decent ladies," he chuckled. "Not wanton naked females lurking in my room."

Ken grabbed Audrey's hand before she could get any momentum into her swing. "Careful, you are going to lose what little you have on," he leered.

"Why are you doing this to me?" The wail ended in a burst of righteous indignation. "Did I interrupt something you had planned with Janet?"

"Jealous?" he teased.

"Not in the slightest!" she said with a toss of her head that sent her long hair sailing past his face.

"Not in the slightest?"

With one hand Ken unwrapped the towel and flung it across the room. His hard, black eyes raked across her naked body, searing her pale, shivering flesh in their smoldering rage that quickly flamed into lust.

"No more games, Audrey," he growled, his voice thick, no longer teasing. "You planned this all along.

Alan had you pegged right. Hero worshipper!" He grabbed a handful of her hair at the nape of her neck and forced Audrey's face up by exerting a steady, controlled pressure that stopped short of pain-inducing roughness. "When I was a nobody, you wouldn't even give me the time of day. Now all of a sudden you're up to all sorts of sordid little tricks!"

"No'" she sobbed.

"Stop it," he demanded, giving her a hard shake. "Tears won't help you this time." He forced his mouth down savagely on hers and crushed her against him.

"No, Ken," she pleaded when she managed to turn her face away. She pushed at his powerful chest.

Ken seized her hand and pressing it flat, slid it slowly down the front of his shirt. "Go ahead," he sneered, uttering the command through tightly clenched teeth as he forced her hand lower and moved it in a sensuous, circular caress, "seduce me. That's what you had in mind, isn't it?"

In a confused attempt to dispel some of his anger, Audrey continued the erotic stroking. With a cruel deliberation and detachment, Ken reached up to caress her breasts, teasing and exciting until an involuntary glaze of desire crept over her vivid green eyes.

"Are you going to deny that you want me?" he jeered, moving his hand down her slim torso to the warm, inner surface of her smooth thighs.

"No," she breathed. Audrey lowered her lids and a huge tear rolled slowly down her cheek.

His eyes swept over the full, uplifted globes of her breasts, taut and aglow in their state of heightened arousal, down to her narrow waist and the graceful curve of her hips, across her flat abdomen to her long, elegantly shaped legs, and he stopped groping her. The hard, cold cynicism dissolved into an anguished contrition that was wrenched from the depths of his soul, for he had rendered that incredibly beautiful body defenseless, stripped it of its dignity, and reduced it to a shameful nakedness that had been barbarically shorn of its eroticism.

"Audrey," he groaned, folding her into his arms in an attempt to encase and protect her from the degradation he had inflicted upon her. "I'm sorry," he murmured into her thick, strawberry-blond hair. "My God, I never wanted it to be like this. I've always wanted you, Audrey, but you never wanted me. Not until Nava del Sol," he said as he covered her head with soft, penitent kisses and drew her closer, his voice uneven and so filled with regret and raw pain that Audrey's heart went out to him. "It has to be what I represent, not me," he said, tipping her face up. His apologetic eyes reflected the deep wounds her careless indifference over the years had caused.

"No." Audrey denied it, wrapping her arms around him, as much to comfort Ken as to seek refuge from the dreadful ordeal that anger and misunderstanding had wreaked on them both. "No," she repeated as she tenderly caressed his face and searched for the words to allay the fears she suddenly recognized. "I...I never noticed you before..."

"That much I know," he groaned with a small, sad smile. "Must you always be so painfully honest?"

"I never noticed anyone but Alan." Audrey bent her head and lowered her voice. "I never dated anyone else, you know that. Not even after the divorce..." Her voice trailed off and Ken gently raised her face to gaze into the luminous, tear-filled green.

"Would...could you ever love me?" he asked with uncharacteristic hesitancy.

"I think I do," Audrey murmured, still lacking the courage to make the irreversible declaration.

"Think?"

"I trust you," she replied simply. "I've always trusted you."

"You never listened to me," he said in a flat tone, arching one eyebrow skeptically.

"I never listened to anyone." Audrey frowned and made a face. "You always made me so mad, I refused to listen to anything you ever said."

"I love you, Audrey." It was a simple, direct statement and its very simplicity stunned her. "But I won't settle for anything less from you."

Her heart sang and in a daze Audrey swayed toward Ken. "I wouldn't expect you to."

"Well, how long do you expect me to wait?" he growled. "With you standing there like that!"

"What? Oh." Comprehension penetrated and a broad grin lit up Audrey's face. "I love you, didn't I just say that?"

"With you who can tell?" he muttered, kissing her with a fierce, growing hunger.

The hands that swept over Audrey's body touched tenderly, lovingly; seeking to console, examine, learn; searching out the most sensitive areas; thrilling with the excitement of discovery.

Audrey had never been touched with such delicacy, as though she were priceless, fragile, adored. Her flesh tingled, swelled, soared to meet and experience the pleasure of his fingers and palms. Her entire soul wanted to leap out to be enfolded and cherished by this man. It was not enough to be the object of his attention; she longed to lavish her tremendous emotion on Ken—the Ken she had been blind to for so long—to repay him for all the kindness, the love he had shown her all those years she suffered from crippling stupidity.

What would have seemed crude had she read it, vulgar to her ears, seemed natural, right, sublimely conceivable. Her hands moved down to his waist, unfastening the buttons of his shirt, the buckle of his belt. She pressed thousands of tiny, fiery kisses to the mat of dark hairs covering his chest. One arm slid around his waist, under the light cotton fabric, drawing the fullness of her breasts to his bare skin while her other hand slid down along the inside of his thigh, caressing in rhythm to the passage of her hardened nipples across his flesh.

Ken's hand spread open to encase her breast, yet uncover the tip to facilitate the erotic course, and the arm around her waist drew her closer. Audrey succeeded in freeing him from the encumbrance of slacks and shorts, and the trail of kisses blazed lower. With a sharp intake of breath, Ken caressed her head, lifting and stroking the thick, red-gold tresses until he could stand it no longer. It had been too long for both of them.

Turning and lifting her onto the bed, he pressed down. Controlling his ardor was no longer necessary. Both gave generously and freely, partaking fully of what was offered in a spirit of unselfish love.

Contentedly exhausted, Ken collapsed across Audrey and she ran her fingers through the hair at the nape of his neck.

"Did I tell you I loved you?" he murmured against her cheek and Audrey sighed in the affirmative. "I lied."

He raised up to trace her lips with one finger while his eyes examined her beautiful features. "I adore you."

A mischievous glint lit up the deep-brown eyes and Ken arched his back slightly. "What a temptress," he grinned down at her, conceding the emotional defeat that belied the physical dominance of his position.

"I've never seduced anyone before," giggled Audrey, making a tiny, wriggling motion under him.

"Keep that up," he exhaled in a sharp rasp, "and you'll get a second chance."

"Promises, promises," she sighed, kissing him playfully.

"None of them empty," he leered, but just then the phone rang. Very reluctantly, Ken rolled away from her to answer it.

"Oh, hell," he swore after listening for a moment, "I forgot all about it. Thanks, Tom. We'll be right down."

"Get dressed," he ordered. "We've got to be downstairs to greet our guests in ten minutes!"

"Ten minutes? We'll never make it."

"Not if you stay there," Ken grimaced, giving her a light kiss before he arose. "I'll take the shower."

Audrey was dressed and made up before Ken had

finished showering and she tapped her foot impatiently while he finished dressing.

"Well," he asked as they left the room, "how do you like this arrangement?"

"Nice." Audrey slipped her hand into his. "I think you were right about this being a setup though."

"Oh?"

"I didn't do it," she hastened to explain.

"Too bad," he grinned. "Not that it matters anymore." He kissed the top of her head.

"Maybe we should leave at separate times, just in case Barney is lurking about. He made all sorts of insinuating remarks yesterday."

"Barney can damn well..." Ken muttered something under his breath.

"Ken! That's disgusting!"

"Sorry, I'll have to learn to hold my tongue around you." When they entered the elevator, Ken smiled at her. "Did I tell you, you look beautiful?"

"No." Audrey stepped away from his impending kiss. "You'll mess up my makeup," she teased.

"You don't need it." He winked at her. He glanced at the lighted numbers as they flashed in sequence above the door. "Tom and Janet should be in the lobby."

"Oh!" Audrey blushed and bit her lower lip. How could she have forgotten about Janet?

"I think I'd better explain something to you," said Ken, but the elevator doors opened and Tom made a point of checking his watch when he saw them.

"We're running late, Ken," he said with a tinge of annoyance. "You look lovely, dear." He smiled at Audrey, studying the effect of her silky-blue, strapless gown with a practiced eye.

"Thank you," she murmured, not daring to look up at either Tom or Janet.

"We seem to have changed partners." Tom offered the brunette his arm, and to Audrey's amazement Janet did not seem the least perturbed. What poise. She was a better actress than Audrey had given her credit.

They stood at the entrance to the magnificent crystal-chandeliered ballroom to greet the guests, many of them foreign dignitaries Audrey had only read of in newspaper accounts. During dinner she found herself seated next to Señor Arevalo, the Colómbian Minister of Energy, with the vice-president of Brazil seated across from her. Thanks to Mike and the Congressional Research Service, Audrey was able to discuss the various solar energy systems and their benefits and shortcomings with some degree of accuracy and intelligence.

"These modern Americanas," teased the minister, a portly, beribboned man who was fully cognizant of his self-importance, plus a generous measure to which he was not necessarily entitled by rank or birth. "There is no end to the information they can store. Little computers every one," he laughed, kissing her hand as they all arose to survey the displays and mingle.

Later in the evening the executive director of a midwestern solar manufacturing plant was brought over to Audrey by Barney.

"This is the little lady you need to be talkin' to," he boomed, and Audrey cringed at Barney's boorish manners.

The thin, nasal-toned, balding man soon launched into a monologue about the merits of his particular system, and while Audrey affected an air of polite listening, her mind drifted back to the hotel room and Ken. And Janet.

"Now what we have to do is get this damned government off our back. We don't need all these useless regulations," he was saying when Audrey's mind wandered back to the current affair.

"Excuse me," she interrupted, "weren't you just saying that the government should be funding and backing these programs?"

"Yes." His eyes narrowed suspiciously. "What's your point?"

"Well, unfortunate though it may be," she stated, although she was not in full agreement as to its undesirability, "whenever the government hands out large grants of money, the natural tendency is to regulate the use, not that that always works out to the mutual satisfaction of either party."

"Let 'em regulate what needs regulating! I know my business," he retorted.

"'Course you do. 'Course you do. Why don't you just get yourself a refill," Barney indicated the executive's nearly empty glass. "We'll be right with you." As soon as the man had melted into the crowd, Barney turned on Audrey. "What the hell do you think you are doing?"

"I beg your pardon?"

"That man expects to be treated real nice. Real nice," he repeated with a suggestive wink. "If you get my meaning. Not get a damn lecture on the federal bureaucracy!" Audrey glared contemptuously at Barney. "If not," he threatened, "that cozy room arrangement of yours is going to get a mite warm. A mite warm!"

"That reminds me, Barney. Mr. Walker would like to go over those expense accounts with you. Due to a mix-up, he is having to share a room. He would hate to discover that he was being charged for a room no one was using."

It was a pointless evasion of the truth, but it was not entirely a lie. Still she hated to start out this way. His manner demeaned her relationship with Ken though, and she saw no reason to substantiate his nasty innuendo. Besides she enjoyed watching the greedy man squirm. She hoped, however, he would not discover her duplicity. Ken approached and Barney hastily departed.

"I didn't think you knew how to lie," Ken whispered as he steered Audrey out to the balcony.

"With Barney it was so easy," she giggled.

Ken's eyes bored into Audrey's. "Just don't start with me, okay?"

"Ken..." Audrey was crestfallen.

"I don't think I could stand it if you did." He pulled her to him and his mouth was demanding and possessive. "There's no way I'm rooming with Tom," he laughed, "so you'll have to stay a dishonest woman. Besides," he bent to nibble her ear, "he has a roommate."

"Who?" she asked when his arms closed securely around her.

"Over there," he said, nodding to his right.

"Janet?" she gasped.

"Yes. Which prominent Phoenix architect did you think they meant in that article?"

"You know very well who I thought!"

"Whom. And, yes, I did."

"Why didn't you tell me right off?" she demanded.

Ken shrugged and bent to kiss her, moving his tongue slowly over her soft, yielding lips, reawakening the total response she had so recently demonstrated. Pressing her to him, he caressed her and covered the side of her head with eager kisses. "Maybe because of all those years you made me suffer," he mumbled against her smooth, soft cheek as he searched for her mouth. "Am I forgiven?" he asked, hovering just above her lips.

"Yes," she answered with every fiber of her soul.

"Isn't it beautiful?" he sighed at last as they looked out across the ocean.

The domed night surrounded and encased them, the navy satin lining of the heavens strewn with a million, flickering jewels, while the ocean murmured its perpetual rhythmic melody and cast its lace edging along the iridescent sands.

"Yes," whispered Audrey, but her gaze had wandered to Ken's finely chiseled, angular profile. Every ounce of her being was alive with the depths of her commitment to him, and the sea and the heavens hummed of the constancy of her love to the accompaniment of the mariachi music.

"The song never ends," he murmured, demonstrating once more how closely aligned were their thoughts.

"Not thinking of ways to harness the tides, are you?" asked Tom, wearing a gentle smile as he and Janet strolled across the terrace to them.

"I'm dedicated," Ken grinned in response, "but I do have some romance in my soul."

Audrey was comfortably enclosed in his strong arms, and she leaned her head back against his shoulder and tenderly squeezed his arm. "I can attest to that," she smiled happily.

Ken bent to look down into her upturned face and his dark eyes smoldered before he grimaced in annoyance. He glanced at his watch and groaned. "Is this thing never going to end?"

"Don't be so ungallant," scolded Tom. "These people are our guests." He smiled at Audrey. "He's such a diamond in the rough. Maybe you can smooth over some of the ragged edges."

"I doubt it," giggled Audrey. "He's a very stubborn man."

"Persistent," Ken corrected her. "I'd better get back to Señora Castegna," he sighed, "before she comes looking for me."

He left and to Audrey's dismay, the midwestern bore was coming toward her.

"Ms. Mathieson," he twanged, "we didn't get to finish our little discussion." He glanced over the railing. "These peasants sure know how to put on a fine display for the tourists," he nodded approvingly at the colorful band strolling along the patio beneath them. "It is much more...pleasant out here, I must admit," he winked at Audrey.

She cast a furtive, pleading glance at Tom and Janet, but they only waved and smiled encouragingly as they departed. It was only a matter of minutes until the nasty little toad was patting Audrey's hand and tentatively reaching for her waist or shoulders. With a casual toss of her hair, Audrey gracefully changed position so often she was beginning to feel like a choreographer. And still, the obnoxious little man persisted.

"Señorita," called the minister. He came out to the terrace and made a sweeping bow when he gallantly kissed her hand. "I have been searching for you all evening."

Audrey introduced him to the American executive and in glowing terms described the system the American was involved with. Preening like a little bantam rooster, the man was soon filling the minister's ear with exaggerated tales of his operation, and the two men stroked each other's egos to their mutual satisfaction. Quite unnoticed, Audrey slipped back inside only to confront Barney with yet another businessman on the make. This rather distinguished-looking man, who upon closer inspection proved equally seedy, flattered and cajoled Audrey, making ill-disguised suggestions for that and subsequent evenings. Janet mercifully rescued Audrey from the two cloying men, and Audrey took the occasion to tell her how happy she was about her wedding plans.

"For more than one reason, I'm sure," laughed Janet.

"Am I that obvious?" blushed Audrey.

"Actually no. But Ken certainly has been!"

"He has?"

"Sure." Janet laughed heartily. "You are probably the only one who wasn't aware of it."

"Are you putting me on?" Audrey asked in astonishment.

"Not in the slightest. Ken has been tripping over himself ever since you started on this project. I swear even if you hadn't been able to do a thing, Tom would have hired you just to shut him up!"

"Ken?" Audrey shook her head in disbelief. "He rarely says two words."

"Don't we all wish!" trilled Janet. She looked around for Tom. "Thank God! They're leaving."

"Is everyone gone?" asked Audrey when they joined the two men at the doorway. She checked the empty room.

"Yes, finally," Ken answered.

"I wonder if we could get a bottle of champagne at this hour?" mused Janet as they filed into the elevator.

"Let's go up to my room and see," suggested Ken.

"Well, what do you know?" he grinned when he

threw the door open wide, revealing the red-rose festooned sitting room.

"How lovely," smiled Janet.

"Where did these come from?" asked an awestruck Audrey.

"Bushes I should imagine," teased Ken. "Like them?" Audrey was too busy blinking back the tears to answer. "I guess so," he grinned, hugging her tightly.

"I'm afraid there are only two glasses," he said as he walked over to the silver champagne bucket, his arm around Audrey. "We'll have to share."

Tom carefully popped the cork with the minimum of fuss or mess. "I think we can manage," he smiled.

"A toast." Tom placed his hand around Janet's and raised the glass she held. "To the success and future of Nava del Sol," his gray eyes gazed fondly at Janet and Audrey, "and everything begun with it."

"Have you told her yet?" Tom asked Ken when they had drunk to the toast.

"No. I've decided to wait until the opening."

"That's less than five months away. Will it be ready by then?"

"I certainly hope so."

"What?" asked Audrey.

"It's Ken's secret," smiled Tom. "We'll see how long he can keep it."

"Judging by his past record, I'd say we'll know by tomorrow!" laughed Janet.

"I've matured with age," Ken retorted smugly.

"You haven't done much of either," laughed Tom. He took Janet's arm. "Come, my dear. We have a long day tomorrow. What do you plan to do with your spare time?"

"Hit the beach, then the shops. How about it, Audrey?"

"Am I free?" she asked Ken.

"Yes," Tom answered. "Ken didn't plan this very well. You're getting a paid vacation. Enjoy!"

"Meet you at ten," called Janet as they left.

"Do you mind?" Audrey asked Ken.

"Why should I?"

"Well, I am working for you..."

"Don't worry," he grinned. "You'll earn your keep." He poured her another glass of champagne and led her into the bedroom. "Just see that you don't earn it Barney's way."

"Ken!"

He pulled her onto his lap and laughed at her irate reaction. "You are ravishing when you are furious," he grinned. "Especially in that dress, although frankly I preferred the towel."

"Ken!" Audrey blushed and her eyes wandered to the huge bouquet of scarlet blooms on the chest of drawers beside the bed. "When did you order all these roses?" she asked with a puzzled frown.

"Last night."

"But..." Audrey shook her head in confusion. "How did you know everything would get all mixed up?"

"Because," that dazzling smile lit up his face, "I made the arrangements."

Audrey stared at his smug expression. "Then you weren't surprised to see me?" she accused.

"Oh, yes I was! Especially like that!" he laughed. "I was planning to surprise you!"

"The best laid plans of..."

"Oh, no! Not another one," he warned, stopping her in midsentence with a playful kiss that quickly increased in ardor. He took the glass from her and set it beside the vase of flowers.

"I didn't get to drink that," protested Audrey.

"And you are not going to. I just remembered that when you drink, you don't get uninhibited, you fall asleep!"

"Speaking of sleep," Audrey looked around the large room, "which bed do you want?"

"Which one do you think, you little tease?" Ken kissed her and leaned forward until Audrey fell over onto her back.

"My brother wouldn't approve," she smiled, tracing

his wide, sensitive mouth with the tip of her index finger.

"That is where you are wrong," he laughed, arching one eyebrow. "Besides, we could take care of that."

"How?"

"We won't tell your brother."

A tiny frown flickered across her brow and settled into a chagrined lift of one eyebrow. "That is not exactly what I had in mind," she said softly, afraid to press him into a premature, or worse, false commitment.

"No?" he smiled tenderly.

"No."

"We'll see." He grinned, running his fingers through her long, silky hair. "First I should make sure I'm going to want you around for an extended period of time, don't you think?"

A tiny edge of white showed as Audrey lightly scraped her teeth along her lower lip. "What if you don't?"

"Won't happen," he confidently asserted, bending to kiss her.

The tender embrace deepened when Audrey opened her mouth and their tongues began the slow, sensuous tasting examination in tandem with their hands that unfastened and explored, teasing, provoking, and enflaming flesh until it cried out for the soothing moisture of mouths, and when that was not enough, the final, tension-releasing union of bodies.

It was a languid, confident mingling of bodies and minds. Love had been declared, accepted, welcomed. Emotional conflict out of the way, they were free to discover and enjoy the intimacy. As the last waves of euphoria ebbed, Audrey nestled sleepily into Ken's arms, marveling at what she had missed all these years.

"Well," he asked, "what about you? Do you want me hanging around you for the rest of your life?"

"Longer," she said, kissing his collarbone. "Why did Janet say you couldn't keep a secret? I never knew how you felt."

"I didn't want Alan to know."

"What?" Audrey raised up to look at him.

"Old rivalry," he shrugged. "I kept throwing girls at him, hoping he'd leave you alone. But, no, you had to keep tagging along after him." Ken cupped his hand on Audrey's cheek, his eyes dark and misty. "I wanted to break your stupid little neck."

"I was so thrilled to have him pay any attention to me, a nothing, little freshman," she shrugged.

"You were never nothing," he huskily asserted, placing her head under his chin.

"But I was a hero-worshipper. Maybe," she said softly, "when Alan didn't turn out to be a hero, I let him down."

"There was no way you could have prevented that. Alan was always insecure. Everything and everyone threatened him." It was a quiet, thoughtful statement, devoid of rancor or pity.

"Maybe I should have tried harder," she sighed.

There was a long silence. "Regrets?"

"Yes." Audrey sat up and caressed Ken's smooth cheek and slowly ran her fingers through his thick, glossy black hair. "I wish I had known how you felt."

"Would it have made a difference?" he asked, pressing her hand to his lips.

"I don't know." She looked away shyly. "I never felt this way about anyone. Not even Alan."

"Audrey," he whispered, rolling her on her back and leaning over her, "I'll never let you go again."

"Promise?"

"I love you," he mumbled as his hands gently and possessively drew her ever closer.

Chapter Eleven

Sleep was refreshingly blissful and Audrey awakened to discover that Ken was already dressed.

"Lazybones," he laughed, knotting his tie. "You must work for a real softie."

"I'm not working at all today," she said, scrunching up his pillow and burrowing into it.

"You'll have to make up for it tomorrow." He bent to kiss her shoulder. "Don't get sunburned," he warned. "I'll be damned if I am going to sleep in the same room with you and not be able to touch you." He plunked the other pillow on top of her head. "Make yourself decent. Breakfast is on its way up and Mrs. Potter is doing just fine."

Suddenly awake, Audrey sat up and looked at him. "You called home already? Is Bonnie okay?"

"She's going to the zoo this morning, so you'll have to call her this afternoon." Ken kissed her lightly. "I'm late."

"Aren't you having breakfast with me?" Audrey asked, disappointment marring her pretty face.

"Can't this morning."

"Ken... thank you."

Ken flashed a broad, teasing leer. "My pleasure."

"I meant for calling Mrs. Potter."

With an agile movement he ducked the pillow she had flung at him. "Someone has to look after the little dickens, what with that jet-setting mother she has," he winked. "'Bye."

Audrey arose and showered, but the radiant glow did

not diminish, bolstered as it was by her boundless love and respect for Ken.

"Where are my sunglasses?" teased Janet, shielding her eyes when Audrey approached her in the lobby. "If you glowed any brighter, you'd mess up all the solar devices," she laughed, pointing to the displays set up outside the main meeting room.

"It shows?" Audrey grinned sheepishly.

"Just a tad," Janet laughed throatily. "I just saw Ken and the two of you could power your own photovoltaic generator. I wonder if Tom can harness any of that into his houses?"

The two women strolled across the dazzling white beach behind two hotel attendants who carried chairs while they selected a site.

"What do you think of Nava del Sol?" Audrey asked after thanking and tipping the two young men.

Janet hesitated, holding the half-opened bottle of suntan lotion in midair.

"I can't put it into words," she said quietly in a voice filled with emotion. "It's Tom's so, of course, I would love it, no matter what. But this is so much more than I had anticipated. Everyone has always been so concerned with squeezing every dime they could out of every inch of land. But not Tom. When Ken showed up with his final plans for the project, I thought Tom was going to break down. He had kept that land untouched for years, wanting to do something like this, never having the time to devote to it, adamant that not so much as a rock be removed until he knew exactly what he would do."

"I know," said Audrey. "That was what attracted Ken to Tom in the first place."

"He hired Ken specifically for this and offered him the partnership to support it."

"They were both taking a big chance," said Audrey. "It's been a constant battle with the administration in Washington to support solar technology development. So many of the eastern powerbrokers think it's a fluke."

"That's because it doesn't require some rare, expensive fuel someone can own or manipulate," Janet stated, giving a short, cynical laugh.

"Congress finally passed that bill allowing federal tax credits for solar installations," Audrey said, smiling proudly at the part her brother had played in securing the legislation. "Together with the Arizona tax credits and depreciation, Ken's solar energy systems are very economical. You should have heard the utilities squawk when the Federal Energy Regulatory Commission required them to buy back the excess electricity generated by these solar-powered systems Ken is using."

"I heard!" she laughed. She shook her black hair back over her shoulders and applied some lotion to her arms. "They didn't mind getting the electricity; they just hated the thought that some poor consumer might turn on a light bulb without having to pay a king's ransom! I don't think they like to see their meters running in reverse," she added with a bemused grin.

"It's never worked that way before," laughed Audrey. She inspected her shiny arms and legs. "Think I've got enough goop on me?"

"Sun's very hot here," Janet shrugged. "I rarely burn and I'm slathered. What's Ken's surprise?" Janet changed the subject as she stretched out in the sun.

"I have no idea," answered Audrey. She put on her sunglasses and adjusted the position of the back of her lounge chair.

"You are probably the only one he can keep anything from," grinned the brunette. "And that's because you are such a perfect foil."

"Was that foil or fool?" grinned Audrey.

"Foil. But be careful it's not the latter."

"What are you getting at?"

"Ken is very special. You seem to have developed the habit of tuning him out, Audrey. He's so transparent where you are concerned, it breaks my heart." Janet was suddenly serious. "Don't hurt him, Audrey," she warned.

Audrey shoved her hair aside and adjusted her sunglasses, grateful for the protective screen the dark lenses provided. "I won't," she quietly vowed.

"What are you doing out here?" boomed Barney's stentorian voice. He waddled over to them, sinking into the soft sand with each step and intermittently shaking it out of his shoes as he walked across the beach.

"Pretend you're asleep," groaned Janet, placing her wide-brimmed straw hat over her face.

"You just trot right on in here with me, gal," he ordered, pulling on Audrey's arm. "I've got a client waitin' for you."

"I'm off duty today," she protested, jerking her arm free.

"You're in my employ, missy, and I'm tellin' you to get in there."

"I thought Mr. Walker made it abundantly clear that I would not be free to work on anything but Nava del Sol until it was completed," snapped Audrey. She wrapped her short beach coat around her to conceal her bikini-clad figure from Barney's insolent inspection.

"There's no reason you can't meet with some prospects," he growled. "Not unless you enjoy giving the impression you're Walker's floozy."

Audrey checked the automatic, indignant retort and answered calmly and coolly, "You are getting very tiresome, Barney. Haven't you worn that out yet?"

He gripped her arm and squeezed it painfully in his meaty hand. "How do you think it looks for me, sweetie? My employee loafin' around like some high-paid chippie when this is supposed to be a business trip?"

Audrey glared at him, her acute animosity barely under control. That was exactly what he was trying to pass her off as.

"We have that meeting at one," Janet interrupted. She poked around in her bag and removed her watch. "I'm sure you can spare Mr. Longworth about twenty minutes."

"What meeting is that?" asked a very suspicious Barney, and Audrey was just as curious.

"Ms. Mathieson and I are due to speak to a number of local merchants this afternoon," Janet explained, her demeanor so calm and reserved Audrey's estimation of her soared even higher, and she suppressed the giggle that threatened to blow the carefully constructed fabrication.

"That so?" asked Barney, looking from one to the other with great misgivings.

"That is so," said Janet, stretching back out in the sun.

"Why wasn't I told?" Barney asked Audrey as he led her to the lobby.

"It came up after dinner last night," shrugged Audrey. "Goodwill tour, that sort of thing. PR." It was not a complete lie. Certainly supporting the local economy could be classified as "public relations."

The executive she had met the night before arose from one of the lattice-woven chairs in the lobby and extended his hand.

"Ms. Mathieson?" he smiled charmingly.

"Mr. Acheson."

"I'm flattered you remember," he smiled, squeezing her hand and placing his other hand over hers instead of releasing it once the conversation had begun.

"It's my job," Audrey smiled, although she did not say it aloud.

None too subtly, he examined her long, lightly tanned legs, which glistened from the suntan lotion. "May I buy you a drink?" he offered as he led her to a table on the terrace.

Audrey rarely drank, so she never knew what to order. What was the name of that drink she remembered seeing in a magazine ad with Mexico in the background? It was someone's name.

"Margarita," she ordered when it came to mind.

Mr. Acheson raised his eyebrow. "Tequila drinker?" He ordered a pitcher and sat back to look at Audrey, who had the distinct impression he was assessing his odds and his best approach.

It was not yet noon, but was already extremely warm.

The breeze from the ocean was soft and refreshing and the margarita was delicious. The salted rim mingled pleasantly with the beach air, and the cool, refreshingly tart drink went down surprisingly easy. So easily, that Audrey finished several as quickly as if they were iced tea, for the salt increased her thirst.

Mr. Acheson was going on about something mundane about which Audrey had not the slightest interest, when he refilled her glass for the fourth time. A waiter approached the table and handed her a note. Audrey stared at the blurry missive and concluded that Janet had dreadful handwriting. However, she had not forgotten the afternoon's excursion, only lost track of the time, so she excused herself and thanked Mr. Acheson for his hospitality.

"I look forward to being repaid," he smiled, rising when she did.

"Yes, of course," she smiled blandly. What the devil was he talking about?

She exited through the lobby and looked around the atrium for Janet, an excessively difficult feat, for her eyelids kept trying to close.

"Oh, Lord!" laughed Janet. "Let's go get you dressed."

"What time is it?" asked Audrey.

"Nearly two. Good thing Ken's not here," she giggled, leading Audrey to the elevators.

"Whatever do you mean?" asked Audrey, drawing herself up primly.

"What have you been drinking?"

"Margaritas," grinned Audrey. "And they were delicious!"

"How many of those things did you have?"

"Lots, I think. But I am not drunk. Just very tired." She yawned.

"Would you rather not go shopping?"

"No, I'm fine. I'll take a shower to wake up." Audrey blinked rapidly. "I can hardly keep my eyes open."

"I'm not surprised." Janet shook her head in amazement. "Those things are lethal."

By two thirty, thoroughly refreshed, Audrey went on a shopping binge. Up the road from the Playa was a complex of open stalls and tiny specialty shops featuring magnificent examples of handblown amber glass from Mexico City and delicately painted pottery from the Tlaquepaque factories outside of Guadalajara, placed beside gaudily decorated earthenware. Cheap costume jewelry vied for the tourist trade opposite exquisite sterling-and-turquoise pieces from Colômbia, and shoddy leather merchandise rested alongside butter-soft suede from Venezuela. In a small shop tucked into an alleyway, Audrey found an array of gaily embroidered linen and cotton pinafores and purchased one in every color for Bonnie.

Five o'clock brought an end to her extravagance when Janet reminded her that Tom and Ken expected them for dinner. When Ken returned to the hotel that evening, Audrey was dressing.

"Have fun, tourist?" he teased at the pile of packages covering one of the beds. "Did you leave anything for anyone else?" he laughed as he turned her around to zip her dress, pausing to kiss her shoulder before completing the task.

"Those wrapped packages are for you," she said.

Ken wandered over to the bed. "What is all this? It looks like Christmas came early!"

"No. Your birthday came late," she shrugged. She ran the brush through her hair and decided to leave the long tresses free. "There are just a couple." She kissed his cheek and handed him the first.

"Almendaro!" he laughed when he unwrapped a coconut that had been carved into a gorilla. "That is the ugliest thing I have ever seen," he chuckled as he turned it around in his hand.

"Yours was uglier."

"Not by a mile!"

"Beauty is in the eyes," she retorted.

"So it is," Ken agreed, gazing deeply into Audrey's laughing green eyes. "What else did I get?"

He opened a long rectangular box. It was a small

chess set and the little metal figures represented various characters from Don Quixote. Ken held up the tiny knight and examined it.

"Do you think I am a dreamer?" he asked. "Tilting at windmills?"

"No. But I do know what an uphill battle this has been," she said gently.

Ken picked up the windmill. "You know this represents our competitor?" he teased.

"Not yours," she dismissed him with a toss of her luxurious hair. "You'd use any source that worked, and you know it. It's your solar suppliers who think they have the only practical renewable resource."

"You think you're so smart," he grinned, pulling Audrey onto his lap. He opened the package containing the inlaid chess board and one that held a brightly embroidered shirt.

"Here," Audrey handed him the last one, a large, flat parcel that proved surprisingly heavy.

"What's this? A paving stone?" He unwrapped a book of recent architectural innovations. "It's in Spanish!"

Audrey opened it to a marked page and pointed to an article about Nava del Sol and some drawings signed "K.W."

"Mike told me you had had some work published in an anthology a few years ago, and I thought that looked like the title he had mentioned. The book dealer thought I was crazy going through it page by page."

Ken gave a short laugh that was followed by a look of amazement. "That was over three years ago. You remembered?"

"Yes," she blushed. "It surprised me too."

A wry, crooked smile put in a brief appearance and Ken surveyed all the presents. "This must have cost you an awful lot, Audrey."

"Didn't I tell you?" she laughed. "I'm on an extravagant expense allowance."

"Audrey," he gently scolded, "you can't afford this."

"I wanted to do it," she said quietly. "Barney was very generous with his bonus... something I'm sure he immediately regretted," she added with a grimace. "Don't spoil it, Ken."

"I would never spoil anything for you." He held her tightly and ran his finger lightly down her profile. "Beautiful little Audrey," he grinned. "You always got your way."

"You always put up a terrible fight, first," she laughed. "Besides, I was never that 'little.' For two years I was taller than you."

"One. And what good did it do you?" Ken stood up and patted the top of her head, which only came to his nose. "What else did you do today?" he asked as he went to change his shirt. "Besides sit on the beach?"

"If you know, why did you ask?" Audrey followed him to the dressing area and touched up her lipstick.

"You're not brown enough to have been there very long."

"Barney insisted I meet some manufacturer who plied me with tequila until Janet rescued me."

"Well, if that's his technique, you're safe enough. What did he do when you fell asleep at the table?"

"Nothing. I didn't."

Ken walked over and tipped her face up. "You're not getting used to that stuff, are you?"

"No," she giggled, putting her arms around his waist. "Now who's being stuffy?"

"I think I'll have a word with Barney," he muttered, kissing the top of her head.

"He thinks I've been shacking up with you to get the account."

"Barney has an evil little mind, Audrey. I can't wait until this campaign is over so you can stop working for that..."

"What will I do then?" she asked, stepping aside so he could see in the mirror to comb his hair.

"You can transfer to any other agency you want."

"Are you sure?"

Ken turned around to face her. "You have to have

more confidence, Audrey." He took a long, slow breath. "I know Alan nearly destroyed yours, but that's over now."

"Yes, it is." She smiled shyly, placing her arms around his neck and his arms closed securely around her.

"I'll do everything I can for you, you know that. But for your own good, you have to learn to stand on your own feet."

"I'm getting better. I can stand up to Barney. Sometimes."

"Sometimes isn't good enough." He held her away. "It won't be for much longer," he promised, kissing her forehead, her nose, and her chin.

"What?"

"This... awkward arrangement, for one thing." He looked steadily into her eyes. "Would you rather have your own room?"

"No," she said, after a moment's hesitation. "I love you."

"Don't worry about Barney," he grinned as he led her to the door. "Everyone knows about us, and they're all jealous!"

"Maybe," she blushed, "we should be a little more discreet."

"Remember how we used to try to hide our lightning bugs in our hands by clamping one hand over the other? And the spaces between our fingers would glow?" he laughed. "Well, I have about as much chance of concealing the way I feel about you. And you, my dear," he kissed her lightly, "I am happy to say, are not faring much better!"

"I thought I was very subtle and circumspect," she said in an affectation of aloofness.

"Well, you're not."

"That's just because you could always see right through me."

"Too bad you weren't as gifted," he grinned, squeezing her hand affectionately as they walked down the corridor.

"And you waited all these years for me anyway?"

Ken laughed heartily. "What a conceited little monkey you are!" He looked at her and shook his head. "Sorry to disillusion you, but no, I didn't. I was well over you years ago." He hugged her to his side as he pressed the elevator button. "Until I ran into your brother and I saw that picture of you and Bonnie, and he told me about your divorce, that is."

"Then what?"

"Then I really knew it was all over!"

"Oh. Just curious."

"Curiosity skinned the cat."

They walked arm in arm to the patio restaurant where Tom and Janet were already seated, and Audrey was delighted to see that it would only be the four of them.

"I trust the day's activities did not tire you too much?" inquired Tom, and from the twinkle in his gray eyes she knew Janet had fully apprised him of her escapade with the margaritas.

"A water and water for the lady," Ken deadpanned to the cocktail waiter when he arrived to take their order.

"No," Audrey laughingly protested. "Those margaritas are delicious!"

"You have had enough for today."

"Am I going to be rationed?" asked Audrey, arching one eyebrow.

"No, your drinking is," said Janet.

The waiter returned with a margarita which he placed before Audrey and she stared blankly at him. The small, red-jacketed Mexican man nodded toward a far table occupied by Mr. Acheson. Audrey frowned and she felt Ken stiffen at her side.

"Excuse me," she said politely, "there's been a mistake." She replaced the glass on the tray without acknowledging Mr. Acheson.

"I understand Ken is an author of sorts," Tom broke the tension.

"I don't know what sort." She smiled at Ken. "I can't read very much Spanish."

"Maybe that's an improvement," teased Janet.

"I don't doubt it," laughed Ken, placing his knee against Audrey's. Her relief at the end of that uncomfortable incident was short-lived, for Barney approached their table.

"I am sorry, Barney," Audrey declined his offer to "talk." "It will have to wait until Monday."

"Business meeting?" he asked sarcastically as he glowered down at her.

"No, dinner." Audrey pointedly checked her watch. "I do not work after five unless I choose to do so."

"I will see you at nine, sharp, Monday morning. In the Terrace Restaurant," he growled before he stalked off.

"He certainly has a lot of nerve," Janet said.

Tom frowned at Ken. "You know why he's acting this way, of course?"

"Yes, and I am beginning to dislike the ground he swaggers on," scowled Ken.

Tom reached into his pocket and removed a card which he gave to Audrey. When she read the name of the prestigious Phoenix advertising agency, she raised her eyebrow.

"He's an old friend," said Tom, referring to the name of the president printed at the bottom. "Go see him."

"Thank you," Audrey said after several moments of indecision. She handed the card back to Tom. "I'll contact him when this project is completed." She smiled broadly. "If you think I'm going to abandon Nava del Sol to Barney, you are crazy! And it would be highly unethical to steal the account from him."

"You'd have to wrestle him," laughed Janet, and Audrey joined her, shaking her head in horror at the prospect.

Tom nodded approvingly and pocketed the card. "That leaves only one alternative," he said to Ken.

"So it would appear." He gave Tom a wry smile. "I have my own timetable, and Barney is not about to dictate the terms."

"What are you talking about?" asked Audrey.

"You're going to have to learn to be a little patient," smiled Ken. He shook his head at Audrey. "Don't you ever see what's going on around you?" he asked when her expression grew more confused.

"No, what?"

"You will soon enough."

"Anyone for a walk along the beach?" asked Ken when dinner was over.

"I'll go," offered Audrey.

"You never had any choice," he grinned, dragging her with him when the others declined.

"Wait until I get my shoes off," she protested when they reached the sand.

"Good idea." Ken sat on the edge of the patio and removed his. "Leave them here," he said, placing Audrey's high-heeled sandals next to his.

It was much easier to walk on the firm, damp sand near the shoreline, and they strolled slowly, arms wrapped around each other's waists. A young couple on horseback cantered along the beach and waved to them as they passed.

"Would you like to do that?" asked Ken.

"It looks like fun. Would you?"

Ken gazed into her upturned face. "I'd rather have you here, close to me," he whispered, hugging her tighter and resting his head against hers.

Audrey slipped her other arm around his slim waist and clasped her wrist to encircle him. She would never tire of walking with him, holding him, matching her stride to his, feeling his lean, muscular movement beside her.

"There's no place I'd rather be," she said softly. "For as long as I live."

"Is that all?" His long, sensitive fingers gently caressed her arm. "That's not nearly long enough."

"How long?" she asked, and his answer was a deep, yearning kiss.

They paused as millions had before, since the dawn of man, to watch the waves roll out, each new edge of the delicate foam imperceptibly curling and meandering further away than the last as the ocean receded, leaving behind its treasures: some, microscopic passengers of the eternal seas; others, secret delights disgorged from the deepest recesses of the tidal basins; still others, objects stolen from the land by raging currents, returned at whim and leisure to alien soil. Ken stooped down and picked up a sand dollar.

"The ocean has opened its safe," he grinned, holding the pearly object up in the moonlight before he handed it to Audrey. "Also, its garbage disposal," he grimaced, stepping over an old, rusted can. "Gifts from the sea." He shook his head and smiled. "You don't get to choose which ones the sea sets before you."

He put his hands in his pockets and stared out across the gently swelling blackness and his voice was soft and shy. "When you married Alan, I figured I could just go out and look for someone else to love. I kept thinking, 'maybe this one,' but it never happened." Ken's profile was etched by the moonlight and Audrey reached out to touch his face. "I came close... once, but when I found out you had divorced Alan..." Ken placed his hands on Audrey's face and gently tipped it up, bringing his forehead down to rest against hers. "I was always afraid Alan would leave you..." His eyes shone softly as he gazed into the dark green depths. "I can't tell you how I felt when I learned you had filed. It meant you were finally over him." Ken's voice was richly ebullient and he grinned happily. "So I barged right in."

"Lucky me," smiled Audrey, and the glow came from deep within.

"Lucky *me*," he whispered, taking her into his arms.

He turned her around to face the ocean and Audrey sank back against the firm warmth of his all-protective body. "There's eternity for you," he murmured, rocking her gently as she flowed against him, relying solely on his strength for support. "Ebbing and flowing, day in and day out, to the same rhythms. Always the same, yet always different. All that boundless, perpetual energy."

"You are thinking of ways to harness it," she teased, patting his arm affectionately.

"Not true," he laughed. "But I'd be a rich man if I could." He kissed her temple and crouched down, pulling Audrey with him. "Watch this," he pointed to the last bubbling remnants of foam which were quickly replaced by the next wave. "No two waves are identical. No two patterns inscribed in the sand are alike. The tides are fascinating." He helped Audrey to her feet. "You could spend a lifetime looking at this," he spread his arm to indicate the coastline, "and never get bored."

"Why, Ken Walker," she laughed. "You are really a beach bum at heart!"

"Nope." He kissed the top of her head and his arms closed securely around her. "It's just that nothing in nature is boring. Man is the only creature who regiments and systematizes everything."

"Man, not woman," Audrey taunted with a grin, and Ken threw his head back and roared.

"True enough," he agreed, pinching the end of her nose. "Am I boring?"

"Never." A wave of elation washed over Audrey and she lowered her eyes self-consciously as she hugged him. "I've never loved anyone the way I love you, Ken. It almost scares me how much I love you."

"It shouldn't. It must have been written in the stars, or the tides, or all over the world! Nothing this wonderful could have been an accident!"

"No, nothing," Audrey agreed, drawing his face close to kiss him with a profound emotion that far surpassed the most extreme physical desire.

"Love is like the ocean," he laughed shyly as he took her hand and started slowly back down the beach, "if I may be forgiven a momentary lapse into triteness."

"Forgiven." A smiling Audrey leaned her shoulder against his arm.

"Forever demanding something, yet always giving freely in return. Never satisfied with what it has shaped, unceasingly and untiringly molding and forming by gentle persuasion as much as by insistent demands."

"And are you molding and shaping me?" asked Audrey, tilting her head prettily and flashing a teasing grin.

"As much as you are, me," he laughed.

"I thought you were already perfect?" she laughed gaily.

"I was." Ken squeezed the hand he held. "Now, I'm better." He paused to tuck a lock of strawberry-blond hair behind her ear. "I didn't think it was possible for you to get better, but now that you love me," that adorably crooked, sheepish grin meandered across his face, "I see that I have accomplished a miracle. I have improved on perfection."

"You are not too conceited, are you?" laughed Audrey. She swung their arms happily as they walked.

"How is Mrs. Potter holding out?" he asked as they resumed their stroll.

"Very well. I spoke to her this afternoon when I got back from shopping. Bonnie seems very cheerful."

"You should have brought her with you. She would have been well cared for," said Ken. "They have a lot of facilities for children and the staff seems kindly disposed to the children who are here on vacation."

"I know. Mexico is one of the few countries I've been to where they seem genuinely fond of children. It's also one of the few countries I've been to," she laughingly clarified her statement. "But women have a hard time being taken seriously," she sighed. "When you bring along a child, no matter how well-behaved, people treat you as a nonentity. You saw how hostile Barney was that day in the office."

"Barney is a hostile man." He stopped and turned to face Audrey. "I know how much you miss her though and how hard it is for you to leave her."

"It won't be for much longer." Audrey absently bit her lower lip. "She took her first steps with Mrs. Haskell."

"This is the longest you'll ever be away from her, I promise. After this project is finished, I'm going to make certain you two are not separated again."

"How?" Audrey smiled curiously, wondering how far she should press him for an answer.

"No patience," he laughed, taking her hand and continuing along the beach. "You're not ready to take on Barney yet," he returned to a neutral topic. "But you're getting there. Can you guess his next move?"

"More harassment," shrugged Audrey. "Why is he doing this? I've never done anything to him."

"He doesn't need a reason. It's his nature. Do you remember Bobby Miller?"

"The paraplegic? Sure, but..." Audrey could not make any connection between Ken's high school classmate and her boss.

"Back when Bobby and I worked for the school paper, Barney was the radio announcer who covered the high school games."

"I remember."

"Good ol' Barney used to put gum wads in Bobby's notes and mash out his cigars in his coffee. But the worst thing he did was set up obstacles so that Bobby couldn't get in or out of the press box without a great deal of difficulty. And he used to place bets with the maintenance man on how long it would take Bobby to maneuver around them." Ken's voice had deepened to a growl of wrathful indignation. "He also did imitations of Bobby when he thought no one was around who'd talk."

"How did you find out all this? About the bets, I mean? You were on the team, not in the press box."

"One day the maintenance man had had a few belts

and he started doing one of Barney's routines outside the gym."

"Wait a minute!" Audrey snapped her fingers. "Did this have anything to do with the press box mysteriously caving in on Barney?"

"Come to think of it," he chuckled, "it might have."

"Walker's Marauders?" she teased.

"I can't remember that far back," he feigned innocence.

"Old age?" laughed Audrey.

"I could never warm up to Barney," he shrugged. "If he spots a weakness, he goes for it with a vengeance."

"And you're my weakness?" Audrey quietly asked.

"Nope." He kissed her cheek. "I'm your strength. However, he knows you are vulnerable." He smiled fondly at her. "You're not that sure of yourself and he can't pass up the opportunity to hit someone who can't hit back."

"I wish I knew how to fight him," sighed Audrey.

"Why? You're no fighter. You never were." His arms tightened around her, protectively enfolding her. "Feisty with a short fuse," he chuckled, "but you never went for the jugular."

"Is that what it takes!" She frowned, dismayed at the ugly thought.

"No." He gazed with enormous affection into her eyes. "You are what you are, and I love you. Just don't be a doormat." He held her face in his hands and his thumbs tenderly stroked her cheekbones. "Do you trust me?"

"Of course." Audrey placed her hands on his. "I love you."

When he bent to kiss her, his lips were warm and moist and Audrey melted longingly against him, her body supple as it responded naturally and lovingly to his touch.

"Audrey, I love you," he repeated.

"I know." She kissed his cheek and clasped her hands

tightly behind his neck. Golden highlights danced off her silky hair. The moonlight that shimmered on the dark ocean imparted a creamy softness to her face and neck and modest cleavage visible at the neckline of her frothy, peach-colored garment.

"Come on," said Ken, his voice thick and raspy, "or I'll ravish you right here and now, public beach or not."

He walked her briskly back to the hotel, pausing just long enough to pick up their shoes, but not allowing her time to put them on.

"Ken," laughed Audrey, running to keep up with him, "what's the matter with you?"

"I'm in love," he laughed, sweeping her up into his arms to carry her into the waiting elevator that fortunately was empty. "I think I'll eat you up," he grinned after he had put her down and pressed every button on the panel. "You look delicious." He immediately began to nibble on her neck.

"Stop that!" she protested with a laugh. "It tickles."

"It's not supposed to tickle. It is supposed to send you into paroxysms of joy."

"Well then, you must not be doing it right."

"No?" Ken stepped back to look at her. "Is that so?" He bent forward and slowly kissed her chin back to the juncture of her jaw beneath her ear. With a feathery lightness his teeth traced the soft flesh that covered her bone, barely scraping the surface.

"Does that tickle?" he mumbled as his lips moved up to capture the thin, fragile lobe of her ear.

"No," she whispered, caressing the back of his head. The pressure of controlled sharpness, teasing, testing, tasting with exquisite care the delicate morsel, sent a silvery shimmer of electricity from the point of impact to the soles of her feet, then soared upward along her thighs, circling her womb as she swayed forward until her lower body was supported by his hips and thighs.

"How about this?" His warm breath was as inflammatory as the movement of his lips along her chin and throat.

"Unh-unh."

"This?" His nose lightly described her collarbone as he inched lower. His tongue darted between his soft, caressing lips and a soft moan was Audrey's only response.

His hands held her hips in place as his mouth moved with excruciating slowness to the low V of her cocktail dress. Flexing his knees, Ken gradually bent her pliant body back, sliding his hands along the sloping curve of her buttocks while his lips followed the swell of her left breast. The airy georgette yielded readily to the insistent pressure of his mouth and fluttered breezily against his cheek as it parted to reveal the pale, creamy treasure he was seeking.

"This?" he asked, the question a tremulous exhalation as his tongue flickered downward to flutter against, stroke, and finally, encase the throbbing tip.

A deep, shuddering intake of breath was Audrey's reply and she would have succumbed completely to the exquisite pleasure of his exploring mouth had the elevator not arrived at their floor. Audrey did not remember how they got out of the compartment, or to their room, but the night itself was indelibly etched in her memory.

Chapter Twelve

Sunday was a blur of sailing, picnicking, strolling, and loving as Audrey and Ken basked in the pure joy of each other's company. The last of the delegates to the Solar Convention arrived and there was a second welcoming dinner that officially opened the meetings.

The phone rang at eight thirty Monday morning.

"Time to get up," Ken gently shook Audrey. He pried the pillow off her head. "What a baby! I'm glad I'm getting to see the real you beforehand."

"Before what?" she mumbled drowsily.

"Hand," he laughed. "Which is exactly what you are going to feel in two seconds if you don't get up."

"What do you care if I meet with Barney or not?" she yawned as she rolled over.

"I care a great deal," he said very seriously. "You are not going to give him any more excuses for his slimy insinuations," he made reference to Barney's cornering her at dinner Saturday evening. He reached out to smooth her hair from her face. "I didn't mean that the way it came out," he said gently. He got up and put on his robe, then went over to his briefcase while Audrey rose and went out to start her shower.

"Here," he said, walking up to stand behind her as she brushed and coiled her hair to keep it from getting wet. He handed her an agenda. "You're going to be very busy," he apologized. "No more shopping sprees."

"Good. I'm broke," she laughed. She gave him a quick kiss then entered the steam-filled bathroom.

"By the way," he said when they were both dressed

and ready to leave, "you handled yourself very nicely the other night about that drink."

"You'd better be careful," she warned. "If I get too independent, I may discover I don't need you."

"I would hope not." He turned to face her when they reached the elevator. "Tired of me already?"

"No. You?"

"No, I'm not getting tired of you, either." He stepped aside to allow her to enter the compartment. "I've got my work cut out with you. Besides, I may never graduate you."

The elevator quickly filled so their conversation was severely restricted.

"Ready to beard the lion?" he asked when they reached the restaurant.

"Yes. I take it I'm going to be on my own?"

"Never in spirit." He glanced at the agenda she carried. "Ten o'clock in the conference room. No fashionably tardy entrances, please."

Barney tracked Audrey as she made her way across the flagstone-paved terrace, but he made no attempt to rise when she approached the table.

"Well, well, all bright-eyed and bushy-tailed," he mumbled between mouthfuls of mangoes.

"Good morning, Barney," Audrey greeted him pleasantly as she sat down.

"Where's Walker?" The heavy-set man peered around Audrey, his calculating blue gaze darting about the broad, palm-lined room.

"I have to be in a meeting at ten, Barney," Audrey wearily informed him, "and I have a very busy schedule today. What was it you wanted to discuss?"

"Mr. Acheson is most anxious, most anxious, to resume his...discussion," he winked meaningfully at Audrey, "and since you have led him to believe you are amenable..."

"I have done no such thing. I made myself perfectly clear Saturday night."

"Now, now, Acheson is no fool," Barney cut her off. "He knows you can't be too obvious in front of

Walker." Ignoring her indignant interruption, he went on, "Barney's not plannin' to stay local forever, missy. Who knows where all this could lead? A few out-of-state contacts and next thing you know ol' Barney's gone national." He gave Audrey a sideways glance. "Listen, I know a workin' girl's got to make ends meet, one way or another."

Audrey glared at him in absolute disgust and loathing. "When this Nava del Sol project is completed, my association with you is terminated." She gave him her notice as she arose to leave.

"Suppose I fire you first?" he snarled, clamping his fat hand on her slender wrist.

"You'll lose the account and Harkness and Walker will sue," she calmly informed him, for the first time confident of her abilities and contributions.

"Got it all figured out, have you?"

Audrey wrenched her hand free.

"Don't be so sure, missy," he sneered. "I can countersue and tie this whole thing up in the courts for years. And then you'll be wishin' you'd gotten a little something for all the mud I intend to sling."

"Barney, there are laws against this sort of harassment."

"You willing to pay the price to test them?" he asked to her back as she turned and left.

No, she realized with a sick feeling, she was not. But she was not about to let on to him. A show of bravado might be all she needed to deflate the bully. She certainly hoped so.

Still badly shaken by her confrontation with Barney, Audrey took a seat at the end of the long speaker's table in the conference room. Without a word Tom placed a cup of coffee in front of her. Before long she was deeply engrossed in the debate over the renewable energy resources, and Ken was magnificent.

She made copious notes for the second phase of the campaign, spurred by both sides of the arguments, and was so involved with her current thoughts she had no time to dwell on Barney's threats.

"Lunch?" asked Ken, appearing at her elbow.

"What? Oh, look at the time!" she cried, gathering up her papers.

"What have you been up to?" Ken asked as he took the pad from her. He read through her first sheet of notes and raised his eyebrow. "Tom," he called to his partner, "can you come over here?" When he did, Ken handed him Audrey's notes.

"From what I can decipher of your chicken scratches," grinned Tom, "you are either a genius or a solar fanatic." He returned her notebook. "I would like to discuss this at lunch. I think we should refine this a little more, then I would like to release some of it at the news conference. I would like to sound out some of our Latin American colleagues, too. Shall we adjourn to my suite?" He offered Audrey his arm. "I don't want any of this leaked prematurely."

Barney met them at the elevator and he took Audrey's other arm.

"I see you are scheduled for lunch with the agency rep, gentlemen," he smiled expansively as he flourished the agenda. "I'm beginning to feel like you three are tryin' to exclude ol' Barney. Cut me out of the herd, so to speak. But, of course, you fine men wouldn't be considering breaching any contracts, now would you?" he winked. "Unless, of course, you had something else in mind, in which case I am duty-bound to protect this sweet young thing." He stepped into the elevator with them, still holding Audrey's arm.

"You were writin' up a storm in there. A veritable storm, little lady. Ideas for the campaign, I hope. I certainly wouldn't want you cheatin' these fine men by writin' letters to Mama!"

"We were going to discuss the next phase of the campaign over lunch, Mr. Longworth," said Tom. "You are most welcome to sit in and give us your ideas." He gave Audrey a piercing glance. "Weren't you going to phone home first, dear?"

His glance included the notebook, and Audrey nodded.

"Yes. Apparently Mrs. Potter was out earlier, and I like to check in with her every day," she smiled.

"I'll come with you," Barney volunteered, but Ken intervened.

"Why, Barney, I thought you were anxious to discuss the campaign?"

The cash register in Barney's brain clicked away, almost audibly, and Audrey suppressed a giggle when he puffed himself up. "Publicity is my middle name. My middle name," he gloated, stepping off the elevator with the two men, Audrey and her personal affairs relegated to insignificance.

Audrey waited impatiently for the international operator to complete her call. She did not trust Barney alone because she feared he might offend the very proper and dignified senior partner. This project was challenging enough without having to backtrack and repair needless damage.

"Mrs. Potter," she greeted the voice on the other end of the line. "How is everything going?" She listened for several seconds, and her happy smile faded into a puzzled, then angry, frown. "When?" she asked, more abruptly than she had intended. "Yes, of course," she spoke soothingly to the ruffled sitter, "I'm sure you can handle anything." She listened again. "Are you sure? I can come back sooner... no, no, Mrs. Potter. I have the utmost confidence in... What?" Relief burst forth in a short laugh. "That ought to have done it," she agreed with the woman. "Okay. But if he shows up again, call me immediately... Fine... Put her on... Hi, baby." Audrey's smile was in her voice and Bonnie burbled happily on the other end.

She finally hung up, but Mrs. Potter's news still disturbed her. Ken would give her good advice, Audrey thought on the way back to the restaurant. It wasn't really his concern though, and she was reluctant to bring it up. Of course, if this relationship had any future... She would have to play it by ear, she decided, putting on her most professional smile as she crossed the dining room to her group.

"Where are your notes?" was the first thing Barney asked her when she sat down.

"Oh," Audrey affected surprise and dismay. "I must have left them upstairs." She immediately covered that lapse of concentration by detailing her conclusions from the morning's debate to allay the irritable man's suspicions. "Essentially it all boils down to communication and education. Or I should say, re-education. As I listened to the debate, I realized that conservation and environmental protection have usually been touted for the purity of their deprivation: suffer for the cause, sort of thing. Actually, there are tremendous financial benefits to be reaped without sacrificing comfort or convenience, which I believe is the main thrust of Nava del Sol. The latest statistics..."

"Don't get boring, girl. Short and sweet and to the point. You don't need to sell any of us," Barney interrupted. "You got to sell the folks out there."

"That is quite true, Mr. Longworth," Tom readily agreed. "And when Audrey has clarified these points, I am sure we can come to a mutually profitable agreement."

"What were you planning?" asked Barney, profit statements rolling through his mind. "TV? Radio?"

"Yes. And an extensive newspaper blitz."

"Similar to those oil company ads everyone is so familiar with," said Ken. "The ones that answer a few questions in an amusingly informative way."

"Good, good," nodded Barney. "But lots more TV. We haven't done much TV so far. Not nearly enough."

"It will be difficult to convey this type of message over TV," Ken cautioned the advertising man. "But I see no reason why we can't coordinate more with PG Productions, who have been handling that aspect so far," he added in an effort to be accommodating.

"After all," Tom picked up that line, "the main theme is generated by your agency. PG has been primarily responsible for the technical aspects, so I foresee no insurmountable problems."

"We can use the little lady here," suggested Barney, as the prospect of having the powerful Phoenix agency check with him went to his head. He jabbed his meaty thumb in Audrey's direction. "Cheesecake sells. No reason not to flaunt what you gentlemen have already noticed."

"That is not the image we are striving to promote," said Ken. His jaw was grimly set and his eyes were cold and hard.

"Listen, sonny," Barney leaned forward onto the arms he had folded in front of his plate, "I know you've got some pretty fancy notions 'bout what you're tryin' to do, but it's the guy who's goin' to have to take out two loans and a mortgage that will require everyone in his family over fifteen to work twenty hours a week who's going to be buying... if you're lucky. And he doesn't know passive from active, and conservation sends him up the walls. I'm tellin' you, sex sells! But," he shrugged and sat back, "it's your loss if you want to play this so damned highfalutin."

"Actually," Audrey intervened, "that is exactly the point I'm trying to make. This should be a re-education process. Make the average man aware of the advantages, and in turn, as desirous of these homes as he has been of those inefficient, extravagant, shoddily built shoeboxes he has been forced to accept for lack of an alternative."

"The man on the street will take whatever he can get, and he doesn't want to be educated, just satisfied," Barney cynically insisted.

"That is because in the past he hasn't been either!" snapped Audrey. "With these homes presented in the proper light he will be both educated and satisfied."

"Can't be done." Barney emphatically shook his head. "You're just gonna waste all their money," he indicated Tom and Ken. "Not that I'm complainin'. If they're happy, I'm happy." He winked at Audrey. "You just see that they stay that way." Barney mopped his chin with his napkin and casually asked Audrey what room she was in.

"Ms. Mathieson is in a private suite," Tom answered for her. "Apparently there was a mix-up with the reservations and hers had been canceled. The hotel never puts inside calls through to those rooms without explicit instructions." He turned to Audrey and smiled. "Just notify the desk, dear."

"Gladly," she replied. "I wasn't aware of the problem."

"If you'd give me the number," Barney persisted, "it would simplify things altogether."

"I am afraid not," said Tom. "You would still have to go through the switchboard."

"I might need to stop by to consult with you," he tried again, giving Tom a peculiar glance. "Besides, I see no reason for a big fancy suite goin' to waste while you're tied up in meetings every day." All three were taken aback and Barney hastened to add, "I'd surely like to impress some of these potential clients I keep running into."

"But you are going to be tied up, too," Ken reminded him. "We want the Longworth Agency fully represented at all times. I had hoped you would find that to your advantage," he shrugged as he slid his chair back in preparation to leave. "But we are quite flexible."

Tom stood up with Ken. "The hospitality suite is at your service at almost any hour," he smiled.

Audrey watched with keen interest as the porcine features of her boss contorted with the effort required to digest this information.

"Fine, fine," he mumbled, not rising with them. He put his hand on Audrey's arm. "We have some unfinished business to discuss."

Tom slid his cuff back and pressed the button that lighted up the face of his watch. "The panel will resume in ten minutes, Ms. Mathieson." He left with Ken.

"What is your room number, and don't get cute,"

Barney glowered at Audrey. "Acheson has been trying to reach you for two days now, and he's getting impatient."

"That's his problem." She stood up and he rose, too, not quite towering over her, although his immense size presented a formidable intimidation. "I'm going to be late, Barney," she protested against his continued interference.

"What's the matter? Walker got you under lock and key?" he sneered. "What makes you think he cares what you do in your spare time?"

Audrey peeled his hand off her arm and walked out.

"Just remember, girl," Barney's booming voice followed her out of the room, "you're still workin' for me."

"Dammit!" she swore to herself. Why couldn't he just leave her alone?

Audrey did not get a chance to speak to Ken or Tom before the meeting resumed, but Tom came over as soon as it adjourned.

"I'm sorry we didn't get a chance to discuss what we had planned. That man is..." Tom gave an expressive shrug. "Unfortunately there is more than a germ of truth in what he said." He frowned at Audrey. "Do you think you will be able to put something together for us by the end of the week?"

"I'll try my best."

"You always do," he smiled, patting her shoulder. He sat down. "I would like Janet to move in with you for a day or two," he said quietly. "Ken can stay with me."

Audrey studied the reserved man, a curious expression on her face. "Okay," she consented without enthusiasm. "When?"

"I've already made the arrangements. I assure you it is not my preference, nor Ken's."

"I'm terribly sorry..."

Tom patted her hand. "I am not blaming you for any of this." He walked her to the elevator and pressed her floor just as Barney entered. The offensive man got off before either of them, however, and Tom gave a friendly wave to Audrey when he stepped off.

Janet was already in the sitting room of the suite Audrey had shared with Ken when she entered. The brunette was doing her nails and her hair was bound in a turbaned towel.

"What are you wearing tonight?" she greeted Audrey with a bright smile, as though there was nothing unusual in the change of roommates.

"Is it formal?" Audrey asked, although she did not evince much interest.

"Always. Tom loves formality." Janet was seated in the carved wing chair and motioned to Audrey. "Sit down, Audrey."

"I feel like an idiot. Worse," said Audrey as she sat primly on the edge of the sofa. "I feel cheap."

"Why? Because of Barney?" shrugged Janet. "He gets his jollies annoying people. If he can get in a cheap shot, he will. Nothing's too low for him." Janet's cobalt-blue eyes darkened and narrowed. "Why do you let it get to you?"

"I don't know," sighed Audrey. She sank back into the sofa cushions.

"Don't you?" Janet crossed her long, shapely legs. "You're so damned insecure, Audrey. Why can't you trust Ken?"

"I do," Audrey defensively retorted. "But Barney can do a lot of harm."

"No, he can't. Not unless you let him." Janet stood up and stretched, then bent over to touch her toes and stretched again. "I'm getting old," she groaned when her joints creaked. "You can have the bathroom; I'm through."

Audrey wore the jade-green dress she had bought for her first meeting with Tom, and Janet complimented her on her selection as she pirouetted in front of the mirror for one last, critical appraisal. "They're going to be sorry."

"Who?"

"Ken and Tom," laughed Janet. "I hope they eat

their hearts out! Maybe this'll teach Tom not to be such a prude."

"Or Ken to make such rash decisions," laughed Audrey, thinking it was Ken's surprise room arrangements that had precipitated all this nonsense.

"How's that?" asked Janet.

"To have made this mess in the first place. I hope Tom doesn't have second thoughts about his judgment."

"We definitely made a mistake," groaned Ken when both women came toward them.

"It's all your fault," sighed Tom. He took Janet's arm and led her into the dining room. "You'll pay for this."

"Señorita, you must come sit with me," insisted the Colómbian official, as he led Audrey away.

"Serves you right," she heard Tom whisper to Ken.

It was a small dinner party, just the four Americans and the South American dignitaries and their wives. Tom directed most of the conversation toward Audrey, and he and Ken nodded approvingly throughout. Before too long she had won over the Argentinian delegation, who previously had been the staunchest opponents of the conference goals.

"Excelente, Señorita," gushed the Colómbian, who had been at his most charming all evening. He did not appear likely to relinquish her until Ken intervened. Making a sweeping bow and gallantly kissing her hand, he bade them all good night.

"I have to watch you every minute," hissed Ken.

"If you did a better job, you wouldn't have these problems," chuckled Janet.

"Why is everyone picking on me?" bemoaned Ken as they walked down the long corridor to the elevators. "How is Bonnie doing?" he asked Audrey.

"Fine," she answered after the slightest hesitation, which Ken immediately noticed. "Alan came by today," she explained when questioned. "But Mrs. Potter got rid of him. Quite dramatically," she added and went on to explain how that indomitable woman had sent him packing. "I'm sure he will not be back," she said, but neither of them was totally convinced.

"If you find it necessary to go back sooner," said Ken, "I'll make the arrangements. In the meantime, I see no reason why I shouldn't make a call or two to increase the surveillance in your neighborhood."

They had reached their floor and both men escorted the women to their suite.

"You will get this nonsense with Barney cleared up soon?" Tom scowled at Ken.

"A day to throw him off the scent ought to do it," grinned Ken. He bent to kiss Audrey chastely at the door. "Just like all the dates we never had," he smiled wistfully. "See you in the morning. Tomorrow will be light. There's nothing important until the afternoon."

"I plan to get a gorgeous tan."

"We're going fishing," Janet announced to Tom's wry grimace.

"This whole situation is ridiculous, you know," Audrey laughed when she and Janet were alone.

"Tom can't stand Barney," shrugged Janet. She kicked off her shoes and stretched out on the bed nearest the balcony. "He likes you."

"Are you angry, Janet?" Audrey paused with her dress half unzipped, but the brunette's brilliant blue eyes lit up when she smiled.

"A little disappointed." She sat up to study Audrey. "What can Barney do to you?"

"Nothing, really. Just make things as ugly as possible. I don't want anything to go wrong." Audrey walked into the dressing room and stepped out of the dress. "Why can't some people just let others alone?" she sighed. "Instead, they pick, pick, pick. Even if you ignore them, they do that, when they don't have any business intruding in your life at all!"

"I understand, if that's any consolation."

"Thanks."

It was well past one o'clock in the morning, and they did not talk again. Silence prevailed until eight, when the phone rang.

"Heads up, Audrey," yelled Janet, who had answered it. She tossed the instrument to the other bed and went back to sleep.

"Hello?" mumbled a groggy Audrey.

"Well, well!" boomed Barney's voice. "I need to see you on the terrace in half an hour."

Audrey staggered out of bed and replaced the phone on the nightstand. She showered and dressed, trying to make as little noise as possible. There was no reason for Janet to have been disturbed and she seethed silently at Barney's rude call. A half hour did not provide enough time for her temper to cool. Barney studied her for a long moment after she had ordered a light breakfast, and his pudgy fingers drummed idly on the white tablecloth.

"How much do you think they'll be willing to go for this next phase?" he asked, starting the conversation on a topic that interested him. "Think we can double the ante?"

"I doubt it. Mr. Harkness makes the final decisions. I haven't even gotten the quotes for the embossing on the first series."

"I have. I'll prepare the cost sheets when I get back to Tucson. Did you turn all those time sheets in to Nancy?"

"Yes."

"What about your time here? You keeping track of all that?" He wolfed down the platter of fruit that had been set before him and started in on the second basket of muffins.

"No. This is a research trip. They're paying my expenses and I have no intention of billing them anything additional."

"What about all that work you did yesterday? Including lunch?" He slathered an enormous blueberry-filled pastry with what looked like a quarter pound of butter. "That was at least four hours spent on this account."

Audrey sipped her coffee, what appetite she had, gone at sight of the gorging that was going on across from her. "I told you, I am not billing any of this.

When I get back and start to work on the second phase, I'll keep track of my hours," she stated with finality.

"Your decision." Barney inhaled the plateful of scrambled eggs. "But it's not a good idea to let personal considerations interfere with business. You gonna eat that?" He pointed with his fork to the untouched walnut pastry that was rapidly cooling. He speared it and it, too, went the way of the other food that was but a dim memory.

Ken joined them and Barney looked up, attracted by the fresh platter of mangoes, strawberries, and bananas that was the standard first course for every guest at breakfast.

"We were just going over the billing for Nava del Sol," said Barney. "I should have some figures ready next Friday."

"Whenever." Ken rested his leg alongside Audrey's, and she pressed her knee against his, enjoying what little physical contact she could maintain with him in public. "The fishing party is getting ready to leave soon," he informed Barney. "Are you planning to go?"

"No. Don't much like boats," replied Barney. "Quite a classy outfit though. Kind of wish I enjoyed fishing," he sighed. "Who all's going?"

"Most of the South American delegation and Tom and Janet. She's quite an aficionado of the sport."

"What are your plans, little lady?" Barney asked Audrey.

"Sun and fun. I'm free until three."

"You?" he asked Ken.

"I'm conducting sailing lessons for the Countess and Señora Castegna," grimaced Ken. He checked his watch and groaned. "Duty calls. Enjoy your freedom while you can," he winked at Audrey. "You'll be lucky if you see the light of day in the weeks to come. Isn't there something we can interest you in, Barney?"

"I'll think of something," grinned the corpulent man, and for a moment Audrey saw a dangerous glint in Ken's eyes.

"I'm sure you will." Ken held Audrey's chair for her and she walked with him to the lobby.

"I don't trust him," he said when they reached the hallway. "Be careful."

"What can he do?" laughed Audrey.

Ken's features relaxed considerably. "Not a thing. See you for lunch at a quarter to one." He glanced down the hall and bent to give her a quick kiss when the elevator door opened.

"Ashamed of me?"

"No," he laughed, rumpling her hair. "But if I did what I was thinking, I'd shame you."

"Maybe not," she retorted, arching her eyebrow and striking a provocative pose as the doors closed between them.

Audrey placed another call to Mrs. Potter. There had been no sight of Alan since the sitter had ordered him off the premises, and Audrey was surprised to learn that Ken had also called earlier that morning. "Such a nice man," Mrs. Potter had sized Ken up after her two conversations with him, and Audrey heartily agreed. He really did care about both of them, she realized, her love for Ken growing with each day she spent in his company. That he seemed so fond of her daughter—and, she could not overlook it, the daughter of a man he held in no esteem—was an added bonus Audrey had not dared hope for this early in their relationship.

How could she have been so blind for so long? Ken was there all the time, and she had chosen Alan instead. "Ken had been right," she thought with a light laugh as she changed into her bathing suit, a striking emerald-green maillot that played up the vividness of her eyes... a minor flattery compared to what the tiny, angled pleats that swept from the bust to her left hip did for her already spectacular figure. "A's have nothing to do with smarts."

Audrey checked her reflection and adjusted the strap of her white leather sandals. With her hair and that suit, Ken could not possibly miss her when he returned from his sailing trip. A deeper tan, though, was definitely called for, so Audrey made certain she had the lotion before she headed for the beach.

She was lounging near the water when a shadow passed over her. "Hello, Barney," she said, opening her eyes and suppressing a giggle at the sight of his flabby pink legs, which protruded from his voluminous shorts. The scrawny appendages did not seem capable of supporting all that bulk.

He pulled over another beach chair. "You're a stubborn little filly," he said as he eased himself into the wooden lounge, which groaned in protest. "But you've been quite an asset. I hate to see you played for a sucker. Now don't give me that look, honey. You're just kidding yourself. Walker's just havin' his fun. He can have any woman he wants and he sure doesn't need some divorcée with a brat and a junkie for an 'ex.'"

Audrey stared at him. Did everyone in Tucson, except her, know about Alan? It was a small town, at least as far as the natives were concerned despite its phenomenal growth, but surely, Alan Mathieson and his antics were not that interesting? Still Barney had covered sports, she remembered, and her high school had been the perennial champion for years, so it was not that odd, she supposed.

Barney glanced at Audrey and rubbed the side of his bulbous nose. "He offer to marry you?"

"I don't see where that is any of your business," snapped Audrey.

"I thought not." He gave an elaborate shrug of bored indifference. "Your life. Mess it up some more if you like. It's nothing to me." He rested his head back against the chair and squinted in the bright light, causing his small eyes to disappear completely in the thick, fleshy folds. "I figure you're serious 'bout leavin' when this campaign is over, but you owe me some loyalty in the meantime."

Audrey did not respond and he continued, "This account's gonna do me a lot of good whether you're with me or not. Folks'll remember Longworth handled it, so you be sure to give it your best shot." He folded his hands and rested them on his expansive belly. "I don't know what sort of deal you and Walker have cooked up, but as an employee of mine, it's your duty... your duty!... to back me up and not go runnin' to him with the inside dope on how I run my business."

"I don't know where all this is leading," sighed Audrey, wishing Barney would say his piece and depart, since it did not appear likely he would do the latter without subjecting her to the former.

"I have my own system for billing. Strictly legal. Strictly legal! I haven't had any complaints. No complaints, at all," he puffed himself up indignantly. Rather like a toad, thought Audrey, trying hard to maintain a semblance of control.

"So? I don't know anything about your 'system,'" she stated calmly, not adding that she had no wish to know.

"That's exactly right. So you keep your nose out of it and your mouth shut!" he warned. He lumbered out of the low seat. "You don't know nothin' 'bout time sheets and estimates and all the rest. When the estimates come in, you give them to me, not Walker, understand? And you don't discuss any of it with him."

"I never have," Audrey indignantly defended her professionalism. "Whatever gave you that idea?"

"This business with the room, for one thing. I don't like you goin' behind my back. That is highly unethical. Highly unethical!"

What did he know of ethics? Audrey seethed, but she covered her ire with a veneer of stoic indifference. "Look, Barney, I don't care what 'system' you use. But for your own good, ease up. You're not dealing with your usual clientele of backslappers and winkers." Somehow Audrey forcibly controlled her facial features to successfully mask the contempt she felt for the man. "Honest people aren't necessarily stupid."

Barney laughed derisively. "There are no honest people. Only stupid ones who don't know how to take advantage, or ones who are too smart to get caught."

Audrey sighed and sank back into her chair. What a

distressingly low opinion he had of the world. And she realized with disdain, himself. Her short temper flared at his insinuations. She did not doubt for an instant Tom's and Ken's integrity. Perspective. Barney was a petty crook at heart, so he assumed everyone else was. She, however, had a tendency to grant too much credence to people. Alan, for one, had been a flagrant example. Just because Ken had not mentioned marriage was no reason to doubt his sincerity or love for her. Her heart constricted at the possibility that she might be only a passing fancy. No, Ken loved her, she reminded herself. But she had thought Alan had loved her, too.

"Damn Barney," she muttered, shaking the sand out of her towel. But the doubts were hers, not Barney's. He had just poked around in the debris that was her self-confidence and brought them to the surface. Ken was nothing like Alan. She felt disloyal to Ken even considering Alan in the same thought. "Trust me," he had asked her. If she loved him, she would have to. And Ken, she knew firsthand, was easy to trust.

She went for a short swim, then when she had baked for another hour, went into the hotel. "One twenty," said her watch. Ken was late.

"Ms. Mathieson?" An apologetic Mr. Acheson approached her when she passed the bar on her way to the elevators. "Let me start out by saying how sorry I am to have placed you in that awkward position the other night. It was unpardonably rude, but," he smiled graciously and made a charmingly broad gesture, "we had had such a pleasant chat that afternoon..."

"Just a misunderstanding." Audrey smiled in dismissal.

"Will you join me for a margarita?" he smiled boyishly.

Audrey hesitated. Ken should be along any minute, and she hated to waste the impact of this suit on him by changing before he had had a chance to see it. "One," she agreed. "I have a luncheon engagement."

The table he selected overlooked the beach and Audrey was confident Ken would have no trouble spotting her. Mr. Acheson was polite and attentive without being presumptuous, and he made no references to any expectations he might previously have entertained. Rather he steered the conversation to the Nava del Sol project and he flattered her with lavish praise of her handling of the publicity. An hour and a half passed and still Ken did not appear. Audrey sipped her drink very slowly, losing track of the number of times she turned away the unobtrusive waiter who persisted in attempting to refill her glass, although she did consent to having a second. Barely stifling a yawn, she finally excused herself, but Mr. Acheson insisted upon accompanying her to the elevator.

"Perhaps you ought to rest before this afternoon's meeting," he suggested, pressing the button.

"Oh, dear," sighed Audrey, looking at but not making out the time on her watch, "is it almost time for that?"

"You have an hour yet."

She rummaged through her bag for her room key and Mr. Acheson casually turned the number toward him then pressed her floor. When he rode up to the top floor of the hotel with her, alarms began to go off in Audrey's fuzzy head.

"Oh, I forgot," she smiled. "I have to pick up some information at the desk." She reached across him and pressed the lobby button.

"I'm sure they'll be happy to send it up," he assured her, stepping out of the compartment and steering Audrey down the corridor.

"Thank you very much, Mr. Acheson," she smiled, placing her key back in her bag when he tried to take it from her at the door to her room. "I appreciate your consideration," she stated calmly as she racked her nonfunctioning brain for a graceful way out of what appeared about to disintegrate into an ugly confrontation, "but I really do have to prepare for this meeting." She blinked rapidly all the while, trying desperately not to yawn in his face.

"You need to lie down," he grinned solicitously, making another attempt to secure her key.

"Perhaps I will." Her smile and voice cooled measurably but Mr. Acheson made no move to comply. Indignation was the only thing keeping Audrey awake and she dared not lean against the inviting wall, lest she nod off. "Good day, Mr. Acheson," she frostily concluded her association with him.

Why didn't he leave? Audrey tried to remember what she might have said or done that would have led him to believe she was going to "entertain" him. Barney. "Damn him!" she swore to herself. But that did not help the situation. A boisterous American family on vacation came clamoring down the hall and Audrey had an idea.

"How was the beach?" she asked the youngest child, a boy of about six, as he careened down the hall.

"We found lots of shells," volunteered his sister, who appeared to be about eight.

"How lovely." Audrey stooped down to inspect the booty, hoping fervently that she would be able to rise again.

"Carl is out fishing," said the attractive woman who was shepherding the children with minimal success. A worried frown creased her forehead. "They should have been back by now."

Audrey had had numerous occasions to speak to the woman for they always seemed to pass in the hall whenever Audrey returned to her room to call home, and she smiled encouragingly at her neighbor. "Would you care to take a look from my balcony? I have a lovely view of the ocean."

The woman cast a furtive glance at Mr. Acheson and was about to demur when she caught Audrey's eye. She smilingly accepted the invitation, and for good measure suggested, "Why don't you children show the nice lady what you've found today."

At that, Mr. Acheson excused himself and Audrey unlocked the door.

"I'll just take a quick peek for the boat, if you don't

mind." She spotted it as it approached the dock and Audrey noticed the look of relief that erased the care from her face. "Thank you," she smiled, leading the children back into the hall.

"Thank you," grinned Audrey, and the woman gave a short nod in acknowledgment.

As soon as she had locked the door, Audrey collapsed onto the nearest bed and fell fast asleep.

Chapter Thirteen

"Wake up, Audrey," said Janet, shaking her none too gently. "Ken is fit to be tied!"

"What?" mumbled the groggy woman.

"You missed that meeting this afternoon."

"Oh, no!"

"Oh, yes." Janet was dressed in a beige chiffon cocktail dress and she stood up and adjusted the skirt. "You'd better get dressed. Ken is on his way up, and I, for one, am not about to play referee." With that expression of apathy, Janet sailed out.

Audrey jumped to her feet and quickly showered and dried her hair. The electric rollers were still in place when there was a sharp knock on the door.

"Just a minute," she called out, zipping her dress as she walked over to answer it.

"You're not dressed," Ken observed, looking at her hair and shoeless feet.

"It'll only take a second," she murmured. She tugged at the zipper and Ken made no move to assist.

"You've got too much blusher on," he commented, peering into her flushed face.

"I don't have on any," she snapped. "It's my natural glow," she answered haughtily.

Ken grabbed her arm and spun her around, his face dark with rage. "Is that so?" he snarled. "And who is responsible for that?"

"Mother Nature!" Audrey wrenched free. "What is the matter with you?"

"Where were you all afternoon?" he thundered.

"Here. When I wasn't downstairs waiting for you to take me to lunch, which you never did," she pouted. "I could ask you the same thing."

"What was Acheson doing up here?"

Audrey frowned at him. How did he know about that? "He brought me to my room," she shrugged.

"That much I figured out," he growled into her bewildered face.

"Then why did you ask?" Infuriated by this cross-examination, Audrey turned back into the dressing room. Ken grabbed her arm as she flounced past him and held her in a crushing, viselike grip.

"Audrey," he demanded, "what has been going on?"

Her eyes flashed green fire at him. How dare he think the worst of her? "What do you think?" she shouted.

Ken glowered at her for another long moment, then sighed and released her. "I don't know what to think."

"Don't you?" Audrey was so angry she could have screamed. She went into the dressing room before she did something rash and began to brush her hair furiously. Seconds later she heard the door slam and her knees buckled. Trembling, she sat down and burst into tears. After a few minutes, she heard a knock on the door and she flew over to it.

"Let's start over." That adorable sheepish grin smiled at her. "You're not dressed?"

"Just give me a minute," Audrey snuffled, wiping her cheeks with the back of her hand.

"I'm sorry I missed our luncheon date. Señora Castegna capsized the boat."

"Oh." Audrey placed her hands on his white dinner jacket and traced the lapels with her fingertips. "I had a couple of margaritas while I waited for you, then I fell asleep and missed the meeting. I'm sorry, too."

"Come here," he said softly, and Audrey fell into his arms.

"What started all this?" she asked, snuggling into his shoulder.

"Mother Nature," he chuckled. He followed her to the dressing room and watched while she reapplied her makeup. "It was almost three when I got back and I ran into Barney. He told me Acheson had left with you sometime after two. I came up here after the meeting and I met Acheson in the hall outside your room."

"What was he doing here at that time?" frowned Audrey.

"That is what I wondered," grimaced Ken.

"And you naturally thought the worst."

"I don't have a good excuse," he shrugged helplessly. "I had tried to call you, but there was no answer..." He tensed slightly as the anger resurfaced.

"But how could you think that of me?" she asked, her face clouded with abject disappointment.

"I thought he had taken advantage of you." He clenched his teeth. "If Janet hadn't been with me, I don't know what I would have done to him. She insisted I go back to my room, and when she called to say you were sound asleep, I knew you had been drinking."

"I only had a couple."

"On an empty stomach?"

"Oh."

"What a babe in the woods you are," he laughed, pulling her into his arms.

"Not true," she rebutted, placing a kiss on his smooth cheek. "I got rid of him very slickly," she proceeded to explain. "I had a devil of a time not yawning," she giggled in conclusion.

"You should have! You're not very sexy that way!"

He pulled back to look into her grinning face. "I could be wrong about that," he murmured as his eyes misted and he bent forward. Her lips parted eagerly and he swayed forward for she exercised no restraint anymore in pouring out her love for him.

Breathless and at a loss for words, Ken held her face in his hands and gazed wonderingly into her adoring green eyes. His gaze traveled slowly across her face as though memorizing every feature. Still disoriented, he stepped back and continued his inspection, including the long, sensuous sweep of her teal blue silk dress in his appraisal.

"Needs something," he concluded, turning her around to face the mirror. He reached into his pocket and removed a smooth, heavy necklace which he placed around her slender neck. It was of sandcast silver, composed of two tapering crescents that were joined at their widest points by a round, perfect piece of finely grained turquoise.

"It's beautiful," she breathed, touching it gingerly.

"Come on," he beamed, "give me another kiss and let's get going."

"I love you," she whispered when she had complied. She started to say something but thought better of it. Her blush, however, gave her away.

"Soon as I find Janet," he grinned, "I'm exchanging keys. To hell with Barney and his ugly little mind."

"He's lost interest," shrugged Audrey. They strolled arm in arm to the elevator, and on the way to the ballroom Audrey filled Ken in on Bonnie's latest adventures.

"No sign of Alan?" he asked.

"Not since that one time." Audrey frowned. "That was so unlike him. He's never shown any interest in Bonnie before."

Ken squeezed her hand but said nothing. He led her to the table where Janet and Tom were already seated and before Janet even had a chance for a closer look at the new necklace, Audrey was whisked off to the dance floor by the Colómbian minister, who seemed to have been impatiently awaiting her arrival. She barely saw Ken for the entire evening, alternating dances between the South American officials.

"Enjoying yourself?" She heard Ken's voice behind her as she tried to extricate herself from her earlier partner. His lips were against her ear and each word he breathed was a gentle caress.

"Actually, no," she said, nestling into his embrace. "I've been stood up."

"The cad!" he laughed, holding her so tightly they moved as one body. "Dump that idiot and come away with me."

"I don't know that I can," she giggled.

"Possessive type!" Ken kissed her cheek. "If he'd abandon you, he doesn't deserve any consideration at all. You just leave everything to me."

"Haven't I always?"

Ken peered into her upturned face and grimaced. "Hardly." The frown dissolved into a broad grin. "But you're learning."

The orchestra took a much-appreciated break and the sudden, blessed silence was disturbed only by the clatter of the waiters serving dinner.

"Just one more day of meetings," sighed Ken. "Then I can get back to work."

"You've got a lot to do if you are going to meet that deadline," agreed Tom. "You're not one to make life easy for yourself," he chuckled. "Does she know?"

"Of course not," insisted Ken, and Audrey's bewildered expression bore him out. "Doesn't suspect a thing," he grinned.

Before Audrey could ask any questions, Señora Castegna approached. The voluptuous Venezuelan seized Ken's arm and expounded in animated Spanish, her monologue ending with a lusty kiss.

"¡Mi héroe!" she proclaimed over and over while her husband, a very reserved, dignified, elderly man, strolled purposefully across the room to them.

"Pistols at dawn," quipped Tom to the totally chagrinned Ken.

The woman rushed over to meet her husband and gushed profusely over Ken when she succeeded in dragging Señor Castegna to the group.

"Ah, the handsome American héroe, my wife has quite casually mentioned," he twinkled. "Mil grácias for assisting her in her little mishap today."

"It was very minor," blushed Ken when the woman threw her arms around his neck and kissed his crimson cheek.

"My wife tends to be demonstrative," he chuckled. He thanked Ken again and gently extricated the woman from her savior.

"If she's that grateful now," laughed Janet, "I would love to have seen her right after the 'accident.'" No wonder you were so late!"

"I've been wondering the same thing," teased Audrey as Ken blushed deeper and looked away. "When I think of the hard time you gave me! It was just guilt for what you had been up to!"

"The truth will out," he mumbled.

"That it will!" laughed Tom.

"Finish your dinner." Ken changed the subject. "I don't want to stay here all night."

"I haven't had dessert," Audrey protested when he pulled her to her feet.

"You don't need it. We're going swimming." He looked at Janet and Tom. "Want to come along?"

"Not me," groaned Janet. "I'm exhausted from wrestling that sailfish."

"Too bad the line broke," Tom sympathized, although there was little enthusiasm. "You children run along. We old folks will take it easy tonight."

"Well?" Ken asked Audrey.

"Sure. I'm dying to hear more about your 'accident.'"

"Don't you trust me?" he grinned, turning to wave to Janet and Tom.

"Of course. I'm willing to go for a long, dark swim with you."

"You can be too trusting," he leered. The elevator stopped at Ken's floor. "Meet you at the pool in fifteen minutes."

In less than the allotted time, Audrey reached the pool to find Ken already doing laps. She crouched near the edge and waited for him to swim over. Mimosa and mango trees lined the pool, providing a screen between the pool and hotel and a windbreak from the beach. Huge pots of succulents and African daisies were interspersed with the umbrellaed tables and bright blue lounge chairs, and the music of the orchestra floated on the breeze. The only other sound was the gentle lapping of the water at the side of the pool...a steady ripple generated by Ken's smooth, even passage.

Ken swam to the edge of the pool and wiped the water from his eyes as he grinned up at Audrey. "Come on in."

"Is it cold?"

"See for yourself." When she leaned over to test it with her hand, he seized her arm and pulled her into the pool.

"It's nice," she said, parting the mass of streaming wet hair that covered her face and pushing it back. "Too bad you're not!" Audrey put her hands on top of Ken's head and pushed him under. Her advantage was quickly lost, for he pulled her down with him.

"You are going to have to learn some new tricks," he laughed when they both surfaced. "You never got away with that one."

"Is that so?" Audrey purred, putting her arms around his neck and kissing him with reckless abandon. As soon as his arms moved to encircle her, Audrey kicked off from the side of the pool. Ken lost his balance and went under as Audrey paddled away. Out of the corner of her eye, she spotted a long, dark shape coming at her and raced to the other end of the pool, only to find Ken resting his elbows on the edge of the pool while he waited for her to reach him.

"I didn't think it was possible for you to get any slower," he grinned.

"You must have gotten faster."

"That, too." Audrey crossed her arms on the pool decking and rested her chin on them. "Having fun?" he asked.

"Yes." Her eyes slowly traced his strong profile, then his broad shoulders as Ken turned toward her. "Did you always have such broad shoulders?"

"Not always," he laughed. "For a number of years though." He tilted his head and flashed that crooked smile. "You never noticed?"

"No." Audrey placed her hands on either side of his neck and slowly moved them across his shoulders. "You'd think I would have noticed such a sexy physique," she grinned.

"I certainly tried hard enough to get your attention," he stated, shaking his head in dismay.

"When?"

He pulled her to him. "Always."

"Why?" Audrey focused on his lips her finger was slowly outlining.

"Because you were beautiful," he said softly. "The most beautiful thing I had ever seen."

"Me?" Audrey laughed lightly. "I was skinny and clumsy, and I had freckles and I couldn't get my hair to do anything!"

"True!" he grinned. "But I had rotten taste in those days."

Audrey cupped her hands and made a wide, sweeping splash that washed over his face.

"Still impossible," he sighed as he pushed her head under water. "Give up?" he asked when he let her surface.

"Yes," she burbled, spitting out the water. No sooner had he released her than she made a leap in an attempt to push him under. But Ken would not budge.

"Cheating's not nice," he said and his powerful arms held her immobile.

"It's not a drowning offense," she pleaded, seeing the look in his eyes as he pulled her toward him.

"No, it's not," he slowly conceded. "But it deserves a suitable punishment."

"Ken!" Suddenly, Audrey changed tactics and lowered her eyes seductively. "Ken," she whispered, going very soft and languid.

He hesitated. "This is another trick," he said knowledgeably, but he smiled and let her curl up against him.

"How can you say that?"

"I know you," he laughed, agilely stepping aside

when she made a lunge for him. "Come on, be a nice girl. I've missed you terribly."

"I haven't been anywhere," she teased as she slid her arms around his neck.

"You haven't been with me," he said and his lips sought hers with unrestrained passion. He clasped her to him while his hands traveled sensuously down her scantily clad body, "I don't like sleeping alone," he murmured into her wet hair.

"Neither do I," Audrey admitted.

"Bad habits are so hard to break." He pulled her closer until she was molded to him, one leg intertwined with his.

"Ones you've developed over the years?" Audrey asked almost inaudibly.

Pressing her head under his chin, Ken kissed her forehead. "Don't ask questions you don't want answered." She did not comment and his right hand slid up her torso along the silky green fabric to her bare shoulder and her chin. "You're the only one who has ever been habit-forming," he mumbled, bringing his face down to meet hers.

The water swirled slowly and gently against them, ebbing and flowing along their backs and arms, as it patted flesh and tiled rim in noiseless ripples. Buoyed by the undulating movement that surrounded them, Audrey glided effortlessly against Ken's firm body, held in place by the strong arm that encircled her, separated solely by the sheer fabrics that robed them... a barrier that was minimized by a combination of delicately persistent fondling and the uplifting, forward surge when Audrey tightened her arms around Ken's neck. Liberated from the restricting, elasticized garment, Audrey's breasts strained against the wet, matted texture of Ken's bare chest. His hand moved to clasp her hip as her breasts grazed his chest in a slow, pendular passage while their legs floated freely, merged from pelvis to knees, the total, blissful union all but complete, its very approximation heightening the excitement.

Water, hands, and sheer wet fabric combined, intertwined, becoming one fluid substance, the motion of which washed away the nylon impediments. The liquid mergence followed, adapting, and finally altering the mellifluous cadence. Pleasure was the tide that engulfed them, waxing to unimaginable zeniths that did not plummet, but waned in a delicious diminution.

A silvery crescendo of distant laughter, followed by the indistinct murmur of voices from one of the hotel balconies, jarred their tranquil isolation.

"I feel as if I am in a goldfish bowl," grumbled Ken, although the pool was shielded from view by heavy foliage. "Let's get out of here."

He did so and dried himself quickly, then threw the towel around his neck while he waited for Audrey. She finished tying the belt to her beach coat and he tugged on the end of the sash, undoing it as he pulled her toward him. When he bent to kiss her, he slid his arms inside the short garment, pressing her against his bare skin while his mouth resumed the probing tasting it had so recently enjoyed. Her suit promptly returned to its former state of disarray.

"Ken," Audrey murmured, her whole body swaying against his demanding form, "not here."

"No, not here," he agreed, holding her away and steadying her. "But definitely soon." He slipped the towel off his neck and draped it over his arm. "In case we run into someone," he explained his action with a self-conscious smile.

"What?"

"What? What?" he laughed, rumpling her wet hair. "Some of us are more obvious than others." He smiled, shaking his head at her naiveté.

"Oh!"

"Oh."

It was a prudent precaution, Audrey could not help thinking with barely suppressed amusement, for the lobby and elevators were crowded. "A damned somnambulists' convention must have checked in!" Ken had remarked in an undertone, but the hotel and its guests faded into oblivion once they entered Audrey's suite, and the sun was high before they awoke.

"What time is it?" Ken asked in the midst of a stretching yawn.

"Mzmphlx," mumbled Audrey, pulling the pillow over her head.

Ken lifted a corner of it and kissed the tangled mess of hair and arms beneath. "What a disaster you are in the morning," he laughed.

He threw the pillow across the room and rolled Audrey over. "Kiss me, you irresistible creature," he teased, pushing her hair out of her face. "I know you're in there somewhere."

"I hate morning people," grumbled Audrey. Her eyes fluttered open and she put her arms around his neck. "But in your case, I'll make an exception."

"What's on the agenda today?" she asked as she curled up beside him.

"You've got a memory like a sieve," he sighed, patting her on the shoulder. "What other dreadful things should I know about you?"

"How much time have you got?" yawned Audrey.

Ken ran his fingers through her hair and massaged the back of her neck. "Forever, metaphorically speaking." He eased out of her embrace and reached for his watch. "At the moment, about twenty minutes."

"You don't have any clothes," Audrey matter-of-factly informed him when he sat up.

Not remembering at first, Ken stared blankly at her and Audrey started to giggle.

"Just shows to go what can happen when you plan ahead and forget the details."

"Audrey," he complained, a tolerant frown creasing his brow, "it is too early in the day for such inanities."

She began to laugh hysterically. "You have a warped sense of humor." He arose and pulled on his swim trunks. "When you have composed yourself, meet me in the lobby," he instructed in an authoritative tone of voice. "Twenty minutes," he repeated.

Audrey arrived in the lobby well ahead of Ken, and

Janet greeted her with a dazzling smile. "You look smashing in that pink sundress, Audrey." She appraised the stunning redhead. "Most people with that color hair can't wear pink. You got a sensational tan, too." Her blue eyes sparkled mischievously. "Where's Ken?"

"Locked out, I believe," giggled Audrey. She studied the attractive brunette in the white sleeveless lace dress that set off her bronze tan to perfection.

"Some of us plan ahead," she grinned in answer to Audrey's questioning expression.

"So I see. Sometimes I feel like I'm a visitor to this planet," grimaced Audrey.

"How's that?" asked Tom. He sat down across from both women who occupied the floral-print-covered sofa. "Have you seen the Tucson papers since you've been here?" he asked Audrey.

"No, why?"

"Mrs. Porter, was it?"

"Potter."

"She hasn't mentioned anything?"

"No." Audrey's lovely face was marred by a puzzled frown. "What did they say?"

Tom drummed idly on the arm of the chair while he watched Audrey, and she saw Janet give a small, graceful shrug before she looked up and smiled in greeting to Ken.

"Good morning," he smiled. He was wearing the embroidered shirt Audrey had given him and dark slacks. The brightly accented neutral colors and that wide, genial expression accentuated his dark good looks.

"Nice shirt," commented Tom.

"Audrey has excellent taste."

Tom's glance darted from one to the other, but he only stood up and extended his hand to Janet. "We'd better go in."

"Anything wrong?" Ken asked Audrey. He gazed in concern at her perplexed face as he strolled alongside her.

"I don't know. Have you seen any of the Arizona papers?" she frowned.

"Yes, why?"

Audrey gave a tiny shrug. "Tom asked me if I had. Was there something in them I should know about?"

"Not that I can think of. There was an article about Nava del Sol yesterday, but neither you nor the agency was mentioned. It was a great article," he beamed immodestly. "They couldn't say enough wonderful things about me."

"That I can believe," laughed Audrey.

"Am I that wonderful?" he grinned.

"No, but I'm sure they could never say enough to satisfy you," and he laughed and put his arm around her shoulder.

"Enjoying yourselves?" asked Tom, ushering them to a table on the patio next to the podium that had been set up, and Audrey had the distinct impression he did not altogether approve. But of what, she had no idea.

She found the possibility disturbing, for she valued Tom's esteem. They were all adults and had conducted themselves with decorum. Janet had said he was very prudish, although he had seemed so pleased with her relationship with Ken from the beginning. Try as she might, Audrey could not come up with a plausible reason for the sudden change in Tom's attitude. It was as abrupt and chilling as the arctic air masses that periodically dipped into the desert atmosphere during the balmy winter days, bringing with them a bitter, unexpected frost that blackened and withered everything in their path. He had mentioned the Tucson papers and she recognized the appropriateness of her analogy: an unexpected cold spell from the north. The first thing she would have to do today would be to get hold of a Tucson newspaper.

"Audrey," she heard her name spoken in an irritated voice and she realized Ken had been speaking to her. "Where are you?" he demanded impatiently.

"What? I'm sorry. I wasn't listening to what you said."

"Listening is not one of your strong points. Did you bring those notes you made for the second phase of the campaign?"

"Yes, I have them right here." Audrey bent down and picked up the leather folder she had placed alongside her chair and handed the notes to Ken.

"Audrey," he protested, "they're not typed. No one can read your handwriting!"

"You told me not to let the information out of my hands." Audrey looked around the table and read irritation and weary resignation on all three faces. "I don't understand," she began in a feeble attempt to redeem herself. "I thought this was supposed to wait until we returned to the States."

"Quite right, Audrey." Tom made a visible effort to be conciliatory, which served to increase her apprehension. "But in yesterday's meeting, it was suggested by Señor Castegna that we present the general proposal at the closing breakfast. He was quite impressed at dinner the other night, and he thought it would be an optimistic, upbeat tone on which to close the conference."

"Why wasn't I told?" She caught herself before she asked the question. If she had attended that meeting, she would not be in the present dilemma. Surely if it were that important, they would have gotten a message to her? She held her tongue. If Ken had been negligent, she was not about to point it out. Tom continued to study her, a thoughtful expression on his pleasant features.

"Can you do it?"

"Do what?" Audrey's eyes widened as it sank in. "Speak on this?" She glanced quickly at the assembly and moistened her lips. There was no alternative. "Yes, I suppose so. I'm not a speaker though. I've never been comfortable in the limelight."

For the first time that morning, Tom smiled affectionately at her. "Now might be a good time to start."

"Why?" she almost asked.

"Were you about to say something?" inquired Tom.

"Only that prudence is the better part of curiosity."

"No, it's not," sighed Ken, "but I'm beginning to believe ignorance is bliss."

"Isn't it?" teased Tom, and Audrey relaxed. Whatever had caused the tension seemed to have been forgotten. If not, it had been relegated to a minor annoyance and she quickly dismissed her concerns.

Ken arose to address the group and Audrey watched him, filled with immense pride. He was always charming and attentive to her, and she was sublimely happy with him. Nothing, she realized, could severely dampen her good spirits when she was with him. Even when he provoked her, and vice versa, there was an underlying respect and affection that prevailed, sustaining the relationship, and she radiated that love and confidence in him.

When the last speaker was finished, Tom graciously thanked the participants and turned to Audrey. Ken squeezed her hand lightly for encouragement before he stood behind her chair and she knew she would have no difficulty expressing her desire for the continued growth and development of this system in which Ken so firmly believed.

"Nothing left to do but rest up and get one last layer of brown," laughed Janet when they had finally run out of effusive congratulations to heap upon one another. "What are your plans, Ken?"

He glanced around quickly. "I want to get out of here before Señora Castegna corrals me into any more lessons."

"You'll notice he didn't say what kind of lessons," teased Janet.

"You'd better be careful, dear," Tom warned Audrey, "he's a pushover for a pretty face."

"Don't I know it!" she laughed.

"Such conceit!" grinned Ken, tugging lightly on a lock of her hair. His expression grew sadly wistful. "Let's call home, then get you on that plane," he sighed.

"See you in Phoenix next month," Audrey waved to Tom as Ken walked her to her room.

While Audrey checked with Mrs. Potter one last time, Ken tried to compact her purchases without ruining them, gave up and squashed them all into the largest suitcase.

"Hey!" Audrey placed her hand over the mouthpiece of the receiver to cover her cry of dismay. "What?" she turned her attention to the party on the other end. "When?" Her pretty features settled into a forlorn resignation. "I get in at three. It shouldn't take more than a half hour to get home from the airport... Okay. 'Bye."

"Something wrong with Bonnie?" Ken was at her side, his arm around her shoulder, his dark eyes filled with unashamed worry.

"No." Overcome by genuine concern she made no attempt to disguise, Audrey put her arms around him. "I love you, Ken," she murmured. "Everything is going to be fine," she smiled sweetly, for all her cares had fallen away when he reciprocated, "I love you both."

She did not want to burden Ken, but after Tom's reaction, she felt she owed him an explanation. Alan was her problem and embarrassment, and she did not want it to affect Ken in any way.

"There was a drug bust in Douglas yesterday, and Alan was picked up. The charges were dropped, but the police want to talk to me."

"There's no need," she gently refused his offer to go back with her. "It has nothing to do with either of us."

"Call me immediately if you have any problems," he insisted. A wry smile distorted his mouth and he shook his head slowly. "I'm going to make some calls." He put his finger to her lips to silence her. "No, I insist. I'll call you tonight from Phoenix."

"But..."

"I'm not going to spend my last few minutes with you arguing," he smiled gently as he pulled her closer.

The cab driver had to tap him on the shoulder to tell him they had reached the airport when four verbal announcements in increasing volume had no effect.

Audrey watched from the window as Mexico disappeared beneath the climbing plane. It had been a wonderful five days and her heart soared in tandem with the jet. Ken loved her, of that she had no doubts, and she loved him completely, as she had never loved any man before. And he loved Bonnie. "Give her a big hug and kiss for me," he had instructed when the final boarding message was announced and he had had no choice but to reluctantly relinquish her.

She opened her purse and removed the small, tissue-wrapped necklace Ken had given her for Bonnie. It was a fragile miniature of the piece he had given her, scaled to the toddler's size and weight. Audrey ran her finger over the smooth, cool metal, picturing it on the tiny throat. It would be so good to see Bonnie, again. Ken was right. She should have taken her to Mexico. What did it matter what other people thought? The only ones whose opinions she valued were Ken's and Tom's, and they would have approved.

The impending reunion was marred by the thought of Alan. He had had so little to do with either of them for so long. Why, now, when her life had taken a positive turn, did he have to come back? Why weren't Carla and his swimming pool and his fancy house enough? What in the world did he want with his ex-wife and the daughter he never knew?

Chapter Fourteen

The sight of Bonnie jumping up and down impatiently while Mrs. Potter unlatched the screen door pushed everything aside, and Audrey bent to catch the little redheaded bundle that hurtled across the porch into her arms. While she dressed and undressed the gleeful child in the rainbow of finery she had brought back from Mazatlán, Mrs. Potter filled her in on Alan's latest escapades.

"Came back twice, insisting he wanted to see the child, that was all," harrumphed the formidable-appearing matron. "I told him to clear off before I called the police and he lit out of here like a jackrabbit with a coyote on its tail! Next thing I knew the police came here, askin' all sorts of questions." Her dark, calculating glance swept over Audrey, arrived at a satisfactory conclusion and she nodded sagely.

"You just tell 'em everything you can about that rude no-account."

"Thank you for everything, Mrs. Potter." Audrey smiled wanly. "I'm sure Alan meant no harm. As for the other," she shrugged, "that's none of my concern."

"You just tell them that, honey." Mrs. Potter patted Audrey's arm, bit her lower lip for a second, then with a comically shy smile, bent to hug Bonnie. "You be a little sweetheart," she instructed, planting an affectionately noisy kiss on the baby. "And you take good care of her, hear," she sternly admonished Audrey. With a loud sniffle, she turned and awkwardly folded her bulk behind the steering wheel of her ridiculously small compact car. "You call me anytime," she waved as she drove off.

The police asked very few, very routine questions, and they apologized for the inconvenience. Ken called her that night, and every night for the next week. After that, he called often, but the conversations were short and dealt primarily with the technical progress of Nava del Sol, although he asked her opinion on a number of things, including color schemes and decorating ideas she assumed to be geared to the furnishing of the models under construction. At the end of the first week, a bouquet of red roses was delivered with a note that read: "One down, three to go," and she was touched by his childlike behavior. The middle of the second week she had lunch with Janet and asked about Tom.

"Terrific!" Janet beamed. "He's so happy, he's like a little kid with a new toy! Ken has threatened to get another office so he can get some work done in peace!"

"Have you been in touch with Ken?" she asked after a brief, contemplative pause during which she noted the change in Audrey at mention of his name.

"Off and on. He's due down here at the end of the month," said Audrey, trying not to reveal how very anxious she was to see him.

Janet sat back and tossed her thick hair in an attractive gesture, a bemused expression on her pretty face. "I didn't honestly think he could hold out this long. You've got some pretty stiff competition," she winked.

"Nava del Sol is his first love," Audrey admitted without malice. "I guess he can't tear himself away."

"I suppose." The brunette smiled enigmatically. "Something up there must certainly be fascinating," she teased. When Audrey gave her a blank look, she burst out laughing. "You absolutely amaze me," she grinned, giving Audrey an affectionate pat.

"What?"

"Do you ever intend to land, or are you always going to orbit on the periphery?" She shook her head. "All those questions about color schemes and floor tiles and you can't put two and two together? Let's go," she sighed, still laughing. "I have to get back to work."

"Are you playing with a full deck, Janet?" asked a mildly annoyed Audrey.

"One of us isn't," she chuckled, and Audrey concluded Janet had been out in the sun too long.

She had little time to dwell on any of the broad hints Janet had given her, for the printer had botched the entire set of brochures that were to be placed in the model homes for prospective buyers. Her next few days were spent arguing over who was at fault and redoing the mechanicals to ensure there would not be a repeat. By Thursday of the third week since Mazatlán, Audrey was in the backyard with Bonnie; she was taking down the laundry from the line, Bonnie clamping clothespins onto her fingers and toes. The fragrant scent of the third bouquet of roses, which had arrived early, lingered in Audrey's mind. They were an even deeper red than the first two bouquets and their smell permeated the small house.

A hand tapped her shoulder, accompanied by a deep voice, and Audrey shrieked and spun in abject terror. She lost her balance and floundered amid the sheets, winding herself in the long, billowing fabric.

"Audrey," laughed Ken, trying to steady and unravel her when she threw herself into his arms, still encumbered by the laundry.

"I didn't expect you," she cried in delight.

"So I see," he laughed, holding her tightly. He smoothed back her hair and caressed her face, his eyes misting as he bent to her. "God, I've missed you," he murmured. His lips eagerly sought hers and Audrey echoed his sentiments by the passion of her response.

A pair of tiny arms wrapped themselves around his leg, and at last Ken bent to pick up the child.

"Hello there." He grinned into the delighted little face.

"No loyalty whatsoever," grimaced Audrey when Bonnie slid her chubby little arms around Ken's neck and kissed him on the cheek.

"They do start young," he laughed, wearing a very pleased expression. He put his arm around Audrey and led her back to the house.

"How come you're here?"

"I got lonesome. Want me to leave?"

"Never."

He kissed the top of her head. "What's for dinner?"

"You're not taking me out?" Audrey feigned disappointment.

"I am not taking you out." He gave her a stern look "You have learned how to cook, haven't you?"

"But, of course," she made a sweeping bow. "What would your little heart desire?"

A change flickered over his face and he made a lascivious wink.

"For dinner!" she laughed, punching him lightly in the arm.

His eyes sparkled teasingly and he tapped the end of her nose. "Anything but oatmeal cookies."

"I'll have you know, I make great oatmeal cookies," she declared with an indignantly haughty toss of her head.

"I remember," he grimaced. "Mike and I used them to build forts."

"You had no taste!"

He put Bonnie down and held the child's hand as he walked to the front door.

"Where are you going?"

"Bonnie and I are going out," he smiled. "You stay here and try to come up with something that won't poison us. One hour?"

He waved to her and Audrey watched them walk down the block toward Himmel Park, one so very tall and dark and dignified, the other so tiny and fair and rambunctious, bouncing and bobbing along at his side.

She was setting the table when they returned, Bonnie draped over Ken's shoulder, fast asleep.

"Oh, no," cried Audrey, following Ken to the bedroom. "How long has she been asleep?"

"Just from the corner." He placed the baby very

gently in the crib, but she woke up as soon as her head touched the mattress, yawned once, and bounced back up.

"Now you've done it," sighed Audrey.

"What? She didn't miss her dinner," Ken winked meaningfully at Audrey, "and she'll settle down for a good night's sleep, right after she eats."

"You think so?" Audrey shook her head. "You don't know a thing about children," she laughed. "She can go all night now."

"Nonsense." Ken lifted Bonnie out of the crib. "I walked her chubby little legs off." Bonnie's feet barely touched the floor when she took off with a boisterous squeal. "Last spurt before she collapses," he asserted, but Audrey knew it was wishful thinking on his part.

The only thing the exercise seemed to have affected was Bonnie's appetite, which was ravenous.

"I'll clean up," said Audrey. "You are responsible for that," she pointed to the noisy toddler careening about the living room. "You wear her out."

She heard peals of laughter as Ken played with the baby, but at the end of an hour, Bonnie was still climbing and rolling all over him, and it was Ken who was worn out.

"I don't get it," he sighed as a gaily laughing Bonnie pitched headfirst over his shoulder and into his lap for the fiftieth time. "She could hardly walk. All I did was carry her for one block."

"At that age, all they have to do is blink once or twice and they're recharged," laughed Audrey. She scooped up the squealing little bundle of motion. "The original renewable energy source!"

"I wonder how you go about harnessing that," Ken sighed as he sank wearily into the sofa cushions while Audrey carried Bonnie into the bathroom and started to fill the tub.

"What did you do? Hit her over the head?" he asked when the house was silent and Audrey came back into the living room alone.

"She's sound asleep."

"Where is it, so I'll know the next time?" he asked, putting his arm around Audrey when she sat next to him.

"Where's what?"

"The off switch."

"You just have to learn how to handle them."

"So much to learn in such a short lifetime," sighed Ken, resting his head against hers. "When does she start all over again?"

"About six."

"Six!" Ken sat up and looked at his watch. "What are we doing wasting time watching television?" he laughed, switching it off and pulling her to him in one smooth motion.

Audrey knew she had missed Ken, but not until his arms closed around her and she felt the pressure of his soft, warm lips as they molded to hers, did she realize how much. Their tongues explored moist surfaces well-remembered yet instantly exciting in renewed discovery as their hands roamed over bodies, delighting in familiar textures in a tactile extension of sight. Not satisfied with the limitations of touch, Ken blazed a trail of demanding, fiery kisses.

"Ken," Audrey murmured breathlessly as he hungrily mouthed her neck and chin. She unbuttoned his shirt and slid her hands along his bare skin to his back and began to trace a path with her mouth, delicately pressing her lips to his warm, muscular flesh, following the descending line of dark, curly hairs while Ken burrowed the fingers of one hand into her thick hair and slipped his other hand inside her blouse as she moved lower until his belt impeded her progress.

He lifted her into his arms and carried her into the bedroom. "Audrey," he gasped, caressing her face and covering it with soft kisses, "I didn't think it was possible to want you more than I have, but each time..." He removed her blouse and unfastened her bra and his eyes wandered to her breasts he held in his hands. Very slowly, his thumbs swept over the smooth, taut flesh, revealing the dark aureoles that surrounded the stiffly aroused tips. "It's been so long," he murmured against the pale skin he had bent to kiss.

"Yes, it has," Audrey breathed, offering herself without reservation.

The weeks apart were relegated to a dim, surrealistic memory by the reawakening of desire and the sublime reunion that banished all traces of loneliness caused by separation.

"I missed you," Audrey murmured sleepily as she stretched languidly beneath him, a sweetly contented smile curling her lips.

"So I gathered," he grinned down at her. He kissed her playfully and propped up the pillow as she nestled into his arms. "Audrey, we have to talk."

"About what?" she mumbled sleepily.

"Us. Move to Phoenix."

"Just like that?"

"Just like that."

Very slowly, Audrey drew a pattern on his chest with her fingertip. "Where would we stay?"

"I know where there's a nice condominium in Scottsdale. Two bedrooms, nice view."

"Do you have any idea what Bonnie would do to that place?" Audrey giggled. "All that glass and chrome would be one big, smeary blur. Haven't you noticed all the finger and nose prints around here?"

"Nose prints?" His eyebrow arched quizzically.

"From little faces peering out windows, not to mention that she wipes it on everything. Besides..." She hesitated. Ken had never mentioned marriage, although he always included her and Bonnie in the vague future he constantly alluded to. Would moving in with him really be so different? Audrey could not make a clear distinction, yet she knew it would change things. There was no guarantee it would be for the better.

"I love you," he filled in the empty silence. He kissed her lightly and pulled the pillow back down. "Do you trust me?"

"Yes," she answered without hesitation.

"Good. Go to sleep." He ran his fingers through her long, silky hair. "I love you."

Ken was scheduled to speak before a lunch meeting of the Chamber of Commerce and he drove Audrey to Mrs. Haskell's house, then to the office. At two, he picked up Audrey and drove back out to the sitter's. But Bonnie was not there.

"The missus went shopping and a man come by t'get her 'bout noon," said Mr. Haskell, wiping his forehead with the back of his hand. "Said he was your boyfriend," he winked. The portly man squinted at the waiting silver sports convertible. "Got another one out there?" he snickered.

"What did he look like?" asked Audrey, turning a ghastly white and swaying against the porch railing.

"Nice lookin' fella. Sandy hair." Ken had come around the car and was hurrying to the porch. Mr. Haskell glanced at him, then Audrey. "You don't do badly for yourself," he winked again.

Ken came up behind her and squeezed her arm. "What's the matter?"

"Alan took Bonnie," she said in a deathly voice.

"When?" he shouted at Mr. Haskell.

"This mornin'. 'Fore noon. I didn't have to work an' the missus had some shoppin' to do..."

"Why didn't you call me?" shrieked Audrey. "Where did he take her?" she cried on the verge of hysteria.

"Don't know. He said he was your boyfriend an' he knew right off which one she was. She weren't scared or nothin'. Went right with him."

Supporting Audrey against his side, Ken shoved past Mr. Haskell and entered the house. "Where's your phone?" he demanded.

"Whatta ya think you're doin'?" sputtered the indignant man.

"I'm calling the police," Ken answered through tightly clenched jaws.

"What's going on...Oh!" Mrs. Haskell bustled out to the living room at all the commotion, and immediately set about the impossible task of placating her irate husband and consoling Audrey. "I didn't know 'til I got back a little while ago," she explained to the distraught mother as she wrung her hands. "Carl said he was such a nice fella, and... oh, Audrey, I just don't know what to say."

Somehow, Mrs. Haskell succeeded in getting her husband out into the kitchen and calmed down. "Well, how was I s'posed to know?" he kept insisting to Mrs. Haskell's sympathetic clucking, and he was able to supply the police with an extremely accurate description of Alan's car.

"Nothing more we can do," said the younger and taller of the two officers who had answered the call. He thanked Mr. Haskell for his cooperation and glanced at his notes. One eyebrow flickered in skepticism. "You're certain he's got no legal claim to the child?" he asked Audrey.

Already pale with fright, the question stunned Audrey, and Ken caught her as she swayed unsteadily.

"Of course, she's certain," he snapped at the officer. "Instead of cross-examining her..."

"Now calm down, mister," the pompous policeman interrupted. "We handle these situations all the time. Likely as not, it's a case of one party refusing to grant the other a fair shake. He is the kid's father, after all."

"This isn't one of those times," growled Ken, but he made an effort to control his temper.

"What's your stake in this?" asked the older, more reserved officer. "You the current boyfriend?"

"I've known Alan for years," Ken calmly stated, startling Audrey by the placidness of his demeanor. "He is extremely irresponsible. Not mean," he stressed, only the tiny, nearly invisible tic in his left cheek and the set of his jaw betraying the iron control he was exercising, "just careless." His dark eyes darted to Audrey, then the policemen and he thought better of expounding upon the dangers Bonnie faced.

Trained to handle domestic problems, both policemen acknowledged Ken's decision with a brief nod and an alteration in attitude that was manifested in a surge of brisk efficiency.

"You go on home," the younger man suggested, his tone professionally solicitous. "Any word will be directed there."

"We'll find her, Audrey," Ken tried to reassure her, lowering his voice to a gruff rumble to disguise the tremor. He drove her home, his eyes riveted on the road, Audrey's hand clutched tightly in his. Neither spoke a word and Audrey woodenly followed him into the house.

Too numb to venture an opinion or voice her fears, Audrey sat on the edge of the sofa and Ken did not insult her by engaging in meaningless platitudes or asinine suggestions that she try to relax. Instead, he put the kettle on to boil and placed a phone call to the police station.

By six, the only thing maintaining their sanity was sheer willpower. How tenuous was that hold was brought vividly to mind when the doorbell rang and both leaped to answer it, trembling legs barely supporting heartsick bodies.

"Well, my goodness," Mrs. Hudson clucked when Audrey pounced on Bonnie and she and Ken began to smother the child with hugs and kisses, "if I'd known taking her to Mrs. Watkins's would have caused this much commotion..."

"You've had her all day?" Audrey was incredulous and Ken had his arms full trying to support her and the squealing baby, who had had enough of this demonstrative exhibition and was trying to escape by crawling onto his shoulder.

"Well, no..." The flustered woman shook her head at all the confusion. "Since this afternoon. Your husband came by with her..." A matriarchal scowl of disapproval settled on Mrs. Hudson's elderly features. "Poor little thing was crying her eyes out, all covered with chocolate and her diaper needing changing..." She clucked angrily. "Said he'd only meant to treat her to some ice cream, but she wouldn't stop wailing, then when she smelled bad he didn't know what to do with her.... Men are such incompetents!" she harrumphed. "I tried to call you at the office, but you'd taken off early," she gave an indignant sniff, "and I'd promised Mrs. Watkins I'd sit with her. She's been laid up for weeks, you know, so I had to take her with me. 'Course I gave her a bath first, and... Well, really!" Mrs. Hudson fluttered her hands and blushed for Ken had given her a bear hug and a resounding kiss on the cheek. "Young folks these days," she sputtered to herself as she bustled back to her house. "Such a fuss over a little outing. Next time," she turned and wagged a long, bony finger at Audrey, "give me a call first!"

"There won't be a next time," laughed Audrey.

"Ever," Ken roundly agreed. He closed the door and turned to Audrey and Bonnie. "Better put her to bed," he suggested as he blew his nose. "Before you suffocate her."

Ken made the appropriate calls and found countless excuses to look in on Bonnie after she had been bathed and fed. Audrey came up behind him while he was looking over the end of the crib, having just straightened the blanket over the peacefully slumbering little girl.

"Ken," whispered Audrey, and her voice caught. She put her arms around him and rested her head against his back. "What would I ever do without you?"

He reached up over his shoulder to rub her head, then very slowly turned and pulled her into a tight embrace. "He had no right," he seethed, pressing Audrey's face into his neck. "No right to hurt you. Not anymore."

"Ken, I love you so much."

He held her face in his hands and his eyes were dark and cloudy. "I love you, Audrey. Both of you. I am not going to let anything happen to either one of you."

His mouth sought hers and his uncontainable love washed over and encompassed Audrey, drawing her into the protective confines of his very soul.

"Now, what?" she asked when they had finally settled for the night.

"You can't let him get away with this, Audrey." His voice was low, cold, and uncompromising, but no longer angry.

"I know." Audrey stared out the window at a lonely star that winked in the somber, ebony void as though it knew a secret answer it would not divulge. "I know," she repeated with a forlorn little sigh, for she did not know how to go about dealing with Alan. Even less, did she want to.

"Pete Santa Cruz," he mentioned a high school classmate, "works for the County Attorney. I contacted him from Mazatlán. The police will pick Alan up, especially after this." There was a long silence. "You have to sign a complaint, Audrey."

"I'll talk to Pete," she finally consented after much tortured indecision. She wanted Alan out of her life, once and for all. But she did not want to have to send him to jail to guarantee it.

Ken tightened his arms around her, and she curled up against him, sensing that he did not approve of her reluctance. "I love you," he whispered, and she knew he would try to accept her decision, however much he might disagree.

Chapter Fifteen

"No, Ken, I can manage," Audrey said with vehemence. "I don't want to get Barney started again—"

"But, Audrey," Ken interrupted, "be reasonable. You need the extra money now with Bonnie in the nursery school."

Audrey knew he was making sense; enrolling Bonnie in the church-run nursery school only minutes from the agency had been a costly venture, but she was determined not to stir up more trouble from the Longworth Agency. As they sat in the restaurant having dinner, she thought back over the few days since the incident with Alan. She would not return Bonnie to Mrs. Haskell, or any other sitter for that matter. Ken even included the child in their dinner plans.

He had been so adamant that Audrey see Pete that she finally had consented. She didn't want to file a formal complaint against Alan, but Pete was confident the threat of one would sufficiently stall any future actions Alan might have contemplated. "He's trying to get his life straightened out," Pete had assured her, and Audrey sincerely hoped he was right.

Ken was not so sure, however, and he kept insisting Audrey have the extra salary so that she could afford to protect Bonnie and herself. When faced with Audrey's vehement refusals though, he always relented. He swore to protect them—they were the most important people in the world to him, and he slept well later that night knowing they were with him.

Early in the morning, a human projectile vaulted

across Ken's shoulder, hurtling across him and wedging itself between Ken and Audrey.

"How did she get out?" mumbled Ken, rolling onto his side. "Audrey, she's all wet!" he cried out as he sat up and hoisted Bonnie out of the bed, holding her as far from him as possible.

"That's the way they are in the morning," said Audrey. "I guess it just takes some getting used to." Audrey pulled on her robe and took the toddler into the bathroom. Ken came to the door to watch her bathe the wriggling child. Periodically, he sniffed the sleeve of his robe and made a disdainful face.

"I'll throw it in the wash," laughed Audrey.

"Hold it, September Morn," he ordered when Bonnie bolted, naked, through the door. He caught her in a smooth, quick movement and handed her back to Audrey. "Are they always that pink and slippery?" he laughed.

When Audrey had dressed her and bent to gather up the clothes, he put his arm out to bar her exit. "Not until you kiss me," he grinned, and she gave him a tiny peck on the cheek. "Is that all the thanks I get?"

"For what?"

"For being simply wonderful," he grinned.

"Are you?" she teased.

"You tell me," he instructed, sliding his hand along her jaw as he tipped her face up, his eyes glowing with a deep inner light.

"Yes," she whispered, shyly averting her eyes that could not conceal the love in them.

"You think so?" He rubbed her cheek with the side of his finger and his mouth curled into a broad grin. "Prove it," he said, relishing the shocked look on her face.

"How?" she blurted unthinkingly and he winked at her.

"Fix me eggs over easy, without breaking them."

"That would prove *I* was wonderful," she sniffed with a haughty lift of her chin.

"You don't have to prove you are," he laughed,

wrapping his arms around her. "I already know that." He deftly removed his robe as he brushed past her and closed the door.

"Ken!"

"Save you a trip," he called out to her. "You were going to the laundry room anyway." He turned on the water.

"Anything I can do?" he asked later, when he entered the kitchen.

"Make the orange juice." While Ken spooned out the frozen concentrate, he watched Audrey gingerly work the spatula under an egg.

"Aha!" she triumphantly exclaimed when the egg rolled over without breaking.

"Bet you can't do two," he teased, kissing her cheek as he put his arms around her waist.

"Not with you standing there," she protested, wriggling her shoulders.

"No control?"

"No room. Weren't you supposed to be making the orange juice?" She gave him a fraudulent scowl. "Make yourself useful."

"Oh, what the harsh light of day does to romance," he tutted, but he did as he was told. When they finally sat down to eat, his dark eyes traveled slowly around the tiny kitchen. "Do you spend much time in here?"

"Not as much as I'd like. Or should. I like to cook, and I'll thank you to keep your smart remarks to yourself," she warned.

"I wasn't going to make any," he protested his innocence. "You don't have much room," he continued. "And when you open the refrigerator, it blocks the door."

"I know. Men should be strung up by their thumbs for trying to design kitchens."

"I wouldn't go quite so far!"

"I would. This is not nearly as bad as some of the ones I've seen. At least I have a decent amount of counter space in relation to the size. And the cupboards go all the way to the ceiling."

"I noticed that. But you're tall." He mentally measured her height to the room. "These ceilings are ten feet high. Even you can't reach those top ones. What good are they?"

"Storage," she shrugged. "Even if I don't use them, so what? The ones that stop at the standard height get all greasy and dusty and disgusting on top. And since they're never finished, they're impossible to clean. Men never think of that!"

"Hmm?" He followed Audrey into the dining room. "What else don't men ever think of?" He caught her mischievous glance and made a face. "In designing kitchens," he grinned.

"They almost never give you enough counter space, and the cupboards are too deep or not deep enough."

"Wait a minute." He put some jelly on a piece of toast and handed it to Bonnie. "They're all standardized, so they can't be both."

"There should be at least one oversized one for large items and shallow ones for cans and stuff. With adjustable shelves. And drawers in different depths. And places for cookbooks, and spices, and pot lids, and..."

"Stop!" He shook his head in dismay. "I think I get the picture. It would cost a fortune to build houses like that."

"So? Economize somewhere else." Audrey wiped the sticky purple jelly off Bonnie's face and hands while Ken stared at her in disbelief.

"Where?"

"I'm not the expert," she protested with a laugh.

"You're certainly opinionated enough."

"Must be catching," she winked. She began to stack the dirty dishes. "You know I'm right," she added. "The first thing every homeowner remodels is the kitchen."

With a weary groan Ken arose. "Let me show you something." He went out to the trunk of his car and returned with a folder. "What's wrong with these?" he asked as he spread the floor plans for Nava del Sol in front of her. He cleared the table while she studied them.

Very carefully Audrey went over each one, occasionally referring back to one or another to compare them as she divided them into three piles.

"This one's not bad," she said, pointing to the one on her left. "This one's okay, and these three," she indicated the last stack, "are a disaster. As for this one," she held one up, not sure where to put it, "some of it is great, and some features are dreadful."

"What about this one?" Ken asked, pulling another floor plan out of a separate folder. It was the Piedra Solana model and Ken was extremely defensive about it.

"There's no place for all the appliances one accumulates over the years. And there are not enough cabinets."

"I think I'll retire," he sighed.

Audrey came around behind him and put her arms around his neck. "Can't you make a few changes?" she asked, kissing the top of his head.

"A few?" He rolled his eyes at her. "They're already under construction. How come I never noticed, and why didn't you say something before?"

"I never looked at them that closely because I was distracted by all the other beautiful aspects. I'm sorry."

"Don't be. Down you go, Bonnie. I've got work to do." He kissed the top of Bonnie's curly little head and put her down, gathered up the drawings, and went out to Audrey's studio.

At noon Audrey brought him a sandwich, but Ken was so absorbed in the revisions, he did not notice her. She left it on the edge of the table and took Bonnie out for a walk. Dinner was nearly ready when he finally emerged from the studio, waving a new set of floor plans.

"See, it wasn't that hard," she smiled up at him after she had inspected each one.

"Oh, no. Not at all," he yawned and stretched.

"You're not half bad," Audrey teased, sliding her arms around his waist.

"I'm damned good!" he asserted, giving her hair a

gentle tug. The teasing glow in his eyes faded into a deep light of desire, and Audrey swayed forward, drawn by their hypnotic power.

"Audrey, I can't stay," he whispered in a thick, uneven voice.

"Dinner's ready," she breathed, not wanting to leave the warmth of his arms. Ever.

"I'm sorry," he said, pulling her closer. His hands began to caress the soft curves of her body. "Will it keep?"

"Until next week?"

"For a little while," he said, nuzzling her cheek.

"I'll turn it off."

While she did, Ken went into Bonnie's room. "Playing quietly," he reassured Audrey, taking her into his arms.

Minutes later, the barriers of shirt and blouse had been removed, Ken teased and provoked her breasts with his fingers, caressing the lace enclosed fullness with the palm of his hand, alternately slipping his long fingers under the sheer fabric to stroke and fondle the straining flesh. Frustrated by this change in tempo, Audrey arched her hips in silent supplication, but Ken made no move to curtail the dallying.

"What's the hurry?" he winked down at her, bending low to continue the caressing with his mouth.

"I thought you were the one with so little time to spare," she giggled, punching him lightly in the arm.

Ken steered her into the bedroom. "I never rush what I enjoy," he grinned, ending on a sharp intake of breath when her hand slid under the waistband of his slacks. "No point in postponing the inevitable though," he conceded through another deep, ragged inhalation as he removed her bra and unbuttoned her jeans, the teasing having gone the way of his patience.

"That'll teach you to play games with me." She smiled sweetly up at him, when both had had a chance to catch their breath.

"Hasn't taught me a thing," he leered, bending to kiss the tip of her nose. "Except that you cheat." The teasing expression faded and he rolled away from her. "Audrey, I hate this. I want you with me."

Audrey stroked his smooth, tan cheek, bringing her fingers up and through his hair along his temple. "And I want to be with you," she whispered.

He kissed each of her fingertips, then her palm. "Come with me tonight."

"I can't. I have a job."

Ken clasped her tightly. "Four more months," he groaned. "I don't know if I can take it."

"What?"

"Your days are numbered, young lady." He grinned. "Are you going to feed me or send me off hungry?" he teased, pulling her to a sitting position.

"I thought you couldn't stay."

"I never pass up a free meal. Besides, women don't own the franchise on changing their minds."

While Audrey set the table, Ken changed Bonnie and carried her out on his shoulders.

"Risky," laughed Audrey, pointing to the diaper that drooped baggily from the middle of the kidney-bean-shaped figure. Audrey refastened the garment securely before placing Bonnie in the high chair, and after dinner Ken carried the baby in one arm, his suitcase in the other.

"Next Friday," he said when he had placed his things in the car. "Is it a date?"

"Maybe."

"Maybe? Do you want to scandalize Mrs. Hudson while I coax you into a definite yes?" he leered.

"No! I mean, yes," she laughed, holding him away.

"Good." He kissed her lightly. "'Bye." He rumpled Bonnie's cap of red curls and kissed her, too. "Take care of your mom," he instructed the baby. A frown flitted across his face, vanished, and kissing both again, he left.

It wouldn't be that hard to move to Phoenix, Audrey reflected as she put Bonnie to bed, the vision of Ken's smiling face strong in her mind. Her father was dead, her mother lived in Texas, her brother in Washington.

She had no ties in Tucson anymore. It would be that much farther away from Alan, too. Love and admiration for Ken swelled within her, for he had not spoken about Alan again, nor asked her about her meeting with Pete. It was an omission based on trust, not disinterest, and that confidence gave her the strength to face the inevitable.

The phone rang. Pete Santa Cruz calling to say he had been unable to reach Alan, who had left the state, but would Audrey be willing to speak to Carla? With great misgivings, Audrey consented and set up an appointment for the end of the month. She had no wish to speak to Alan's current, or any other, wife. Nor to Alan.

Friday, there was a foul-up in construction at Nava del Sol, and Ken could not come down to Tucson, nor could he get free any of the next three weekends. During the middle of the fourth week, he called, and he sounded extremely harassed and out of sorts.

"Audrey," he demanded, "get up here this weekend, or else!"

"Or else what?" was Audrey's indignant reply. Working night and day to finish the series that was scheduled to run the next week and meeting with Carla had done nothing for Audrey's disposition, either. "You'll fire me?" she sarcastically asked.

"I'll go out of my mind," he confessed.

"What about Bonnie?" Audrey's voice quavered, and her pulse raced at the undisguised longing in his voice.

"Bring her. I'll get a sitter and take you out on the town," he promised.

"What do you know about babysitters?" laughed Audrey.

"I'll learn," he insisted. "But get up here!"

"I don't know," she stubbornly resisted acquiescing too readily. "Will I even get to see you? You've been so busy all these weeks," she grumbled, although her mind was already made up.

"I do get home nights, though that's been none too comforting," he said in a woebegone voice, and Audrey clucked in false sympathy. "As for my being busy," he chided her, "you'll thank me someday. When will you get here?"

"If I leave at five, Friday, I can be at the site by eight."

"No." The adamancy of his tone surprised her. "Go straight to my condo. I'll be there."

"Okay. 'Bye."

"Audrey," he said petulantly. He waited for her to continue.

"I love you," she said softly.

"It's a good thing, too. 'Bye. I love you," he added very gently.

Ken bent to kiss her while she was still seated in her station wagon. His mouth devoured hers, and still kissing her, he pulled her out, leaning her against the car for support.

"Ken," she gasped when he finally gave her a chance to breathe. "What will people think?"

"Who cares?" he muttered, nibbling on her ear and chin as his mouth again sought hers. And he was right. She certainly didn't.

Bonnie began to protest her confinement in the car seat. "Saved," he grinned at Audrey. "For the moment." He bent into the car and released the child. "At last she's happy to see me," he beamed, hugging the broadly smiling child who wrapped her little arms around his neck and planted a very wet kiss on his cheek. "Oh, that's so nice," he sighed, patting her little back after he had dried his cheek with the back of his hand. "You could teach your mommy," he teased. He put his arm around Audrey while he carried Bonnie into the condominium.

"Put your grubby little paws all over everything," he laughed as he put the baby down. "So I'll have something to remember you by. As for you," he said, drawing Audrey to him, "did you miss me?"

His eyes were dark and misty. One arm was around Audrey's waist, holding her against his hips, the other hand undid her blouse and slid under the sheer fabric to enclose her breast. His fingers gently massaged the soft flesh under her bra, and Audrey swayed forward as she yielded to the pleasure of his touch while his hips rocked steadily and rhythmically against hers.

"Yes," she softly moaned as she pulled his face down to her yearning mouth.

Bonnie began to tug on his pants leg. The longer she was ignored, the more persistent she became, and Ken finally groaned in defeat.

"Hello, squirt," he smiled down at the tot. "Isn't it past your bedtime?" He bent to pick her up, reaching out to steady Audrey as he did so. "Careful," he grinned, guiding her along at his side.

"I thought you were going to get a sitter?" mumbled a very disoriented Audrey.

"I don't like crowds," he chuckled with a mischievous wink. "Tomorrow night and all day Sunday," he whispered. He kissed Audrey soundly and nudged her into a chair in the study. A crib had been set up in front of the desk, and he put Bonnie in it.

"That won't even slow her down," observed Audrey who had gradually regained her bearings.

"What do you mean?" he asked as he walked over to Audrey.

"The desk."

"What about it? I took everything off it that might hurt her."

"Watch."

Ken turned around in time to see Bonnie climb adroitly out of the crib and onto the desk.

"Okay, munchkin," he laughed, putting her back. "You're going for a ride."

To Bonnie's delight, he wheeled her into the living room and surveyed the area. Everything fragile, sharp, dangerous, or valuable had been put away.

"So, she's a climber now, is she?" he said as he removed the glass shelves from the chrome étagères.

"No." Ken turned, a bewildered frown on his face. "Down, not up," explained Audrey. "I can't keep her penned in anymore, but she's never climbed up onto anything."

Not convinced, Ken shoved the loveseat in front of the étagères as a barrier. "Even if she gets on it," he tested it by pulling forward on one of the horizontal slats, "she can't tip it over." He put the glass shelves in the closet.

"I certainly hope this is worth all the trouble you're going to," laughed Audrey.

"I have every confidence it will be," he leered, taking her keys as he went out to her car for the luggage.

Ken insisted upon putting Bonnie to bed, and he entertained the child by reading to her, in French, from an enormous picture book, dramatically acting out all the roles in "Les Trois Petits Cochons," modifying the wolf to a harmless clown, and the pigs to little wisenheimers.

"What a ham!" teased Audrey, throwing her arms around Ken when the performance was over. "Where did you ever find that?" she pointed to the dog-eared book.

"It's mine," he grinned, coloring deeply. "My aunt gave it to me when I was three."

"She didn't understand a word," laughed Audrey.

"Who? My aunt?" he teased. He rumpled Audrey's hair and put the book away. "Of course, she did," he beamed smugly, "I showed her all the pictures. Now," he turned to Audrey with a lurid grin as he closed the cabinet, "where did we leave off?"

And Audrey proceeded to demonstrate.

Chapter Sixteen

"Two down, three to go," Ken sighed contentedly, Sunday afternoon.

"What are you always babbling about?" asked Audrey, resting her chin on the forearm she had placed on his chest.

"You'll see, soon enough." He wore a smug smile as he traced a meandering line from her shoulder, down her spine to her hips, then ran his palm along her smooth derriere.

"Penny for your thoughts," grinned Audrey.

"I should have punched Alan's lights out years ago," he calmly stated. "Then you would have had no choice but to love me." Audrey absently drew her teeth over her lower lip. She did not want to think, or talk, about Alan. That meeting with Carla had been... revealing. But it had left her with a dilemma. Ken brushed aside the lock of red-gold hair that fell across her cheek and tucked it behind her ear. "You do, now, don't you?"

She was surprised by the glimmer of uncertainty in his eyes and she hastened to reassure him. "I've never loved anyone more," she said, pulling herself up to gaze into his eyes.

"What about on a day-in, day-out basis?" he frowned. "Do you think you could put up with me?"

"Yes." The corners of her mouth twitched gleefully. "Think you could stand me?"

"I'm willing to try. Although," he tickled her and turned her over so that he was lying above her, "I'm sure you will do everything you can to make it difficult."

"How can you say that?" she protested with a broad grin.

"I know you."

"You do not," she countered.

"Oh, no?" His fingers knowingly traced her ear and his thumb and index finger teased the soft, delicate flap of her earlobe before moving along her chin to the tissue-thin layer of skin that covered her vocal cords, exerting a pressure that did not quite tickle but electrified every nerve ending. A small, triumphant smile curled the corners of his mouth at the sudden, shallow intake of breath when his fingers reached the hollow between her collarbone, then descended slowly along the center of her rib cage, his fingers expanding laterally to fan the swell of her breast, then closing, thumb circumscribing the lower arc, as they converged on the dark-pink tip, expanded again and swept slowly across to her other breast where they repeated the caress.

"Two can play that game," she warned in a breathy whisper.

"Be my guest," he grinned, and her hand roamed across his flat, pectoral muscle, curling the short, dark hairs around her fingers as she moved them in ever widening, ever lowering circles. Each inhalation expanded his chest cavity, bringing him closer in slow degrees while he continued to tease and coax, first one, then the other, of her hardened nipples. A gradual, imperceptible arching of backs, and a progressive, languid stretching of long legs decreased the meager distance remaining until the slow, steady caressing culminated in the deep, harmonic rhythms that were as old as time.

"You can't leave!" Ken stated with finality when he lay beside her in complacent satisfaction.

"I have to," Audrey quietly stated. "What about my job? If I get fired, I won't even have these few excuses to see you."

"That is patently untrue," he scowled. He stared at

the ceiling for several moments. "Is Barney still giving you a hard time?"

"No. He pretty much ignores me. In fact," she laughed lightly, "he could almost be described as generous. For Barney," she clarified that remark.

"That would mean he was paying you minimum wage," grimaced Ken. He caught her glance and emphatically denied the allegation in her eyes. "I never said a word to him. I want you to learn how to deal with him, on your own." Ken spoke sternly, but he was running his hand through her hair, watching it sift through his fingers. "Why didn't you open your own agency?"

"What?" Audrey sat up. "Where would I have gotten the money?"

"How much did you pay for your house?" he asked thoughtfully. When she told him, he sat up in surprise. "Audrey, you've been sitting on a gold mine! It's easily worth three, maybe four, times that now."

"I have to have someplace to live!" she exclaimed, wondering where his common sense had strayed.

"You could have taken out a second mortgage."

"I couldn't have made the payments."

"Sure you could. All you had to do was first line up your accounts and get a percentage up front." Ken looked at her in astonishment. "Don't you have any idea how your business works?"

"Not really," she admitted with a small shrug.

"It's time you did. You'll never be happy working for someone else, Audrey. Unless it's me, of course," he teased, bending to give her a quick kiss. "It's too late to get a second mortgage now, but if you sell your house, you could be ready by the opening of Nava del Sol. Who knows?" He bent to kiss the tip of her nose. "I might even decide to retain your services."

"But..." This was going over her head way too fast. "Why is it too late?"

"You'll get hit for points and prepayment penalty clauses." He stared at her confused expression and burst out laughing. "It would be much more practical to sell outright and move to Phoenix."

"Oh!" Several possibilities popped into her mind. "Will you explain all the details?"

"When I come to Tucson next week, I'll bring some of Barney's statements."

"I'm not sure I want to know anything about Barney's 'system,'" she scowled.

"It's strictly legal, if somewhat padded. The principle is what you need to learn. Stop worrying," he smiled, smoothing her brow with his finger. "I won't ask you about any of the charges, and don't volunteer anything." He smiled wryly. "That's the first lesson. Never volunteer."

"I have to think about this," she hesitated.

"I'd think you were an idiot, if you didn't." He grinned. "And you are definitely not an idiot."

"How can you be sure?" she asked, not fully in concordance with his assessment.

"Because you love me."

"Yes, I do."

"So? Get dressed," he ordered with a laugh. "I'm going to retrieve Bonnie from the sitter. I want to spend a little time with her before you take her away from me again."

Audrey gazed at him with tender affection. "You really do like her, don't you?" she smiled.

"She's yours," he said softly, gently running his finger down her soft cheek. "But," he said, grinning sheepishly, "I'd like her anyway. She's the cutest thing I've ever seen. With the possible exception of her mother," he added, bending to give Audrey a loving kiss. "She likes me, don't you think?"

"Nope." Disappointment and uncertainty flickered in those tender brown eyes and Audrey immediately regretted teasing him. "She's crazy about you," she smiled up at him. "Haven't you noticed how her face lights up around you?"

"Just like her mother."

"Just like her mother," Audrey agreed, reaching up to draw his face closer.

A second mortgage? Well, the equity, actually, was

what Ken had meant. Audrey mulled over the possibilities while she showered and dressed. She almost discussed her plans with Ken before she left. It would be better to work out the details first, she counseled herself.

Ken came to Tucson as promised and took Audrey to lunch high in the Catalina Foothills at the Westward Look Resort, where he spelled out the basic premises behind the billing process Barney used.

"It isn't all that complicated," he assured her, realigning the stack of papers he had taken from his briefcase.

"So I see." The amounts Audrey had seen had astounded her, and she had been sorely tested to hold her tongue.

"I could have covered the figures," he said, seeing her distraught face, "but I wanted you to make a mental comparison of the actual costs, and by deduction, understand how Barney arrived at his amounts. Every agency uses a standard formula and multiplies the costs by whatever factor will maximize the profits without unduly antagonizing the client. Barney pads everything in case he has to negotiate later. It makes him look generous and he still comes out way ahead."

"I don't think I've got the brass to do that."

"Then, don't," smiled Ken. "Set your fees and stick with them. Just don't set them so low you can't afford to compete. A mistake you made when you were freelancing."

"What do you mean?" she asked defensively.

"It's typical of women starting out. You think because you weren't paid before, you only deserve the minimum." He patted her hand and brought it to his lips. "You didn't have a very high opinion of yourself after the divorce, either," he gently added.

Audrey glanced out at the Catalinas, watching the cloud shadows drift and change form as they crossed the ridges and hills. He was right. That was why she had been so quick to accept the position with Longworth.

But that all seemed so far away. "That was centuries ago," she whispered. Her green eyes were steady, bright with confidence in herself and Ken, and the love she felt for him shone on her face.

"But start my own agency?" Audrey frowned and moistened her lips. "I don't know if I'm ready yet. I don't want to bite off more than my eyes can see."

Ken screwed up his face at her distortion and pulled out a yellow pad, which he handed to her.

"Write down everything you owe. Then underneath, everything you are committed to, in perpetuity: utilities, clothing, food, everything." When she had finished, he studied it closely. On another sheet he regrouped the figures.

"You owe very little," he smiled approvingly. "Pay these off first, and here's how much you have to make to meet expenses and survive." He circled the figure. "It depends on how many clients you can handle and at what rate."

"I don't know," said a still-skeptical Audrey, "It always works on paper, then once a month the bank and I come up with different amounts."

"How do you handle that?"

"I use whichever amount is smaller."

Ken put his head in his hands and peered out through his fingers. "Why do I know you are not joking?" He went back to her list of expenses and added "accountant" to her perpetual debts column. He frowned at her in disbelief. "You never try to reconcile your figures and the bank's?"

"They're always right," she stated the immutable truth.

"Let's go," he sighed. "I need some fresh air." They strolled out into the clear, blue, desert air and Ken checked his watch, a disappointed expression settling on his attractive features. "I was hoping I would get to see Bonnie."

"You're not staying?" Audrey could not conceal her dismay.

"I have to go to Maryland. They've developed a

new, faster system for developing solar crystals. If I can't find what I need there, I'll have to go to Denver, then on to Amarillo."

"Why?"

"We can't get the parts for the photovoltaic unit on schedule. Our main supplier is trying to fill orders for NASA, and if we can't locate another source in a hurry, Nava del Sol won't be ready for the opening. We have to halt construction, as it is, without those devices."

"How much of a delay are we talking about?"

"If I'm successful this week, it won't. We're ahead of schedule. Fortunately, in this climate we don't have the weather on our backs." He held the door open for her.

"I wish there was something I could do to help," said Audrey, studying his worried profile as he started the car.

He put his arm around her and kissed her with carefully controlled passion, then held her close, heaving a deep sigh of regret. "I was looking forward to this weekend."

"These things happen," Audrey tried to sound cheerful. "How long will you be gone?"

"I don't know. Could be a week, maybe longer." He trained his dark eyes on hers. "Will you miss me?" he asked against her lips.

"What do you think?" she mumbled, kissing him with all the love she no longer made any attempt to hide.

"It won't be for much longer, I promise." Ken hugged her to his side as he drove off. "Damn deadlines and delays," he muttered.

He left Audrey at the agency and was gone for most of three weeks, during which time Audrey conferred with Pete Santa Cruz. Alan's wife had been so unlike anyone Audrey had expected that she had relied heavily on Pete at the initial meeting. The meek, mousy, very pregnant woman had proven to be a strong negotiator for Alan. She assured the deputy prosecutor and Audrey that he was not involved in the sale of drugs, but was the victim of years of his own bad example.

"He wants to set himself up in his own realty firm," Carla had said. "But he can't get a loan. He's got a lot of pride. Maybe too much," the quiet woman had stated what Audrey knew to be the truth. "He knew you were doing all right," she said to Audrey, keeping her pale gray eyes focused steadily on Alan's ex-wife. "When it came right down to asking..." Carla gave a resigned shrug. "As for your baby..." She took a slow, measured breath. "He...he's having a hard time adjusting. He wasn't any good with yours...his first," she pointedly corrected herself. "He just wanted to be with her for a little while to see if he could take it..." Her voice faded away and she stared at her slender fingers that were making nervous little pleats in the gaily flowered maternity smock that seemed too festive for the sad, frail woman it covered. "He wants to come home," she said in a whisper. "But he doesn't want to go to jail."

The relief Carla very nearly concealed behind a facade of remote indifference when Audrey instructed Pete to drop all charges haunted Audrey. If she had had any money to give Alan or his wife, she would have. Yet she knew neither would have accepted the crippling shackles of charity. Ken's suggestion, however, was the perfect solution. If she split the equity in the house that had belonged to both of them, Alan could retain his dignity, and she could start afresh in Phoenix, near Ken, yet not dependent on him.

The house sold more quickly and for more than she had estimated, and Audrey accepted the position with PG Productions that would guarantee her a steady income while she got on her feet. She was bursting with the good news but, when Ken called, decided to save her announcement for the grand opening. Ken, after all, was not the only one who could keep a secret.

Ken worked night and day in a frantic attempt to make up for lost time. Audrey did get to Phoenix on four occasions during the next six weeks, but only for two-to-three hours at a time to meet with Tom, for Ken could not get free but two of those times. She was distressed by how tired and drawn he looked, and he was almost caustic about what he would allow her photographer to cover at the site.

"Sorry," he wearily apologized on the way to the small, private plane that was to take her back to Tucson. "Trust me, Audrey. I don't want to spoil the effect of the grand opening," he smiled wanly, and Audrey agreed to comply with his wishes.

But she continued to worry about Ken. She had not had a chance to tell him of her decision, and a nagging doubt resurfaced. He had not pressed her about moving to Phoenix and she was concerned that, in the end, he might well resent the intrusion she and Bonnie would be on him.

Whenever he found a moment though, he called. He sounded so tired and haggard, she longed to be with him. But he did not ask. Not until two weeks before the opening.

"I'll be down this Thursday, no matter what," he promised. "This whole place can cave in, but I am still coming down!"

"I can hardly wait," Audrey whispered breathlessly, vividly picturing his lean, tan features, her heart soaring at the uplifting tone of his voice.

"Hold that thought. Still love me?"

"You know I do."

"Not as much as I love you," he said quietly. "You couldn't."

"Could too," she happily rebutted him.

"We'll see," he chuckled.

It was a moot question as both discovered Thursday night, and the answer was mutually satisfactory.

"Audrey," he sighed happily, "I can barely concentrate on anything. You're on my mind all the time. I thought it would never get here."

"The opening?" Audrey rubbed his cheek and kissed him tenderly. "Then what will become of me?"

"Haven't you figured that out yet?" he frowned with a bewildered shake of his head.

"You told me not to guess, so I didn't."

He laughed lightly and pinched her nose. "I expect you to come to Phoenix, for one thing."

"Maybe." She smiled secretively. "You're not the only one who can plan surprises."

"Meaning?"

"No guessing," she grinned, stopping him with a soft kiss.

"Audrey, you know I hate surprises." He thought a moment. "Maybe I should tell you."

"No, I don't want to spoil it." She wriggled closer. "Hold me," she whispered. "I feel so safe with you."

"You should." He gave a contented sigh. "Two more weeks."

The next afternoon Ken returned from Himmel Park to find Audrey had a visitor.

"Here's my baby," laughed a delighted Elaine Mathieson. She scooped up Bonnie with a happy grin. "What a big girl you're getting to be."

The flighty-appearing, gray-haired woman cooed and grimaced at the baby, hugging and kissing her incessantly while Ken stood awkwardly by, and Audrey's heart went out to him. She squeezed his hand and kissed his cheek. "I love you," she whispered and he patted her hand.

"You look good, too, Ken," smiled Elaine. "I'm so grateful to you, but you were always such a good friend to Alan." Audrey stared at her, wondering what moonbeam she had resided on all these years. "Alan will work things out," she smiled confidently at Audrey. "Promise me you won't keep this little angel away from me," she pleaded, her pale blue eyes watering with tears. They were so vacuous and confused, but so filled with love when she gazed at Bonnie, Audrey could only shake her head in confusion. "Oh, I knew you'd feel that way."

Alan arrived at the door and Audrey felt Ken go rigid at her side.

"It's getting late," he said to his mother, after stiffly greeting Ken and Audrey.

Audrey gently pried Bonnie from Elaine, who gave her one last, noisy kiss.

"You come see us, real soon," she waved to them until Audrey waved back.

"Well?" Ken asked when they were alone.

"I've...I've decided to take your advice." Audrey decided to tell him everything once she had put Bonnie in her room. "About the second mortgage...that is." Ken's hard, cold glare was confusing her and she was not explaining this coherently. "I'm going to give Alan the money—" To her utter dismay and shock, Ken launched into a tirade.

"You are going to do what?" he roared, and she repeated it, getting no further the second time, and it did not have the soothing effect she had hoped for.

"I thought you were going to start a new life for yourself? I thought you were finally through with Alan?"

"I am," she countered, thoroughly confused by his outburst.

"You're taking on a fifteen-year debt for him!" he raved. "How are you going to pay it off? Work for Barney for the rest of your life? I thought you had some brains!"

"I do!" Audrey shouted back, furious that he had not bothered to hear her out. "You were the one who insisted I learn how to make my own decisions!"

"Well, I was wrong! You're not capable of it!" He stormed into the bedroom and gathered up his things. "Not where Alan is concerned," he said bitterly. "Never where Alan is concerned!"

"Ken," she cried, following him to his car.

"Even when he loses, he wins!" he yelled, slamming the door. He roared off and Audrey went slowly back into the house.

She called his number after two frantic hours and he finally answered. "K-Ken," she stammered, "I...I was worried about you..."

"I'm perfectly able to get myself home," he said in the coldest voice she had ever heard, and it chilled her to the bone. "You needn't concern yourself about me."

"Please, Ken," she begged, sensing he was about to hang up on her.

"Why can't you learn to trust me?"

"It works both ways!" she cried, suddenly furiously indignant. "When you are ready to open your narrow mind, call me!" She slammed the phone back on the hook.

He did not call her back, nor did she hear from him the rest of the week, and she was devastated. Tom called once to remind her of the opening gala, but he was cool and distant.

"Men," she muttered to herself. "They all stick together!"

As though to bear her out on that premise, her brother called to let her know when he would be arriving. When she broke down and told him everything, he counseled, "Go see him, Audrey."

"I can't," she stubbornly insisted, hoping he would supply a reason that would override her pride. "If Ken can't trust me, there's no point," she sighed dejectedly.

"Audrey," Mike appealed to her knowledge of their history, "he's got a blind spot where Alan is concerned."

"That's his problem."

"It's yours, too."

But all Audrey could think of was that Ken had not trusted her enough to give her the benefit of the doubt.

Saturday morning the door bell rang at eight, and when Audrey looked up from her coffee, she was astonished to see Janet on the porch.

"I've had enough of this," she announced, pushing past Audrey. She grabbed her arm and led her into the bedroom, where she opened the closet, selected a pretty blue voile dress Audrey had worn in Mazatlán, and thrust it at the younger woman. "Get dressed!" she ordered.

"Have you lost your mind?" Audrey stared at her in horror.

"Do you have any idea what has been going on up there?" Bonnie came toddling in and crawled across the bed to sit on Audrey's dress. "Tom has worked all his life for a project like this. If you think for one minute, I'm going to sit by and let you two stubborn, pigheaded mules destroy his dreams, you're the one who has lost your mind. Now, get dressed; the plane is waiting!"

"What plane? What are you ranting and raving about?" cried Audrey.

"Ken is planning to dissolve the partnership and pull out of Nava del Sol, that's what I am talking about," shouted Janet. "I warned you, Audrey, I wouldn't stand for this."

Audrey was shocked. Ken wouldn't pull out of Nava del Sol. That was his life's work, too. "What makes you think Ken will listen to me?" Audrey asked as she picked up the dress.

"He's in love with you."

"Maybe not," Audrey very quietly disputed her.

"There's only one way to find out."

"What about Bonnie?" Audrey asked, still stalling.

Janet thought a second. "He's crazy about her. Take her with you. You're going to need all the help you can get." She carried Bonnie into the other bedroom. "I'll dress her, and for heaven's sake, hurry! I don't know how long Tom can keep Ken out at the site this morning."

"I don't know," Audrey repeated at the door to the plane, her meager self-confidence rapidly diminishing. "If he doesn't care anymore... He hasn't called..."

Janet handed Bonnie into the plane. "He's been too busy cancelling contracts right and left." She flashed an encouraging smile. "You've got about an hour and a half to think of something in your favor."

There was a car waiting for Audrey in Phoenix, and when she reached the entrance to Nava del Sol, her heart swelled with pride. The townhouses and condominiums were nearly completed, as were the individual models, but all appeared deserted. She drove slowly down each of the streets, her eyes peeled for any sign of his car. How could Ken abandon this? So much of him had gone into it. She owed it to him to at least talk to him. If it was not too late, she thought with mounting fear. She had reached the last street that curved up and around behind a high lot and almost made a U-turn. But she had come this far, so she slowly climbed the steep grade.

A house she did not recall seeing in any of the plans was nestled into the back side of the ridge, and yet, it seemed vaguely familiar. Curiosity brought her nearer and she saw Ken's silver sports car in the driveway. Clinging to Bonnie for moral support, Audrey entered the house.

"Ken?" she tentatively called out.

There was no answer.

Audrey wandered down the long, skylight-lit hall. What if Ken had heard her and chose to leave without speaking to her? She did not know the layout of this house, and it would be easy enough for him to leave unnoticed. "Ken?" she called again as she entered the light, airy kitchen. She saw him. His back was to her and he continued to stare out the window, not acknowledging her presence.

Bonnie began to squirm and wriggle. No sooner had Audrey set the child down than she ran straight to Ken and rubbed her face into his leg.

"Don't wipe your nose on my pants," he gently reprimanded the child.

Unabashed, Bonnie promptly ran off, noisily careening around the corner of the cooking island. "Don't let her do that," ordered Ken. "This has to go on the market and we don't need a lot of smudgy prints all over everything."

"Stop that!" commanded Audrey. She made an unsuccessful grab for the little dynamo who ran giggling through the empty house. Taking a deep breath, Audrey slowly walked toward Ken. "I was just following your advice," she said softly, forcing herself to look into those hard, unrelenting black eyes.

"Even *you* can't believe that convoluted distortion of the truth?" he sneered.

Audrey looked down at the patterned tiles on the cooking island. "You said I should pay off all my old debts before I incurred any new ones."

"Is that what it was? An old debt?"

"Yes." She looked up and Ken glared at her for a long moment.

"You were willing to pay a very high price," he said coldly. He turned to look back out the window.

"I hated him for so long," she said in a barely audible voice. "There are always two sides to everything. I...I probably could have helped him, if I had wanted to." With a small shrug, Audrey shook her hair behind her shoulder. "It was conscience money. It may not be right, but I am free of debt. Alan has a chance to work things out." Audrey twisted a lock of hair around her fingers and stared at the glazed, quarry tile floor. "I hope he does...but it isn't my problem."

Ken turned slowly and sat on the edge of the sill. "You'll be a long time paying off that loan."

"There was no loan." His eyebrow flickered in surprise. "I sold the house." Audrey lifted her head to a proud angle. "I'll be working for PG Productions." She idly traced the grouting on the counter while she let that sink in. She did not look at him but felt his eyes on her.

"When did you do that?" he asked in a flat, unemotional tone.

"Two months ago. I thought if I came to Phoenix to work, I could get better acquainted with the area," she gestured vaguely, "the clientele...and," her bravado faltered, "I could be near you."

Bonnie came tearing out of the hallway and crashed into the refrigerator, putting her hands out to stop herself.

"Stop that!" Audrey sharply chastised her, giving Bonnie's arm a rough shake. "Do you want to go sit in the car?"

Bonnie's arm a rough shake. "Do you want to go sit in the car?"

"Leave her alone," said Ken. He came over, rubbed the curly mop of hair and stooped down to give her a big hug before he released the bundle of energy who proceeded to hurtle across the carpeted dining room. "She's not hurting anything," he said as he stood up. He was practically on top of Audrey, and she looked away from the black, mesmerizing orbs, but they seemed to be everywhere.

"Audrey," he whispered, "do you forgive me?"

She did not need to reply in words and Ken held her securely. "I must be the world's biggest idiot," he said into her hair.

"Get in line, buster," she laughed, wiping a tear from her eyes.

"How did this happen?"

"You wanted me to make my own decisions. I told you you'd have to graduate me one day."

"Maybe I'll make you do postgraduate work."

Audrey looked over his shoulder at Nava del Sol and a worried frown crossed her face. "How can you give all this up?"

"Give what up?"

Audrey stared at his blank face. "Aren't you dissolving the partnership?"

Ken let out a deep, raucous laugh. "Is that what Janet told you?"

"Yes." Audrey paused, deep in thought. "How did you know I talked to Janet?"

"Who do you think asked her to prevail upon your hard little heart?" he chuckled. "Who do you think sent the plane?" Her eyebrow rose to uncharted heights and he could barely contain his glee.

"Wait a minute." She backed away from him. "Are you telling me I've been set up?" He grinned amiably and came toward her with outstretched arms. Audrey put up her hand to stop his advance. "Why didn't you call me?" she asked in rising indignation.

"You told me to contact you when I was ready to

listen. You didn't specify how. You were the one who hung up on me," he reminded her.

"Don't confuse me," she protested, backing into a cabinet.

"Audrey," he sighed, still grinning, although he had stopped. "If I waited for you to figure things out, I would die of old age!" He reached out to her. "Now, come here," he ordered, pulling her into his arms. "If Mohammed can't come to the mountain—"

"Can't or wouldn't?"

"I've been very busy around here," he said, swinging his arm in a wide arc, "in case you hadn't noticed."

Audrey glanced around the kitchen. "What's wrong with this house?" she asked, trying to ascertain what was familiar about it.

"What's wrong with it?" he asked in a horrified voice, holding Audrey at arm's length. "What do you mean, what's wrong with it? This is my masterpiece!" He scowled at her. "Don't be nasty because I got the better of you."

"I'm not." Audrey walked slowly around the kitchen and out the door to the back where she studied the house from every angle. Ken watched in fascination as she went back inside, all through the main floor, and out the front, and again studied the elevation.

"All right," he grumbled sourly, "what's wrong with it?"

"Not a thing. It's perfect."

"You sound surprised," he said peevishly.

"No," she laughed. She went back out to the front entry. Biting her lower lip, she counted her steps as she entered the hallway.

"What are you doing?" he asked in amazement.

"Sh!" She looked all around mumbling to herself and pointing blankly.

Ken grinned. It was obvious she had figured it out.

Audrey went back into the kitchen and opened the cabinets and inspected the drawers. "I know which one this is," she laughed and clapped her hands gleefully. She spotted Bonnie's fingerprints on the refrigerator and her elation dissipated. He had said this was going on the market. "I would imagine this will be very expensive," she said quietly.

"Yes," he readily agreed. "It took three crews working consecutive shifts to finish it in time. It may be impossible to sell," he sighed as he walked slowly over to her.

"Oh, no! How could you possibly think that?" She turned those huge, emerald eyes on him.

"Because," he stood scant inches from her, "it's a package deal."

"What?" Audrey was trying to concentrate on what he was saying, the task made nearly impossible by his nearness.

"It comes with noseprints," he grinned. "And a stubborn strawberry blonde, with a very opinionated architect. Who'd want all that?" he asked, his lips brushing hers as he spoke.

"Me," she replied, her eyes glazing as she leaned toward him.

"I don't know." He pulled back and placed his arms on her shoulders to steady her. "Are you willing to pay the price?"

"Yes," she whispered.

"Don't you want to know what it is?" he teased.

"If you don't kiss me..." she mumbled in exasperation, but he did not let her finish. "Whatever it is, I'll pay it," she murmured as she snuggled closer.

"Tsk-tsk, such a gambler." He took her hand and slipped on an emerald-cut solitaire. "Audrey, will you marry me?"

"Yes," she beamed, throwing her arms around him. Bonnie raced by and he caught her and swung her up onto his shoulders.

"When do you want to move in?"

"After the wedding," she said with a prim lift of her head.

"Tomorrow?"

"I can't be packed to move that soon."

"Bring or buy anything you want," he cavalierly

offered, and Audrey gasped. "Don't get too excited. If this doesn't take off, we'll be eating beans for months."

"Not true," she smugly reminded him. "I have a great job."

"That's comforting." But he gave her a slightly perturbed frown. "Don't you think I can support you?"

"Of course. All this working was your idea. Having second thoughts?"

"Nope. It'll be good for you," he smiled fondly. "Too bad you won't be spending more time in that studio I designed for you."

"But I will. It's strictly free-lance, didn't I tell you that?"

"You never tell me all of anything," he grinned. He put Bonnie down and watched her scamper off, an affectionate smile complimenting his strong, good looks. "I'd like to adopt Bonnie," he said very quietly. "If you have no objections."

"None," she breathed, blinking back tears of happiness. "Oh, Ken," sobbed Audrey, hugging him tightly, "I love you."

"I know," he smiled, bending to her.

Just what the wom[an] on the go needs!

BOOKMATE

The perfect "mate" for all Harlequin paperbacks!

Holds paperbacks open for hands-free reading!

- TRAVELING
- VACATIONING
- AT WORK • IN BED
- COOKING • EATING
- STUDYING

Perfect size for all standard paperbacks, this wonderful invention makes reading a pure pleasure! Ingenious design holds paperback books OPEN and FLAT so even wind can't ruffle pages—leaves your hands free to do other things. Reinforced, wipe-clean vinyl-covered holder flexes to let you turn pages without undoing the strap...supports paperbacks so well, they have the strength of hardcovers!

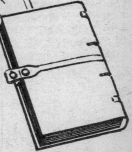

Snaps closed for easy carrying.

Available now. Send your name, address, and zip or postal code, along with a check or money order for just $4.99 + .75¢ for postage & handling (for a total of $5.74) payable to Harlequin Reader Service to:

Harlequin Reader Service

In U.S.:
P.O. Box 52040
Phoenix, AZ 85072-2040

In Canada:
649 Ontario Street
Stratford, Ont. N5A 6W2

MATE-1